MORE PRAISE FOR
RONDA THOMPSON!

PRICKLY PEAR

"A sure bet. High-tension desire and quick tempers between Wade and Cam make for an exciting, delicious read. Especially fun and engaging, this one is an unexpected surprise!"

—*Romantic Times*

"Ronda Thompson's *Prickly Pear* holds the flavor of a true western historical romance skillfully seasoned with sexual tension."

—*New York Times* bestselling author Jodi Thomas

COUGAR'S WOMAN

"Ronda Thompson has a gem here."

—*Romance Communications*

"[Thompson's] warmth and humor breathe life into the story and keep a reader turning the pages, long past time to go to sleep! Bravo!"

—*Under the Covers Book Reviews*

SCANDALOUS

"Ronda Thompson is not to be missed. An innovative writer, she is not afraid to take chances. *Scandalous* is a juicy Regency which will have you smiling over the foibles and fancies of the period. Wonderful as usual."

—*Affair de Coeur*

"*Scandalous* is a fast-paced romp readers will find difficult to put down until the last page is read. Strong characters provide high quality entertainment, while the chemistry between Christine and Gavin sizzles."

—*Under the Covers Book Reviews*

THE MORNING AFTER

Jason opened his eyes. His bleary gaze focused upon the ceiling. It appeared to be made of rock. Blue sky floated past a small opening above and weak light filtered down.

A woman sat beside him. Her long hair hung past her shoulders. Her cheekbones were high, her mouth full and sensuous. Her dark eyes sparked a memory of . . . the night before.

"Where am I?" he rasped.

"At my mercy," she answered.

He tried to rise but couldn't move. He was staked out, spread eagle and stark naked. Not a position a man liked to wake up in—not unless the circumstances were right.

"Look, lady," he said. "I don't know what you're into, and I've never been one to balk at a little harmless bondage, but—"

Suddenly, a knife pressed against his throat. The woman brought her face close to his. "I am not harmless, *Wapiskisiw*."

He wanted to swallow but, all things considered, held back the reflex. Where in the hell was he, and who was this? "You must have me confused with someone else," he managed. "I don't know who Waneta is. The name is Jason. Jason Donavon and—"

She dug the knife's point deeper into his neck. "I do not need to know who you are. I know *what* you are. *Wapiskisiw*—shape shifter. Skin walker. Werewolf."

CALL
OF THE
MOON

RONDA THOMPSON

LOVE SPELL NEW YORK CITY

To Amanda Ashley and Christine Feehan.

LOVE SPELL®

November 2002

Published by

Dorchester Publishing Co., Inc.
276 Fifth Avenue
New York, NY 10001

ISBN 0-505-52515-1

The name "Love Spell" and its logo are trademarks of Dorchester Publishing Co., Inc.

Printed in the United States of America.

Visit us on the web at www.dorchesterpub.com.

CALL
OF THE
MOON

Chapter One

Sirens wailed in the distance, and Jason Donavon fought the urge to throw back his head and howl. The high-pitched sound hurt his ears. The flash of blinking neon lights hurt his eyes. People hurried along the streets of Edmonton, bumping against him, most too impolite to mutter an apology. Some, he noted, went out of their way to avoid him.

He couldn't blame the leery. Catching a glimpse of his reflection as he passed a storefront, Jason saw that his hair now hung past his shoulders in a tangled mess. He'd paid for a shower earlier that day, but he hadn't felt like shaving. A week's worth of whiskers covered his cheeks. His clothes were ragged and torn. He looked like something wild and wondered why he'd bothered to visit the city at all.

Months of searching the Canadian wilderness had gotten to him, he supposed. He had yearned for companionship, the sight of a friendly face—or at least a human one. But the noise, the lights, the smells, and the press of bodies against him were all too much for his sharpened senses. He hurried along, head bent and eyes downcast.

The wind shifted—brought the smell of rotting trash and unwashed bodies. The crowds melted away as he entered the seedier section of town called Boyle Street, but there Jason recognized another scent: the smell of cheap perfume. He closed his eyes and inhaled deeply. It wasn't the perfume that struck a human chord within him; brought visions of cool sheets and tangled, sweat-soaked bodies; made him long to be a man again—it was the smell beneath. The scent of a woman. A musky combination of sex and sweetness. God, how he missed that.

A few prostitutes and their pimps lined the streets. None gave him more than a once-over. His worn jeans, thin T-shirt, and scruffy appearance made it clear he had no money—nothing that would appeal to them. But one girl in particular drew his interest; he supposed it was because she looked out of place. Rather than displaying her womanly wares as the others did with vulgar thoroughness, she wore a cape wrapped tightly around her. While her counterparts used the dim streetlights to show off their bodies, she stood in the shadows. *Odd.*

Jason moved on. A different woman fell into step beside him. "You look like a man who could use some company," she said. The tall blonde's skirt barely covered her rear end. Her large breasts bounced beneath her top as she walked.

"I don't have any money," he said, hoping to get

rid of her. The alley where he'd taken up residence for the past week wasn't far. He didn't mind sleeping outdoors, anymore. He didn't even mind the smell of garbage or the sound of rats shuffling through the trash. Both held a strange appeal.

The blonde wet her lips, showing her tongue in a slow, suggestive manner. "Sometimes it doesn't take money for the right man to get what he wants." Her darkly penciled eyes roamed his body. "Beneath all that hair, I see a good-looking man."

Beneath his hair, his skin, she wouldn't like what she saw. Not at all. He kept walking. "I'm not interested."

Her spiked heels made loud clicking noises against the pavement as she tried to keep up. "Give me five minutes, and I promise to get you interested."

Jason hadn't had intimate contact with a woman for so long, one could probably get him aroused in five seconds. But he didn't consider prostitutes his style, even now that his choices had been taken from him.

"I don't want any trouble." He looked over his shoulder. "I know your pimp isn't going to let you give anything away for free."

She snorted. "He indulges me once in a while—if I see something I really want."

"Believe me, lady, I have nothing you want." He ducked around a corner, hoping to lose her. She dogged his heels. His alley was deserted, as usual. That's why he'd chosen to take up residence there for the past week; he no longer considered himself good company for the civilized. The woman's pimp, he noted, did not follow.

He sighed. "Look—"

The woman grabbed the thin material of his shirt and shoved him against a brick wall. "*You* look," she said in a husky voice, then rolled up her skimpy top.

Jason did look. He couldn't help himself. Her breasts were large and round. Even in the reflected light of the streetlights beyond the alley, he saw her nipples, erect from the cool night air. He shook his head and tried to move past her.

"Impressive, but I'm still not interested."

She shoved him back. Hard. "I think you are. Mind if I check?" Her fingers slid down his chest toward the front of his jeans.

Snatching her groping hand, Jason snarled. "Hey, watch it. Don't you understand the word 'no'?"

The blonde's eyes narrowed. The smile disappeared from her painted lips. "Now you've gone and ruined my fun. I could have at least made things good for you before . . ."

The hair on the back of Jason's neck prickled. The woman's eyes had begun to glow. The shape of her face looked longer than it had.

"Before what?" he asked.

She opened her mouth, and her teeth looked different, too. Elongated. Sharp. Canine. "Before I tear out your throat and have you for a midnight snack," she growled.

Jason stumbled back. The woman's voice was gravelly, deep and distorted. She grew taller before his eyes. Her body thickened and patches of dark hair sprouted from her skin. He stared at her, horror taking the place of his earlier annoyance. Could this be real? Nightmares were no strangers to him; he had experienced them for a long time. But while part of him hoped he was dreaming, another part prayed that he wasn't. He'd been searching for three years and hadn't come close to finding what he was looking for. Until now.

"What are you?" he asked.

A noise registered—a popping and grinding. He knew the sounds coming from the woman's body: bones stretching, rearranging themselves beneath flesh. She didn't have to answer his question. Jason knew what she was. He knew what he'd soon be, too. Prey.

Instinct for survival took over. He shoved the blonde beast aside and made a run for it. At the end of the alley, a figure blocked his escape. The pimp's eyes glowed in the dark like those of a cat. The man growled low in his throat, raising goose bumps on Jason's arms. He was trapped. Tangled in either a nightmare or a more frightening truth.

He chanced a quick glance at the sky. A quarter moon hung suspended in darkness. This wasn't right. The prostitute and her pimp couldn't be what he thought they were. The moon was not full.

"Get out of my way," he warned the man.

Another growl made Jason spin. Behind him was the blonde, all traces of her humanity disappeared. She stood on two legs, but fur covered her body. Saliva dripped from yellow fangs, and her head looked too big. She smelled worse than the nearby trash bins. He backed away, but what waited at the end of the alley wasn't any less frightening than the monster the blonde had become; the pimp had also turned.

Warring emotions tugged at Jason. He'd been searching for three long years, had left everything be-

5

hind: his life, his career, his family. He was dead to the world, would remain that way unless he found the answers he'd been seeking. Now, two creatures stood before him. One might be the key that unlocked a curse; but either could be the death of him. Should he stay, or should he run?

Both creatures closed in. As he stared into their soulless eyes, Jason knew he wouldn't get answers from either of them. Not tonight, anyway.

The female lifted a furry hand, flexing long, deadly claws. She swiped at him. Jason jumped back. He felt the male's hot breath against his neck and doubled up his fist. Spinning, he dealt the creature a blow. The punch didn't faze it. "Shit," he muttered, then tried to dart around and away. The creature's sharp claws grazed his back. His face met the pavement.

Rising, Jason turned and kicked out. His foot connected with the male—and in a place that obviously hurt regardless of what form the pimp took. His attacker howled and stumbled back. The female was on Jason, pinning him in an instant. Her foul breath gagged him.

"Leave the human alone," a voice rang out.

The female's head jerked up, flecks of saliva splattering Jason's face. He watched the glow in her eyes intensify. She sniffed the air like a rat that had just gotten wind of danger . . . or a meal.

"Do you know me, Unma Kin Sica?" he heard the voice ask. "I am Tala Soaringbird. I am *'ashi'doltii*—the one who has been chosen—and I am here for your head."

The female snarled and rose. Jason rolled out of the way. He inched up beside the brick wall of the alley.

As if he hadn't been already a witness to enough strange sights, he was treated to another.

A petite brunette stood a few feet away. She lifted her arms and the blanket wrapped around her slid to the ground. A flash of steel caught the streetlamps. She held a knife in each hand, which soon sliced the air with a skill that left little doubt in Jason's mind that she knew how to use them.

Regardless of her skill, she had to be out of her mind. "Get out of here!" he shouted. "Run!"

His would-be rescuer ignored him. Her dark eyes never faltered from the inhuman face of her growling assailant. Then the male joined the female, and her odds looked worse. Even with knives, she'd be no match for such predators. The woman stood only half as tall as her foes. She was small, delicate and beautiful. Jason's eyesight was abnormally good in the dark, and he saw her clearly, but he had trouble believing what he saw. A dark ribbon of hair hung down the woman's shoulders nearly to her waist. Her clothes were strange. Buckskin. Not an expensive suede suit, but what appeared to be traditional Native American garb. Her eyes were almond shaped and dark as the night. They were the gentle eyes of a doe.

The woman began to chant—a strange language Jason had never heard. The beasts growled and snapped. The female lunged forward, tearing a long jagged streak in the woman's sturdy buckskins. The woman lunged, too. She dug her knife into the creature's chest. It let out an inhuman cry, then the other, the male, howled and knocked the brunette backward. She hit the building on the opposite side of the alley with a thud, then slid to the ground.

Jason knew his would-be savior was about to become a meal. What in the hell was she doing here? Panic engulfed him as the creature moved in for the kill. Then something happened—something that had never happened unless the moon was full. Jason heard the sound of popping and grinding, but this time he more than registered the sound: He felt it.

Pain shot through his mouth, long canine teeth forcing through his bloody gums. His fingertips pulsed, ached. He cried out as claws broke through them. He knew his eyes had taken on a glow, and he felt the humanity within slipping away. But, for once, Jason didn't fight the change. Embracing the beast was the only chance he or his rescuer had of making it out of here alive.

He growled low in his throat. The male's large head swung toward him. Their eyes fused.

Then Jason glanced at the woman. She had roused herself and now stared at him, her skin struck pale by the artificial glow of the distant streetlights. He wanted to help her, wanted her to know that his intentions were honorable. But he could never predict exactly what would happen.

"I'm sorry," he whispered. And he was, because when the beast ruled him, Jason could never remember what dark deeds he committed. Would he fight against these monsters to save this woman's life? Or would she become his next victim?

Chapter Two

The strong smell of incense roused him. Jason opened his eyes. His bleary gaze focused upon the ceiling, which appeared to be made of rock. Blue sky floated past a small opening there, and weak light filtered down. Bits and pieces of the previous night drifted to him. He felt a presence and turned his head.

A woman sat beside him. Her long hair hung well past her shoulders, her cheekbones were high, and her mouth was full and sensuous. Her dark eyes sparked a memory. He'd seen her last night. She was the woman in the alley. The woman he'd meant to protect then feared he'd end up killing.

"Where am I?" he rasped, his throat dry from the thick cloud of scent that hung around him.

"At my mercy," she answered.

He tried to rise but couldn't move. Jason glanced down. He was staked out, spread-eagle and stark na-

9

ked. Not a position a man liked to wake up in—not unless the circumstances were right.

"Look, lady," he said, trying to laugh. "I don't know what you're into, and I've never been one to balk at a little harmless bondage, but—"

Suddenly, a knife pressed against his throat. His captor brought her face close to his. "I am not harmless, *Wapiskisiw*."

He wanted to swallow, but all things considered, held back the reflex. Where in the hell was he, and who was this? "You must have me confused with someone else," he managed. "I don't know who—whatever you said is. The name is Jason. Jason Donavon and—"

She dug the knife's point deeper into his neck. "I do not need to know who you are, *Wapiskisiw*. I know *what* you are. I saw *what* you are. I saw you change last night."

His secret had been discovered. Jason had figured it would be only a matter of time before someone witnessed what the bite of the beast had done to him—someone who lived to tell the tale, anyway.

"So you know what I am. You're lucky to be alive, then. What happened last night?"

The woman drew back, taking her knife from his throat. "The evil ones escaped. Two roam free to spread their curse, but I have captured you."

She had not only managed to capture him, but she'd bound him like an animal. Of course, since she had witnessed the change, that would be what she thought he was—and Jason couldn't blame her. He'd once been a normal man, lived a normal life, but a hunting trip with his brother in the wilds up here had changed

10

all that. Now he and Rick were both cursed.

What did this woman want? He figured he knew. She'd want the same things most people wanted, even if she didn't exactly look like most people. He said, "Wait, don't tell me. Let me guess. I imagine the police are on the way or the reporters? Maybe the nearest freak show? There might be a nice book deal in this for you, or at least an appearance on Letterman."

Her smooth forehead creased. "Letterman?"

"Well, he's not my favorite, either," he agreed.

The woman's expression didn't soften at his joke, so Jason suspected she lacked a sense of humor. Last night, he'd compared her eyes to those of a doe. This morning, her dark gaze was more that of a beast.

"I should have killed you," she said. The woman flipped her knife and slashed it through the air. "I am Tala Soaringbird. *'Ashi'doltii*. It is my sacred duty to hunt the bad ones and plunge my knife into their dark hearts. Their kind are a plague upon this earth."

The dramatics involved in her speech, along with her impressive weapon-wielding, were a little much for Jason so early in the morning. He was hungry, tired, and just plain sick of living. "Go ahead and do it," he grunted. "Put me out of my misery."

His words must have taken her off guard. Confusion clouded her hard eyes. Then she straightened, placing her knife again against his throat. "Is that what you wish?"

Yes, Jason might wish it—had just wished it—but what had happened on that hunting trip three years ago hadn't only happened to him. It had happened to Rick. And being the more skilled at hunting and living outdoors, Jason had vowed to his brother to find the

11

monster that had attacked them and kill it. That was the only way to break the curse. Well, he hoped it was the way to break the curse. He'd seen enough movies where killing the werewolf that bit them returned its victims to normal men.

"Do I get a choice?" he asked.

After a moment, the brunette eased her knife from his throat. "I should have killed you already . . . but I have questions."

Jason stared at her. "That makes two of us. If you're going to ask me how a man can turn into a—"

"No," she interrupted. "I understand what you are, and how you to came to be. I do not understand why you fought to protect me. Why you turned against your own kind to see that I escaped harm?"

His kind. Jason remembered the creatures' glowing eyes, large heads, and protruding fangs. He shuddered over the memory. He'd always hoped he turned into something less vile. "I didn't know I looked like them. And if I act like them, you should kill me."

A surprising hint of compassion flickered within her dark eyes. It softened her face and made her appear ethereal. "You did not look the same," she said. "You took a pure form—which is why you are not dead, slain by my knife. The beast has not fully claimed you." The woman cocked her head. "Why do you fight what you have become? Most of your kind surrender easily to the darkness."

A pure form? Not fully claimed? He had no idea what she meant, and her question was ridiculous. "Why wouldn't I fight it? Every day I struggle to hold on to my humanity. I don't want to be some kind of freak. I want my life back!"

"What is a . . . 'freak'?"

Now that Jason's head had cleared, more of the strangeness of his situation registered. The woman with the knife was truly odd. Not just odd-acting, but she looked as if she'd fallen through the cracks of time. Her beauty was natural, unassisted by makeup—though her skin was a shade women spent fortunes in tanning salons to maintain. The clothes she wore were downright primitive. He glanced around. She lived in a cave for God's sake!

"Freak. One who is different," he explained.

Her gaze widened. "Oh. Yes, I understand."

"Well, I sure as hell don't." He tested his bonds and found them secure. "What am I doing here? What do you want from me?"

The woman moistened her lips, brushed a hand through her hair. The dark strands sifted through her fingers and fell into her face. "I owe you a debt. That is why you are here and not slain as you might be. I saw the female in a vision, but not the male. Had I known there were two, I would have taken a warrior with me. I could be dead or worse, had you not fought by my side."

Her people? A warrior? This woman was starting to creep him out—which was not an easy thing to do to a guy who turned into a crazed dog-man and howled at the moon! "I don't remember fighting for you. I don't remember anything after the change. Just let me go."

Her knife stopped his struggles, poised once more at his throat. "I cannot let you go. Two have already escaped their fate. My thrust did not penetrate the female's heart. She attacked, and I had to fight her

13

while you—in your other form—fought the male. I cut her again—I hope deeply enough to have killed her. When she fell, the male took her and escaped."

Jason felt his gut twist. A sour taste rose in his throat. He had no stomach for killing, or for being a monster himself. "What's wrong with you?" he asked. "Whatever else those two might be, they were once people."

"No." She shook her head. "We call them *Sica*, bad ones. They have allowed the beast within to rule them, and have lost their humanity. They are only animals now, beasts without human souls. Had those two last night not eaten of human flesh and drank of human blood, their form would have been pure, like you.

"I do not see a *waneta*, shape shifter, skin walker," she explained, "in my mind unless it has taken an evil form. When I do see one, and I know where to find the creature, it is the sacred law of my people, the duty given to me, to hunt and kill it so that it will not slaughter the innocent or spread its evil to others."

A persistent ache throbbed behind Jason's skull, and her strange explanations weren't helping. "Your people? Sacred laws? Visions? I don't understand any of this."

The woman rose, moved to a corner, snatched up a colorful blanket and threw it over his lower half. "I will explain, but you may find it hard to believe."

He laughed. "Lady, there isn't much I find hard to believe these days."

Settling beside him again, his captor said, "I do not understand why you laugh. How can you find humor in what you have become?"

Jason sobered. His sense of humor was at least one human trait he'd tried to maintain during the past three years. "You know the saying: Sometimes you have to laugh to keep from crying."

She frowned. "I do *not* know the saying. My ways are different from yours. My people do not mix with the outside world."

Jason found himself a bit miffed. "What exactly do you consider the outside world?"

She lifted her hands, as if encompassing all her surroundings. "The *outside*. The world beyond this place. My people are decendents of a race many years upon this earth. We follow the old laws, the old ways, and we do not allow outsiders among us, or go to live with them in their world. Our race must be kept pure. We are special and chosen for a great duty—to keep not only our blood pure, but to kill those who would taint the world with evil."

And Jason had thought *he* was weird! Maybe last night had been a nightmare after all, and this was still part of the dream. "Pinch me," he said. "I'd like to wake up now."

Of course, he would have liked to wake up to find the past three years only a nightmare, but the woman did not pinch him. Instead, she lifted her knife and slashed his chest.

The white man groaned and arched his back as she cut him. He struggled against his bonds. The wound from her knife was only superficial, but Tala did not enjoy making it. Pain filled her captive's light eyes.

"What in the hell is your problem?" he asked between clenched teeth. "If you're going to kill me, get it over with! Stop playing with me!"

Tala took a calming breath. "I must cut you," she explained. "Under normal circumstances, it is forbidden to bring an outsider among us. You must appear hurt, wounded, if I am to help you."

"Help me?" The man glanced around the cave. "How is what you're doing going to help? I think you're crazy!"

Crazy was a word Tala understood—and maybe the white man was right. She had shown weakness where he was concerned: She had defied the laws of her people and brought an outsider among them. She had defied her own duties by not killing him the night before. He could not know her reasons for doing so— or the shame that lived deep inside her.

The man had shown courage. He had fought for her; and the form he had taken, a pure one, had been that of a great black wolf. She had known him, had seen him in her visions. He was the only one of true form that had come to her in dreams. And she knew why. They were connected by the past. Past sins. Past shame.

"I will tell you how I plan to help when I return. Now, I must go and greet my people or they will think something is wrong. They will send someone to see, and no one must see you. Not yet. You are in great danger here. Do you understand?"

Slowly, the man nodded. Tala did not believe that he truly understood. He had the look of a captured animal. Likely, he would try to escape. But she could not let him go free. She must either try to help him battle the beast within, or kill him. Which she would do, depended upon him.

"Stay here," she said. Rising, she prepared to face her tribe. "When I return, we will talk more. I will give you food and water." She nodded to a place behind her. "I found a small bag in that alley. I assume it belongs to you."

His gaze followed her nod. "Yes. Those are my things. What little I have."

"They will be returned to you," she assured him. "Rest while I am gone."

Tala hated to leave him tied, but she could not trust the man. At the cave entrance, she pushed the vegetation aside and left.

The incline that led to valley floor was steep. Tala had walked it hundreds of times, but never had her feet wanted to move so slowly. She was a fool for bringing the man among them. To survive in secret, as they had done for centuries, outsiders must not know of their existence. Her people were kind, but they could be harsh. Disobeying any law, however slight, could lead to punishment . . . sometimes death. If she had not had a high social standing among the members, if she were not the chosen one, she would have never dared bring the white man to her people's secret encampment.

Reaching the bottom of the incline, Tala moved through the forest. By night, the caves protected her people, but by day they needed sunshine. There were lodges here, gathering places where her tribe worked and held meetings. As she approached them, she saw her uncle throwing bones with a few older men. He spotted her, rose, and hurried to catch up.

"Haidar said that you went to find a bad one you saw in a vision. Did you kill it?"

"If I went, there is no need to ask, Uncle." She wet her suddenly dry lips and kept her gaze averted. "But there is a problem. I must speak to Haidar and The People. Will you gather them for me?"

"A problem?" her uncle echoed. Then he nodded. "I will bring everyone to the meeting lodge."

With a sigh of relief, Tala continued. A child darted from behind a tree and nearly collided with her. Another followed fast upon the first's heels. Both came to an abrupt halt, their eyes wide. The young boys lowered their gazes and bowed respectfully.

Tala smiled and tousled the first boy's hair. "Watch where you are going, Noshi. I could have been one of the elders, and you could have harmed me."

The boy glanced up. "I will watch where I run next time, Tala. As always, we bow to your wisdom."

Her insides twisted. She did not feel wise or deserving of respect at the moment. "Go to the meeting lodge," she told the boys. "I have news that I must give our people." The youths raced off ahead of her, then remembered themselves and slowed to a walk.

Tala smiled. She loved children, but she would never have any of her own. She was the one chosen. Her destiny had been decided years ago when her gifts first developed. But her purity fueled the great powers given to her by Mother Earth, so Tala could not mate and have children like the other women of her tribe.

It was not the same if a man were the chosen. Tala had never understood why, but she supposed it was not for her to question. From the beginning of time, women had been given one set of rules to follow and

18

men another. Tala's gifts had let her cross boundaries—had made her equal, if not above every man in her tribe—but she paid a price for the power. Tala wondered if she would pay a higher one for her foolishness concerning her prisoner.

It was a moment of weakness, having allowed human emotion to overpower common sense. Had it been shame and guilt alone that spurred her to spare Jason Donavon? Even with his tangled hair and unshaven face, the man was uncommonly handsome. She feared that deep inside, none of her reasons for sparing him was honorable. The man was forbidden to her by simply being a male, twice as taboo for being white. To make matters worse, he had a wolf beneath his skin—a wolf that could easily claim him, destroying all that was good.

Her knees trembled when she reached the meeting lodge. Tala prayed for the strength to tell Haidar the truth. The leader would kill Jason Donavon, and he would no longer be her problem—or her shame.

But fate had surely brought the man to her. She had not been stalking him. Tala had simply stood among the vulgar street girls, waiting for the female Sica to choose her victim and lure him to a deserted place. Tala had not even recognized Jason Donavan from her dreams; not until he turned into the black wolf. His turning had startled her, sent questions racing through her mind. Her distraction had allowed two werewolves to escape her knife—monsters that would not have appeared to her had they not posed a threat to those she loved.

Her nervousness grew as she reached the meeting lodge, and saw the others coverging. There were few left among their sacred tribe; keeping their strain pure had taken a toll. Because the tribe's bloodlines had become closely intertwined, only a handful were allowed to mate and produce children.

"Why have you called a meeting?" Haidar, the leader of her band, asked.

Tala had trouble forming the words. Although Haidar was her brother, he was too fair to show her favoritism. She swallowed the lump in her throat.

"I have brought a man among us from the outside. He is ill, hurt defending me against two Unma Kin Sica last night. Long ago, it was our tradition to trade a life for a life. I feel that it is my duty to see this man mended before I send him back to his world."

Shocked silence followed.

Finally, her brother spoke. "Our laws have changed since the days when we were many. It is forbidden to bring an outsider among us. You knew this, Tala, and still you brought him here?"

As her gaze swept the stunned faces surrounding her, Tala tried to justify her actions—both to herself and to her people. "I had no choice. I could not stay away. You may have need of me, of my powers, but this man needed me as well. Our lives have changed, our ways have changed, but should we not honor at least the spirit of our ancestors' laws?"

"But this man will know of our location," Haidar persisted. "After you have healed him, it would be dangerous to release him back into his world. Not with the knowledge of our people upon his lips."

Tala had made a decision, and perhaps a foolish one, but she vowed to see her mistake through. She owed the white man a debt. She owed him more than her brother knew. More than The People knew. "When it is time for him to go, when he is healed to my satisfaction, I will cast the sacred spells. He will not remember being among us."

Her uncle stepped forward. "The council agreed long ago that our sacred spells should be used sparingly by the one chosen. And spells are sometimes weaker than a person's mind. They do not always erase a full memory. Today this man, tomorrow another might venture into our camp. You cannot cast your spells upon the whole world, Tala. Your powers are great, but not so great."

Tala lifted her chin. "Then we will not allow him past the perimeters of our camp while he heals. Even if the spells do not erase us from his mind, he will not know where he was taken."

"That will not quiet his tongue," Haidar pointed out. "He could make others curious. Our safety has always been our secrecy. What a man does not know, he cannot wonder at."

Haidar's concerns were well founded, but he did not have the final say. Tala depended on that. "Is this decision not one for Council to decide?" she asked.

Her brother frowned. He did not like a woman, even his sister and the one chosen, questioning his authority. But Tala knew that if the Council decided in her favor, he would honor its decision.

"Yes," Haidar relented. "It is a matter for the Council. Elders." He turned to address the group. "Join us in the meeting lodge."

"Can we see the man?" a member asked.

"No!" Tala winced at the shrill sound of her voice. "He is very ill. He tried to help me fight two Unma

Kin Sica and one slashed him with its claws. It hurled him through the air and he landed against a hard wall. It—"

"It did not bite him, did it?" Haidar interrupted.

All heads swung toward Tala. "No, there are no teeth marks upon him. I made certain. He needs rest and strong medicine from the old ways. He is very weak, very ill, and I must be allowed time alone with him before he can see visitors."

When she glanced at her brother, Tala expected another rebuke, but he was not looking at her. Haidar stared off into the distance.

"Is this ill man—this *mortally wounded* man—the same one I see running like a deer into the forest?"

She followed the direction of her brother's stare. It *was* the same man. He had not obeyed her. And how had he gotten loose? The *wapiskisiw* would get himself killed on his first day among her people.

"He has a fever," Tala explained. "He is out of his head."

"I will catch him for you," her brother said.

"No," Tala blurted, then tried to calm her racing heart. "I brought him among us. He is mine—my responsibility," she quickly amended. "I will secure the man and return to the meeting lodge to speak with the Council."

"Be quick," Haidar ordered. "If your friend is out of his head, it would be a good time to return him to his people. He will think he has been dreaming."

A murmur of agreement followed. But Tala could not take Jason Donavon back to his world! Not until she taught him how to control the beast within him. Not until she knew for certain that he would not turn.

If the Council decided he must leave, Tala would kill him. No matter the sins committed against the white man, she could not let another enemy go free.

"I will bring him back," she assured her tribe. "Then we will talk."

Jason cursed his lack of shoes. His hands throbbed, and pain shot up his arms. To get the ropes off of his wrists, he'd been forced to stick them into the fire the woman had left burning. Then, since he'd lost his clothing the previous night, he'd dug inside his sack of meager belongings and pulled out a pair of threadbare jeans. Getting into them had nearly killed him. Despite his burns and the rocks now digging into his feet, Jason ran as fast as he could. He glanced behind him. There was no sign of the crazy woman.

He didn't expect to see her. The three years in which Jason had searched for the wolf that attacked him—as well as the curse itself—had made him lean and muscled. He felt at home running wild through the forest, leaping over fallen logs and slipping like a shadow through trees that grew too close together. Although he had no idea where he might be headed, away from his crazy captor was enough for the moment.

A figure suddenly appeared on the path before him. Jason skidded to a halt. Tala Soaringbird stood a short distance away, and he couldn't imagine how she'd managed to catch up with him, much less get in front of him. He supposed she knew these woods better than he did.

Sure that he was the faster of the two of them, Jason darted to the side and took off. He didn't make it far when something hit him from behind and knocked him to the ground. The woman pinned him the moment he turned onto his back, her trusty knife poised again at his throat.

"I told you to stay where you were!" she said.

"I don't always do what I'm told," he shot back. "I don't want your help, okay? I just want you to let me go."

"I cannot," she said. "I have told you this already."

Her breasts heaved beneath her buckskin dress. Jason didn't know why he'd notice given the circumstances, but he observed more than that. She straddled him; her dress hiked up around her smooth, slender thighs. She obviously liked taking the dominant role in a relationship.

"Is this your idea of foreplay?" he joked.

She shoved her hair back over her shoulder and stared down at him. "I do not understand," she said.

Looking at her in broad daylight, Jason noticed the smoothness of her skin, but she wasn't *that* young. Maybe midtwenties? Plenty old enough to know about foreplay. He snatched her wrists and rolled on top of her, pinning her arms over her head.

"If you weren't crazy, and I weren't cursed, I might like to introduce you to the word." He paused to catch his breath. He obviously wasn't getting through to the woman. "Listen, you can't help me. *No one* can help me. Last night was the closest I've come to finding answers to what happened to me three years ago. Do you know what my chances are of locating those two again?"

"You must release me now!" She growled up at him. "Do not force me to hurt you."

He almost laughed, but his sense of humor was fading. His ego had been batted around enough for one day. "You might have gotten the drop on me a couple of times, but—"

His words were choked off. Someone from behind clutched a handful of his hair. Another knife pressed against his throat.

"No!" the woman beneath him shouted. "Do not harm him! He does not know what he does."

Jason couldn't see his attacker, but he was pulled off Tala. With a shove, he landed in the dirt again. In the time it took him to turn and sit, Tala was on her feet. She stood posed as if she meant to protect him. The scene looked as ridiculous as a rabbit trying to fend off a grizzly.

The man who had attacked him was close to Jason's height, but he had a chest any World Federation wrestler would envy. His thighs were the size of tree trunks. The man was Native American, like Tala. Maybe she *was* part of a secret tribe. A cult of crazies. Jason might be able to escape Tala, but the man was another story. The situation called for an equalizer. He groped around on the ground, found a good-sized rock, then shot up, intending to thump the man's skull.

A fist shot out, punched him in the face, and knocked him down. Spots danced before Jason's eyes. His last coherent thought was a disturbing one: A woman had knocked him out.

A while later, he stirred to life again, feeling as if he'd just come off of a three-day drunken spree. Jason managed to open his eyes—well, one of them. Same smooth rock walls. Same opening above, only it was dark now. He turned his head. Same woman, too, except she sat with her back to him. She was naked from the waist up.

He started to say something, but she lifted her arm and drew a wet cloth down her side. Who was he to interrupt a woman's bath? Besides, he wanted a moment before he had another knife poised at his throat, or anyone was chasing or beating him up. This was the same scenario of that morning. He was bound again. The skin on his arms didn't sting as much, and he smelled something, maybe some type of medicine she'd rubbed on his burns.

Questions shot through his mind. What had he gotten mixed up in, and why had he changed last night? Before, at least he'd had the peace of mind believing that he wouldn't be killing anything or anyone except during a full moon. That small comfort had allowed him windows of opportunity to travel, to hunt for the beast that had cursed him and his brother. What would he do if he lost that small assurance?

It had occurred to Jason after a while of hunting—snooping out towns that bordered wildernesses where a wolf by night, and a man by day, might live—that he was faced with an awful dilemma. If the wolf that had bitten him only changed during a full moon as well, how in the hell would he ever find it?

The realization had left Jason with the difficult task of wandering the streets, looking for people who acted strangely—he'd discovered the whole world acted strange if anyone cared to stop long enough and notice. Some people even looked like wolves in human form. But all his suspected monsters had turned out to be people who lived seemingly normal lives. Most of them had dogs, which was a surefire clue they weren't werewolves. Dogs hated Jason. He imagined if his brother, Rick, still practiced veterinary medicine, being a werewolf had become a definite drawback for his practice.

His captor drew her long hair over one shoulder, distracting his train of thought. Marks were cut into her arm: Crescent shaped symbols of some sort. Five of them. His attention shifted to her back. Her skin was smooth and bronzed, but on one side he noticed a small puckering—some type of wound.

"What happened to your back?"

She jumped and spun around. Unfortunately, she had a shirt pressed against her breasts. "You are awake."

"I'd like to think I'm still dreaming," he muttered. "The fact that my eye is throbbing and swollen half-shut leads me to strongly suspect that I'm not." His good eye devoured her. "Besides, if I were dreaming, you'd accidentally drop that shirt about now."

He couldn't swear to it, but he thought she blushed. She also turned around and drew the shirt over her head, ending any interesting possibilities that such an accident might occur. When she again faced him, she was all business.

"You must not try to escape. It will be difficult to convince the tribe you are ill when you dart through the woods like a rabbit. You do not realize how dangerous it is for you to be among us. Or how hard I had to fight to keep you here."

If he could have rubbed his throbbing eye, Jason would have. "I think I'm getting the picture. I'm just not understanding all of it. Who are you? And who are your people?"

"Do you wish to eat? Drink?"

He wouldn't be distracted again, even if his stomach was empty and his throat felt so dry he could hardly manage the spit to swallow. "You didn't answer my question. Where is this place? What—"

"The stew I prepared will grow cold," she insisted. "We will talk while you eat."

Tala Soaringbird was obviously a woman used to having her own way. Jason's stomach grumbled when she removed the lid from a pot resting over a small fire. His accommodations weren't five star, but they beat a dirty alley.

"I can't eat with my hands tied," he complained. "And I've been humiliated enough for one day. I'd prefer not to be spoon-fed."

She stared at him, her full lips pursed. "I will release your hands, but that is all." She then dipped him up a bowl of stew, sat some type of container next to the bowl, and reached forward to cut the ropes around his hands.

Jason stifled a groan as he was freed. He moved his arms. The only good thing about being a werewolf was the fast way his body regenerated. His burns would almost be healed by tomorrow . . . if he lived that long.

He lifted the bowl of stew, glanced up, and noticed the woman had scrambled away. She held her knife in front of her. The sight annoyed the hell out of him.

"In case you've forgotten, I tried to help you last night. I'm not going to hurt you."

"One must always be wary of the enemy."

The stew was venison. To a starving man, it tasted like heaven. "If you're so scared of me, why'd you bring me here?" he asked, tipping the stew into his mouth.

She straightened, tilting her chin. "I am not frightened of you. I am cautious. Can you change forms whenever you choose?"

Jason picked up the strange second container and peered down its spout. He sniffed the contents. Satisfied it was only water, he took a drink. "I didn't think so. Last night—that's never happened to me when the moon wasn't full. I panicked when I saw the monster moving toward you. I guess the situation brought it on."

The woman scooted closer, but she didn't put down her knife. "That is the way it begins."

He laughed. "It began three years ago."

"No," she insisted. "The way the loss of control begins. First one incident, then another will bring the beast forth. Soon, it becomes more difficult to control the part of you that is more animal than man. Before long, the man is gone and only the beast remains."

A chill raced up his spine. Being controlled by the moon was creepy enough. He hoped she was crazy, spouting nonsense. Still, he couldn't help being curious. "How do you know these things?"

"My people have been hunting your kind for centuries. But only after the human side is gone and evil has taken over the human soul. I want to know if hope exists for those still trapped between the moon and humanity. I need to know this." She leaned closer to him, her dark gaze intense.

"Why?"

29

As if she realized how close her face was to him, she drew back. "If we can save those who have not turned, they are enemies we do not have to hunt. I believe if a man . . . or a woman is strong enough, they can fight the beast within. They can tame it, control it, turn a curse into a gift."

"A gift?" Jason sat his empty bowl aside. "Yeah, right. I can't see where howling at the moon and running wild, never knowing what I've done the next day—"

"But I believe you *can* know," she interrupted. "I believe that if you are strong enough, you can learn to think like a man, even while in the form of a wolf. If you are strong enough, you can control when you change."

God, she was insane. He was still rational enough to know that . . . yet he was desperate enough to want to believe her. If he could think like a man, even when the change happened, he could control what he did, know what he'd done the next day. And if he could control changing, he might live a fairly normal life. But that couldn't be possible . . . could it? He narrowed his eyes.

"If your people only hunt werewolves and kill them, what makes you think what you're suggesting is possible?"

The woman ran a hand through her hair. She glanced away from him. "For many years there have been legends, stories told of those who could shift, become an animal, or even become another person. In these legends, there are good and evil among the shifters. The good use their abilities to help and protect their own. But the evil ones have no loyalty, no love, only hate and the need to destroy others. I have heard that a pure heart can save one from the beast. I have heard that if Unma Kin Sica bites one who can fight the call, the one bitten can save not only his own spirit, but the spirit of the one who bit him."

Jason had hoped she might not be crazy, but her mumbo-jumbo wasn't doing anything to convince him of that. He'd always thought of himself as a good person before the wolf attack, but he wouldn't go as far as calling himself "pure." To his knowledge, he'd never killed anyone in wolf form, certainly never anyone while human. He'd never messed around with married women, although he'd certainly messed around with his share of unmarried ones. He'd worked hard at his boring position as a CPA in a Dallas accounting firm, but he'd played hard, too. He supposed he wasn't a bad person, not before the accident, and he didn't think since. During the past three years, he'd worked at odd jobs to support himself, always on the move, always searching, always aware of the promise he had made to his brother.

"I was once a Boy Scout," he mumbled. "Maybe that will count for something."

"You were a scout?" Her dark brows arched. "You tracked boys?"

Jason sighed and rubbed his throbbing eye. He reached toward one of his feet. Tala's knife flashed toward him.

"Do not release your ankles."

It was back to business as usual. "My foot itches, okay?"

She relaxed. "You may scratch it, but no sudden moves."

31

Reaching down, he scratched his foot and bit back a groan as pain from his burns registered. "I have another problem. Nature calls. Maybe you can teach me to control that, too. It would save me a lot of wasted time."

"Nature calls?" She frowned. Her eyes widened a fraction. "You wish to relieve yourself?"

"Now you're catching on. Speak English much?"

She shook her head. "No. We have our own language. Passed down through the ages. But we are taught English and other languages from childhood as protection. If we are forced out into the world, we must be prepared."

He'd been joking. Her English was good; she just seemed uneducated about slang. "So . . . you said something this morning about being the one chosen. What does that mean?"

" *Ashi'doltii*. It means 'I have been chosen.' I have been given special gifts. It has been many years since one like me has been born among The People."

Jason still wasn't positive that the woman and her cave might not be a hallucination. Maybe he'd eaten bad mushrooms during the last full moon, and they were just now kicking in. "What kind of 'gifts'?"

He thought she wouldn't answer. She fingered the knife she held and stared at him for a moment. "It is wrong to speak of it with outsiders, but I think you do not believe the things I tell you. I have visions. I can sometimes look at a man and see the wolf within, or at a wolf, and see a man staring back. I can find the evil ones before they find us. I am the huntress."

Despite the far-fetched garbage it seemed she fed him, Jason's interest was piqued. "Then you can find the one that attacked me and my brother? There can't be that many werewolves roaming around Canada."

Her gaze darted away from him. She shifted, as if uncomfortable with the conversation. "You are wrong. There are many. The visions only come to me if they pose a future threat to my people, or to someone I care about. The woman; I saw her in a vision. I saw where she stood, under the lights to tempt men. Then I saw her stalking our camp. I had to stop her before the vision came to pass."

Jason moved closer to her. "Is it true that if I kill the one that bit me, the curse will be ended? I will go back to being a normal man?"

Slowly, her gaze wandered back to him. "Yes. That is true. When the source of the evil planted within you has been slain, the beast can no longer live inside of you."

Suddenly, Jason realized he shouldn't hope he was dreaming or hallucinating. He'd been roaming around for the past three years searching and had turned up nothing. This woman might lead him to the one that attacked him and his brother. She might be his only hope! Of course it was ridiculous to believe her, but then again, it had seemed ridiculous to believe in werewolves a few years ago. A little show of power would soothe his skepticism.

"What else can you do besides find werewolves and see into the future? Can you move objects with your mind? Show me these powers you claim to have."

She rose. "My gifts are not for all to see." The woman walked over and cut the ropes from around his ankles. "Come, I will take you to the forest to attend your personal matters. Do not try to escape again," she warned. "You know I can catch you."

She had caught him once. But that didn't mean she could catch him again. Yet . . . did he want to escape? If he wasn't at the mercy of a crazy woman, Tala Soaringbird might be Jason's best hope of finding the monster that bit him. If she couldn't find the beast, she'd said she could teach him to control it in himself. It sounded too good to be true.

Jason followed her out of the cave, down the steep incline and into the forest. He might be taller, but he had to hurry to keep up. "I do get some privacy, right?"

"I have no desire to watch you," she assured him. "But remember, if you run, I will catch you. There is no escaping."

A woman shouldn't be so confident, he decided, or goad him; it brought out his competitive side. He was half-tempted to run just to prove her wrong. But then again, he wasn't sure that he wanted to escape. Should he run before the crazy woman ended up killing him? He didn't have long to make his decision.

Chapter Three

Tala expected the man to flee. He would have trouble believing her, believing she lived the way she lived, held the powers she held. Even if he'd been forced to accept that not all things were as he'd once thought, the human mind had trouble embracing what was not familiar, or seemed illogical. When confronting Haidar, the white man's instinct had been to fight. With her, it would be to flee. He considered his strength and intelligence superior. It was a fault of most men.

She waited, her senses alert, ready to spring into action the second she heard his footfalls. But he did not run as she expected. He reappeared a few moments later.

"All right. I'm done."

"You will not try to run away?"

He drew a hand over his forehead. "Not right now.

I want to hear more about your tribe, about your powers, and about you."

The night darkened his eyes, but she knew they were the color of a lake in winter. Despite their frosty shade, they sent out heat. She felt the warmth of his gaze move over her. It was an odd sensation. Tala was not used to men looking at her as if she were a desirable woman. There were no men in her tribe not related to her by blood, and even if that were not the case, she was forbidden to consider them.

To still her thoughts she said, "The hour grows late. We will sleep tonight and talk tomorrow." She started back toward her lodge, then caught wind of a familiar scent. "Stop." She placed an arm in front of the white man. "There is one waiting, watching. You must place your arm around my neck and act as if you need help to walk."

"Who is it?" he asked softly.

"Haidar. He does not want you among us. He is the leader of our tribe. If you want to stay, if you want to live, you must do all that I ask."

The man did not immediately acquiesce. She suspected he did not readily follow orders, from women or anyone else. Finally, though, he put his arm around her. She felt the heat of his bare skin through her shirt. His breath stirred her hair. He did not lean heavily upon her, but walked slowly, shuffling his steps as if he were weak.

His touch burned her skin. Tala felt like she'd been running a long way by the time they reached her cave and went inside. Flustered by her reaction to the white man, she scrambled from beneath his arm.

"I must bind you again," she said. "We both need rest."

"Look, I'm not going anywhere tonight," he argued. "I can't sleep that way. You're going to have to trust me."

Trust him? Tala could not. The beast within might not have fully taken over, but this was an outsider, a white man, one who had tried to escape her once already. Yet, since he did not wish to be bound, it might take great effort to subdue him. She hadn't slept for three days. Her journey to the city and tracking the evil one had exhausted her. She threw more wood on her small fire and lit some incense.

Snatching up a blanket, she moved to the entrance of her cave and sat with her back against the wall. "You may sleep on my furs," she told him. "I will watch you."

He moved to the hides spread on the ground and sat. "I hope I don't drool in my sleep or anything," he muttered. "It's not very polite of me to take your bed either. How about we switch places, or better still . . . share the bed?"

Tala had trouble understanding whether the man was serious or trying to make a joke. "It would be foolish of me to let you guard the way out, and more foolish to share the bed with you."

He laughed. "You need to lighten up."

She glanced down at her body. "You believe I am heavy?"

The white man laughed again, shook his head, and ran a hand through his long, tangled hair. He flung one of the furs back and crawled underneath. "Have it your way. For now."

The incense she burned would soon have a lulling effect on the man. Beneath her breath, Tala began to chant—to cast her spell. She saw her captive's eyes grow heavy, watched his chest rise and fall with steadiness. A moment later, he was asleep. She rose and sat before him. His face needed to be washed. Tala took a cloth and gently cleansed the day's exertions from him. She traced the strong line of his jaw. He needed to remove his whiskers. She lifted up a strand of his hair. It felt different than hers. Not as coarse.

Her gaze moved over him and she frowned. The burns on his arms and the slashes she'd made on his skin with her knife were already healing. She must replace them. The man would not like that. But as the Elders had remembered the old ways and agreed that Tala should honor her debt to the man, the outsider would be allowed inside their camp only until she had healed him. Then Tala would be forced to cast the sacred spells to erase her people from his memory.

She had lied when promising that last bit, though. She could not erase his memory of them. Doing so would erase what she planned to teach him as well. The hole she dug herself for this man kept getting deeper. She owed him a debt, but her people did not know that. The night of the attack, she had let their enemy escape. Even if she had killed the female, the male might want revenge against Tala. He might seek her out. She might have placed her tribe in danger— had already placed them in danger simply by bringing the white man here.

"Why have you haunted my dreams?" she whispered, staring down at the man. "Why can I not kill you and be done with it, with all of it?"

His lips did not speak an answer, but along with the rest of him, they intrigued her. His mouth was well-shaped. She ran a finger over those lips. Slowly, she lowered her face to his, her heart pounding. She tasted him, felt the firmness and texture of him. Then suddenly his hand gripped the back of her neck and pulled her down onto the furs.

Jason's mind felt foggy. He couldn't seem to open his eyes, but he did register sensation. Wonderful sensation. Human sensation. The soft feel of a woman beneath him. The innocent press of her lips against his. He might be dreaming, probably was given the fact he hadn't kissed a woman, or anything else that he knew of, for three years. Dreaming was all right; he'd take whatever he could get.

The sweet taste of her mouth made him groan. He coaxed her to open to him and explored her with his tongue, drank from her like a man who'd been stranded in the desert and had fallen upon an oasis. She didn't fight him, which also strongly led him to believe that he was dreaming. He knew who she was, who he would conjure in his mind, and Tala Soaringbird would as soon gut him with her sharp little knife as kiss him.

"Kiss me back," he instructed. "Taste me like I'm tasting you."

Her tongue dipped into his mouth; her arms went around his neck. He felt her tremble beneath him, but did she shake with fear, or with passion? Since it was his dream, he decided upon passion and moved atop her. His hand closed over her breast—not naked flesh as he had hoped, but still, a nice handful even if she did wear a shirt. A moment later, pain exploded inside his head. The dream slipped away—*she* slipped away—and all he had left were the dregs of morning.

The sun over the opening above beat down into his eyes. With a groan, Jason flung an arm over them. "Why in the hell does my head feel like it's going to explode?"

"Too much sleep. It is not good for a person."

He managed to sit, but the pounding grew stronger. When he cupped his head, he felt a knot on the back of his skull. "Where'd I get this bump?"

Tala said nothing, so he glanced up. She sat before the fire making something that smelled delicious. "You might have banged your head on the floor while you slept," she offered, her expression blank. "It is made of rock."

Jason sighed. "Yeah, I know it's made of rock. Why do you live in a cave?"

"We all live in caves," she said. "We have meeting lodges in the forest below that are hidden beneath thatched roofs so that your people who fly in the air do not spot us, but these caves offer us more protection. There are many caverns on this side of the bluff, and one very large one where we sometimes gather; and lower there is a special place."

"How many of you are there?"

She glanced down, stirring whatever simmered in the pot over the fire. "Not many. Once, we were a great people, but many have died, and our numbers grow smaller still. We do not seek mates from the outside. Too many in our tribe have the same bloodlines, and we do not join with those of the same ancestry. It is forbidden."

"In my society, too," he said and smiled at her.

When she smiled back, he thought her mouth looked different. Her lips looked red, swollen. Snatches of a dream floated to him—touching her, kissing her—then as quickly floated away.

"You wish to eat?"

"Smells good," he admitted.

"First, you must remove the whiskers from your face and the tangles from your hair." Her gaze moved over him, and by the pinch of her lips, she didn't like what she saw. "Even an animal cleans itself."

Jason wasn't dirty. He'd paid for a shower the day he'd met Tala in the alley. So he hadn't shaved for a few days, hadn't combed his hair. He did make it a point to brush his teeth on a regular basis, especially during a full moon when he had no idea what he might have eaten the night before.

"I'll need my bag, and some water."

The woman reached behind her and handed him his belongings. He could tell she'd searched the bag's meager contents. Jason wished he had another T-shirt, but the one he'd been wearing the night the two creatures attacked him was the last of his limited supply. "My razor?" he asked.

"This?" She held up the blade. "It has a sharp edge. It is like a knife, a weapon."

"I can't shave without it," he pointed out.

She fondled the knife at her belt, as if to remind him that her weapon could do far more damage than his razor; then she surrendered the item. She poured him a bowl of water, laid a thick slab of soap beside the bowl, and gave him a rag he assumed he should use as a towel.

Shaving without a mirror might prove tricky, but he'd done it before. He brushed his teeth first. She watched him while she tended their breakfast. His razor was dull, but he managed to scrape off his whiskers. He dug an old brush from his bag and wished he hadn't been so lax in his appearance. It hadn't seemed important while tracking down werewolves. Once the brush moved smoothly through his hair, he returned his toiletries to his bag.

"Better?" he asked.

She stared at him, then slowly nodded. "Yes," she answered. Then, as if she'd forgotten her business, she filled a bowl with food and handed it to him.

The meal looked like some kind of stew again, but there were berries melted into the mixture along with meat. He tried a spoonful, and thought it tasted very much like sweet and sour . . . something. He ate a few more bites. "What is it?" he finally asked.

"Skunk."

Jason spit the last mouthful he'd chewed back into the bowl. "What?"

Tala frowned. "You do not like it?"

"Maybe if you hadn't told me what it was," he answered. He set the bowl aside.

"You asked." She pointed out. "And we must make due with what is given to us by the forest."

He felt tempted to grab his toothbrush again. "I don't understand why you live the way you do."

Snatching up his bowl, she ladled its uneaten contents back into her pot. "I have told you. We do not mix with the outside. We live by the old ways. It has served us well since the beginning of time."

Jason was confused regarding more than one issue. "You don't go to the grocery store, but you have a car stashed somewhere so you can drive to the city in search of werewolves?"

"I did not say that I had a vehicle." She rose and stretched. "You assumed so."

Of course he assumed so. And the way her movement pulled her buckskin shirt tight against her breasts proved distracting. "If you didn't drive, how'd you get there and back?"

"There are other ways to move from one place to another." She turned, and she had her knife. "But enough of this talk. I must prepare you. My brother and my uncle will visit today. You must appear very sick, wounded."

He scooted back. "Oh no you don't. You're not carving on me again."

"It is necessary."

He rose, hoping the fact that he towered over her would change her mind. She didn't make a move toward him, but stood staring . . . waiting. A moment later pain ripped through his stomach. He doubled over, then fell back down to the furs. The pain was sudden, came out of nowhere, and was suspicious.

"What did you do? Poison me?"

"It will pass," she assured him. "I thought that you would fight me about the cuts I must make."

Jason bit back a groan as another sharp pain tore through his belly. A sweat broke out on his forehead. Damn her, she was crazy. He had to get away from her before she killed him! His vision blurred when he

43

glanced toward the cave exit. Jason tried to rise, stumbled, and fell to his knees.

"I do not wish to hurt you," the woman said softly.

"So you keep telling me." Jason felt trapped, helpless. It wasn't a good combination. More than pain clawed at his insides. He felt the change coming. His flesh itched, his gums hurt. "I guess you were right. It is happening more often. It's even daylight. I don't want to hurt you, either. Get the hell out of here!"

Instead of obeying him, she stepped closer. "Fight the beast's power over you. Hold it back."

"I can't," he growled. "Run!"

Her chin lifted. "I will not run. Fight the beast within you, or fight me. Those are your only choices."

Tala Soaringbird might be crazy and a sadist, but she was still a woman. And Jason wouldn't hurt a woman, intentionally. "I don't know how to fight it!"

"Focus," she commanded. "See yourself as a man and only a man."

He closed his eyes. While his stomach twisted into knots, and sweat ran down his temples, Jason tried to picture himself as a man. The man he once was. A human, and nothing else. He couldn't stop the other visions from clouding his mind, though. The couple who'd attacked him in the alley. Wolflike creatures that walked on two legs; red, glowing eyes; fangs bared. "No!" he shouted, his body trembling. He would not become one of them. He'd die first.

"You have two arms," he heard Tala say, then felt her fingers slide down them. "Two legs." Again, he felt her hands move down his limbs. "You are a man."

Afraid if he opened his eyes, she would see them glowing in the dim lighting of the cave, Jason kept them closed. He tried to focus on her, on the sound of her voice, on the warm touch of her fingers moving over his skin. He was a man. She was a woman. He didn't want to hurt her, didn't want her to see him as anything but human. Slowly, the pain subsided. His teeth retracted. Exhausted, he fell to his knees and crawled toward Tala's furs.

She helped him beneath their thick covering, saying, "Among us, there are many from different cultures. Once, we all came together for the shared cause of survival. Our ceremonies and our language are a mixture of who we once were. There are those among us who have survived the Sun Dance. A few shallow slashes upon your skin are nothing compared to that. You must learn to endure pain, control it just as you will control the beast."

Chills wracked Jason's body. Even through the churning in his stomach and his exhaustion over fighting back the wolf, he understood her persistence.

"Give me the knife," he said. "I'll do it."

She frowned at him. "It would be foolish of me to trust you with a weapon."

God, she annoyed him. "Well, haven't you ever done anything foolish in your life?"

The question pricked Tala's conscience. She *had* done something foolish: She had brought this man among her people. She had lied for him—and worse. If he took her knife and used it against her, she would deserve her fate. Fear had risen in her when the change began to take Jason, and again she realized the danger in which she had placed both herself and her tribe.

"If we're going to be roommates, I need a show of

trust from you," the man said between gasps of pain.

Tala had never trusted an outsider. She had been raised to be leery of all but her own kind. She had drugged the man's food because she knew he did not take his life or his situation seriously. The effects would soon subside, but she felt bad that she had tricked him, worse that she must cut him. But as a warrior, a protector of her tribe, her heart could not be bigger than her duty. Personal feelings were not hers to command; they were dictated by her destiny.

The man extended his hand. He had long slender fingers and short clean nails. His hand had touched her the night before, had cupped her breast and sent forbidden sensations through her. She had panicked and clubbed him over the head to escape. But he did not remember. Her spells, along with the incense meant to fog his mind, were strong.

Slowly, she slid her knife's handle into his open palm. Then Tala held her breath. The white man set his jaw and made a shallow wound across his chest. He did not cry out. He did not hesitate to open another cut upon his arm. She saw a flare of defiance in his light blue eyes before he handed her the knife and turned away. Soon, he would be unconscious, which was how she wanted her relatives to find him. If a man could not speak, he could not bring trouble upon himself.

In a tired voice, she heard him say, "You know, if you could just find me a shirt, you'd save us both a lot of trouble."

She gave him a rare smile. Of course she would borrow a shirt for him, but first, Haidar and her uncle must see his wounds. She reached forward and touched his shoulder. He did not turn toward her. Tala's fingers lingered on his skin. Smooth, warm flesh stretched over muscle and bone. White man though he was, his flesh held the kiss of the sun. With his long dark hair, he might pass for one of her tribe—except for his sky-colored eyes.

"How is the man?"

Tala jerked her hand away. Her brother and uncle had entered without her notice. Normally anyone entering would announce their presence and ask permission, but the visit had been arranged during the council meeting. Again, her preoccupation with the white man had caused her to be careless. She should have heard the men approach.

"He is not well," she answered. "As you can see."

Her relatives moved closer and stared down at Jason Donavon. Tala could not see the white man since he had turned away, but she hoped his cuts still dripped gore and that a sheen of sweat still coated his body. He groaned and pulled his knees up to his chest.

"The cuts do not look deep," Haidar observed. "What is wrong with him?"

"Infection," Tala answered. "I will need the healing waters later tonight to help him sweat the poison from his body. It may take many nights to see him healed."

The news made her brother frown. "You will do all in your power to make certain this man leaves us as soon as possible?"

"Of course." Tala lowered her gaze. "He is a burden. Why would I want him among us?" When Haidar did not respond, she glanced up and met his dark stare.

"Keep him from the others," he commanded. "We

would not want him to spread his sickness, the way his people have done among ours for centuries."

She lifted a brow. "That was many years ago, brother."

"Time does not change the lessons learned. His kind and ours do not mix. The white man smiles at us while clutching a knife behind his back. We live by the old ways, so we must not make the same mistakes our grandfathers and theirs before them made."

Tala had been taught these lessons, too. The whites were her enemy in more ways than one. Still, she would argue: "Is it not the same among all things that there are good and bad? Should all be judged by the actions of a few?"

"Your sister is right," her uncle said to Haidar. "We may live by the old ways, but this a new world. Our duty is not to judge the past mistakes of men, but to live as we have always lived. To fight the evil we understand and leave the rest to those who live in the world without shadows."

Haidar bowed in acknowledgment of their uncle's wisdom. "Heal the outsider so he can be gone," he said to Tala, then left the cave.

Her uncle settled across from her, nodding toward the white man. "The people are talking."

She was not surprised.

"They are curious about this man. Most have never seen an outsider up close."

"Nor will they, by my brother's command," she said. "Maybe it is best to keep him from them, and they from him."

"The Elders have decided otherwise," he reminded her. "You were right before: Our world is shrinking.

48

We must learn to fit in. This man could teach us ways that are more modern."

"But Haidar—"

"—Takes his role as leader seriously," he finished for her. "Just as you take your duties to heart and stand by them. We will see what kind of man the outsider is, then decide." Her uncle sniffed the air. "Now fix your old uncle a bowl of what smells so good."

Tala's heart lurched. She had not made much of the stew, only enough to disable the white man for a short time. She could not feed her uncle something that would make him sick, or explain why she had ruined the food.

"It is skunk," she said weakly.

Her uncle wrinkled his nose, then shrugged. "Not my favorite, but an old man who can no longer hunt for himself must take what is offered."

The way of the tribe was to feed those too old or too young to fend for themselves. Tala and her brother took care of their uncle. They had lost their parents at a young age, and their uncle had taken in three children. Now Tala and her brother repaid the kindness, though their sister no longer could.

"It does not taste good, uncle," she argued. "I will make you something better and bring it to you later."

"You worry too much," the man grumbled. "This will be fine. Pass me a bowl."

Tala had lied too many times for the white man's sake. She would not make her uncle ill for him. She lifted the pan.

"The stew, uncle, it is—"

Suddenly the white man turned over on the furs and

flung his arms out, knocking the pan from her hand. Its contents splattered across her shirt and over the floor. Her patient mumbled something and settled back down.

"Now see what he has done," she complained. "He has made a mess and wasted the meal."

Her uncle sighed. He lumbered to his feet, his motions slow with age. "You will bring me something later?" he asked.

"Yes, uncle," she promised.

"Take care, little one."

She smiled. It was a name he had called her as a child. Fondly, she watched her uncle hobble toward the cave entrance. Tala began cleaning up the mess. After removing the stew from the floor, she glanced at her stained shirt. She rose, went to the baskets that held her clothing and removed a clean tunic. She slipped the stained one off over her head.

"You owe me one."

His voice started her. Tala wheeled around, but clutched the tunic to her breasts. The white man's eyes were open.

"Owe you one?" she repeated, unsure of what he meant.

"For making sure the old man didn't eat that crap."

How did he know the words she and her uncle exchanged? "We were not speaking your language. How do you know—"

"It didn't take a genius to figure out that he wanted something to eat and that you didn't want him to have it," he explained. "What were you speaking? Cree?"

"As I have told you. The language is our own." Tala turned away and slipped a clean shirt over her head.

50

"One derived from many cultures. We call ourselves *Oyate Ba'cho.*"

"Never heard of it," he muttered.

After pulling her long hair over one shoulder, Tala poured a bowl of fresh water and found a cloth. She bent before her patient and washed the blood from his shallow cuts. "None have heard of it. That is because we have remained a secret for many years. The old man is my uncle."

"Your uncle?" Jason Donavon lifted a brow. "So your parents are here, too? And brothers and sisters?"

Sadness found her. It had been many years, but she remembered her parents, and she missed them. "No, my parents are dead. Haidar, he is my brother, and I have a sister—but she is gone from here."

"That goon is your brother?"

Tala frowned. "That word does not sound like a nice one. Yes, he is my brother."

"I'm sorry about your parents. What happened to them?"

He did look sorry, sad for her. Tala wondered why he would. He did not know her; she was a stranger, an enemy to him. Her grief had been locked inside for many years: Her people believed one did not speak of the dead, or it would bring them from the spirit world.

"My mother died of a weak heart when I was seven summers. My father . . . he could not live without her. It was like asking the moon to go without the stars, the sun to go without the sky. He took his life so he could be with her. He loved her more than anything."

A strong hand closed over hers and stopped the unconscious motion of cleaning blood already gone from his chest. "That must have been hard on you. Losing them both."

The pain had dulled with time, but as a child, she could not understand. Nor could she as a woman. She had tried to make what her father did an honorable act in her mind; but still, he had made her feel unimportant to him by taking his life. It was as if because her destiny had been decided, he had believed she did not need anything else . . . or anyone.

"It *was* difficult," she admitted, then snatched her hand from beneath his. "Is your sickness better? If it is not I can give you—"

"No thanks," he interrupted. "You've given me enough for one day."

Tala glanced away from his wry expression. "I told you why I tricked you. And I told you the sickness would soon pass." When he said nothing, she asked, "What is the 'one I owe you' for knocking the pan from my hand before I was forced to explain the drugged stew to my uncle?"

"It just means that you owe me a favor."

She felt his eyes move over her. It made her uncomfortable. "What would you ask of me?"

"I assume you mean within the limits of what you would consider reasonable?"

She glanced back at him. "Yes. It must be reasonable."

"I could use a bath." His eyes moved over her again. "So could you. You're wearing splatters of stew on your face."

Her first instinct was to wipe the food away, but then the man would think she cared how she looked to him. "A bath can be arranged," was what she said instead.

Chapter Four

They had left the cave, moved down the incline, and entered the bluff at a lower level. Jason was glad he wasn't claustrophobic. He was also glad that he could see exceptionally well in the darkness, because the tunnels Tala led him through were narrow and pitch black. There were some places he could barely squeeze through. The walls became damper as they moved lower into the caverns, and he was beginning to think they'd never reach their destination when he saw the proverbial light at the end of the tunnel. A few feet more and he stumbled into paradise.

The cavern was huge. At least, compared to the tunnels they'd taken to reach it. Flaming torches were mounted on the walls, casting shadows around the large enclosure. The light bounced off stalactites above. Below, steam swirled around his legs. He caught the scent of sulfur.

"This is one huge underground hot spring."

"It is a sacred place," Tala said as he followed her through the mist. "A place for healing. A place to cleanse impurities from one's body, and from one's mind. Take my hand. I will lead you down to the water. There are rocks, and the steam makes it difficult to see them."

He took her smaller hand in his. A current passed between their fingers. She jerked back a little, and he knew she'd felt it, too. He grasped her hand more firmly and she led him down the rocks. He stumbled a couple of times, but once they reached the water the steam thinned somewhat. The pool was crystal clear. It bubbled.

"The water is hot," Tala warned. "You must allow your body to adjust by degrees."

"It doesn't seem to matter if I get burned, remember?" Jason asked, showing her his healed arms as proof. "Doesn't the fact that my body regenerates itself mean that I'm immortal?"

Tala removed her moccasins and her leggings. Her shift hung to the tops of her smooth thighs. "No," she answered. "You can die the same as any other man."

"The heart, or the brain," he guessed. "Those are my weak spots. I've read that they are the only two organs that can't regenerate themselves in ... well, someone like me."

She slid her feet into the water. "That is true. And there is another way to die."

"I'm sure you can't wait to tell me what it is," he said dryly, eyeing her legs. They were long and slender.

She spoke: "Although your body will heal itself

when you are young and strong, you cannot turn back time, or make it stand still. You are not immortal. I have found the carcasses of those like you who have died of natural causes. Of old age."

He'd never thought of growing old as a werewolf. Of suffering his curse for that long. It was too upsetting a possibility, and too difficult to accept. "That doesn't make sense to me."

Tala shrugged. "It may not make sense, but does what you have become make sense?" She glanced around. "Does this secret place make sense? Do I?"

She had him there. And under different circumstances, she could have him anywhere, Jason thought as his gaze ran the length of her legs. He sat beside her.

"No," he answered. "None of this makes sense to me."

She rose. "In time, maybe it will. Do you wish to bathe?"

The steaming pool looked enticing. Almost as enticing as Tala did, standing bare-legged before him. Jason figured he was pretty bad off if he could feel attracted to a woman who'd taken him prisoner, cut him up, poisoned him, and planned to do who knew what to him next.

"If you'll join me," he found himself saying.

To his surprise, she nodded. "I am here. It would be foolish not to take advantage of a bath." She moved away, disappearing into the steam. "I will be watching you."

Jason didn't know how she'd watch him. The vapor rising from the pool was so thick that an instant later, he couldn't see her. "I wish I could say the same," he muttered, then rose and stripped off his jeans. He climbed down the smooth rocks and eased his body into the warm water. It swirled around him, embraced him like a wet, willing lover. He moved deeper, the water rising to his waist, then higher to his chest. He sighed. It felt almost better than what he remembered sex to be like. He couldn't see her, but he heard Tala enter the water farther down to his left, near where they had entered the cavern. She would place herself between him and escape.

Was she naked? Of course she would be if she were bathing! Jason wondered why she trusted him enough to place herself in such a vulnerable position, but then, there wasn't much about the woman he considered weak.

"Are you still here?" he asked.

"I am here."

Her sultry voice floated to him through the steam. She didn't sound that far away. Jason waded toward her. He was drawn to her. Maybe he would be to any woman who knew what he was and who would still sleep in the same room with him. Strange, but it almost felt good to have someone know, to have his secret exposed. It was a hell of burden to carry around.

"How about you scrub my back, and I'll scrub yours?"

Silence.

"Hello?" he called.

"I do not think what you ask is proper for two who are not mated."

"Of course it's not proper. That's why I suggested it. A big bad wolf should act like one."

Silence again.

Then, "I do not understand your words at times. I do not understand you."

Jason kept moving, sensing her closeness even if the steam made seeing her difficult. "It's hard to tease someone who doesn't laugh at my jokes."

"I do not find you amusing. And do not come closer."

He stopped. She must have excellent hearing. "I—"

"Be quiet," she suddenly ordered. "Listen."

A steady dripping noise where the water trickled down the walls and into the lake was the only sound he registered . . . at first. Then a subtler noise: the light brush of feet against rock floors.

"It is my brother again. I told him to give me privacy. He is suspicious of you."

The mist suddenly parted and she stood before him, her dark hair wet, her bare shoulders gleaming with moisture.

"Quickly, move to the bank and climb out. Lie upon the rocks and be still, as if you are resting."

His gaze strayed lower than her shoulders. He saw her shape beneath the water: her full breasts, her slim torso, even her long legs.

"Hurry," she hissed. "Do not forget that your life is in danger here."

Jason found it difficult to concentrate on anything but the fact that she stood before him naked. Maybe she was right and the beast *was* taking over his humanity. He stared into her eyes, felt his nostrils flare slightly as he caught her scent—wildflowers, earth, sky. Nature's subtle gifts, not the heavy perfume he was used to smelling on women.

"Please."

Her whispered plea cleared his head. He hadn't thought she knew what that word meant either. So far, all she'd done was order him around. He fought back his natural instinct to defy her, his animal instinct to defile her, and moved toward the bank. He climbed out of the water, grabbed one of the blankets she'd brought along, and spread out on the warm rocks. A few minutes later, her brother appeared. Jason closed his eyes.

Tala made a pretense of bathing, her back toward the bank. When she felt her brother's regard, she dunked down in the water and turned.

"Why do you interrupt my privacy?"

"Why do you place yourself in such a vulnerable position with a stranger?"

She glanced over to the white man. He lay wrapped in a blanket, his eyes closed. "He is weak and no threat to me. Bathing has depleted all his strength."

"If he is weak, how did you get him to the Sacred Waters by yourself? I came to your cave to offer help in moving him. When you were not there, I came to see if you had moved him by yourself."

"I am stronger than I look," she reminded him. "Because you and I are of the same blood, I think you forget sometimes that I have powers the rest of you do not have. That *you* do not have."

He sighed. "You are the chosen one, Tala, but you are still a woman. I do not think it is right, you caring for this man, being alone with him. When he grows stronger—"

"It will be time for him to leave," she interrupted.

"Until he is able, again, I must ask that you let me care for him. It is my duty. The Council agreed."

Her brother threw his arms in the air. "The Council is made up of old men. They have forgotten the passions of the young. This man will see you as a woman, not as the rest of our tribe sees you. As they *must* see you. He may not respect the gifts given to you. He may try to steal them."

The possibility caused her heart to leap traitorously. A man had never pursued Tala. She had never really felt like a woman, maybe because of that fact. Her brother believed, like himself, she only needed her destiny to make her feel whole and happy. He was wrong. Perhaps if she had not romanticized the love her parents had felt for one another, she would not long to experience the same.

"I will be careful," Tala said. And she would. All knew the lesson about playing with fire. She must not get too close to the flame—but that did not mean its warmth would not draw her.

"Do you wish for me to stay and help you return the white man to your lodge?"

Tala shook her head. "After he is rested, I will help him return. I wish to finish my bath."

"Be careful. You know that our blood, the blood of our parents, is weak. Our sister has proven so."

They had not spoken of their sister for three years, but always the pain had been fresh inside of Tala. Meka had shamed them. She had turned her back on her own kind. She had turned her back on Tala. Once they had been close, almost of one mind, one heart. Now Tala bore the burden of her sister's shame. She carried the girl's sins within her.

"I am not like Meka," she said. "I am stronger, as are you, Brother."

He nodded, and for the first time, she saw that his heart also hurt over their sister's actions. Haidar turned and disappeared into the steam. Tala did not relax until she knew he had gone.

"He is gone," she said.

The white man opened his eyes. He stood, tying a blanket around his waist. "Your big brother doesn't like me, but aren't you old enough to get into trouble without his interference?"

She did not understand. "What trouble?"

He shrugged. "Any trouble you'd like. I bet he's run off all your boyfriends. Men who would call upon you," he clarified.

The conversation made her uncomfortable. "I told you, I am the one chosen. There have been no men in my life . . . not in the way of which you speak."

His dark brows rose. "Are you telling me you're a virgin?"

"Keep your voice down," she whispered. Sound bounced off the rock walls and carried up to the chambers above.

"Well, no, it's not anything to shout about," the white man agreed in a flat tone. "Twenty-something-year-old virgins are probably easier to find these days than werewolves."

"Do you make fun of me?" she demanded.

He raised his arms, as if in surrender. "Calm down, Warrior Princess. I just find it hard to believe. Look at you. You're beautiful, perfect. I can't believe a man hasn't noticed that before now."

A hot flush spread through her body. Tala did not

believe it had anything to do with the warm water that surrounded her.

"My powers are fueled by my purity," she whispered. "I am forbidden."

His cool eyes roamed her face. "Well, you know what they say about forbidden fruit."

That was one she did know. It was said to be the sweetest. She noticed how muscular Jason's body was, how chiseled his jawline now that he had removed the hair from his face. "Yes, I know what is said about forbidden fruit."

He smiled. "Of course, they wouldn't say that if it weren't true."

She could not speak, could think of nothing clever to say to ease the tension suddenly between them. This man could make her feel breathless, a longing for what she knew nothing about, with only his eyes. He was bold. He did not look away from her or try to hide what she knew to be only a physical attraction he felt toward her.

"We should return." She broke eye contact with him. "I wish to get out of the water now."

He shrugged. "Who's stopping you?"

Tala hoped the man made another joke. "You are stopping me. I need my blanket."

Bending to retrieve the object, he asked, "This blanket?"

Her skin had started to shrivel. "Yes, that one."

"You're sure? This is the blanket you need? Another blanket won't do?"

"I do not have another blanket," she said, but felt an exasperated smile tug at her mouth over his silliness.

61

His teasing grin faded. "God, you should smile more often." He shook his head, dropped the blanket where she could reach it quickly upon climbing out, then turned his back. "On second thought, maybe you shouldn't."

Tala hurried toward the bank. She snatched the blanket and wrapped it beneath her arms. "Thank you for allowing me my privacy." He turned, and she realized they stood too close, both wet, both naked beneath their coverings.

"I haven't lost my manners . . . at least not when I can help myself."

"The gift I have offered is to help you help yourself. Will you take my gift?"

He frowned. "What was the alternative again?"

The truth was always better than a lie. "Death."

Jason Donavon ran a hand through his long, damp hair. "Well, you drive a hard bargain. Become your slave or die. I can just escape you know, any time I feel like it."

The man did not respect her powers because he'd seen nothing of them. "Come to my lodge. I want to show you something."

One of his dark brows lifted. "Beautiful, exotic, half naked woman lures man to his death by promising to show him something. Did you ever see the movie, *How the West Was Won*? This reminds me of Jimmy Stewart going to look at the varmint with that half wild looking girl."

Tala sighed. She had no idea what he was talking about. She started to tell him so, but he lifted a hand.

"I know. You don't watch movies, and you don't know who Jimmy Stewart is. That's okay. Lead the way. Like Jimmy, I'll always want to see the varmint."

Chapter Five

Jason wished he had a pair of decent jeans, or maybe some of those leggings like Tala's brother wore. Since he'd roamed around so much, he'd kept his luggage light . . . real light. There were times during the past three years when he'd been so homesick, he'd only wanted to return to America. Of course, he couldn't. His parents, along with everyone else he knew, thought he had died in that hunting accident. For a time, Rick, his brother, had thought he'd died, too.

The family had buried an empty casket. Jason supposed the hospital hadn't wanted to admit to the family that they'd lost his body. That would spell a big lawsuit. While he'd been roaming around half out of his mind, unsure what had happened to him, his brother had returned to America with a nasty bite, a curse he wasn't aware he suffered, and the pain of burying a younger brother who was worse than dead.

Once Jason had understood what he'd become, and once he'd realized Rick was likely infected, as well, he'd gone home and told his brother what had happened. Rick had nearly passed out upon seeing him. The news that they were both werewolves hadn't been much easier for him to swallow. Where was Rick now? How was he coping?

"You have gone to another place in your mind."

Tala's words recaptured his attention. Jason sat upon the furs, her across from him, a small fire burning in the grate that separated them.

"Sorry," he said. "My mind wandered. Well? What did you want to show me?"

She drew a deep breath. "I should not reveal any of my powers to you. They are not meant to be shared with the outside world—with those who do not understand that there are those in the world different from themselves."

He laughed. "I don't think I'm included in that group. Not any longer."

"Watch the flame," she instructed.

He'd rather watch her. The firelight danced upon her dark skin, brought out the blue highlights in her hair. Reluctantly, Jason lowered his gaze to the small flame. It suddenly leapt to life, flared high and made him jump back. He swore it singed the hair on his arms. A moment later, the flame died again. His gaze snapped to Tala's face.

"Did you do that?"

"Would you like for me to do it again?"

Skeptical, he nodded.

Her dark eyes lowered to the fire. It flared, grew higher and higher. Jason had to scoot back again. He might be impressed, but he was also analytical.

"How do I know you're not over there throwing something to make it flare up like that? Heaven knows you've got enough strange potions around here."

"Shall I move to other side the cave and control the fire again?"

"Yeah, far enough away that you can't toss something into it."

She rose, moved to his side of the fire, then backed away until she stood almost at the cave's entrance. Jason waited. Tala seemed to focus entirely on the flame. He watched it climb almost to the ceiling.

"Damn," he whispered. "Can you control other things?"

Moving toward him, she settled on the furs. Jason sat beside her.

"What other things?" she asked.

"People."

"No," she answered. "It is forbidden to try. Man is given free will. It was written long ago that the one chosen could not take free will from another."

"Mine has been taken from me," he reminded her.

"This is true," she agreed. "Taken by a selfish act. I am sworn to use my powers for only good. I can also use them to fight evil, but the mind of one that is more beast than human cannot be controlled. There is not rational thought in the mind of the beast."

"I don't want to become one of them." He'd only meant to think the thought, not share his fears with her.

Her hand touched his. "I do not know if I can help you, but I would like to try."

When he turned to look down at her, he realized

how close they sat to one another. "Why?"

She lowered her gaze. "To see if I can maybe help someone else. I mean, someone like you."

He snorted. "Oh, I see. I get to be your experiment? Your lab rat?"

Her gaze snapped back up to his face. "I could have left you. I could have killed you. I chose to spare you."

Jason leaned closer. "And all this because you owe me some type of debt for fighting beside you that night in the alley?"

"One kind act for another. An eye for an eye. A tooth for a tooth. It took many words to convince the Elders to apply the old ways to the life of an outsider."

"What happens if you can't help me?" When she refused to look at him, he gently turned her face toward his. "You have to kill me, right?"

She nodded.

Well, here was another thing to add to his list of what *not* to look for in a girlfriend. Jason's hand dropped from her face. "I'd want you to," he found himself admitting. "If you couldn't help me, if there was no way I wouldn't turn into one of those monsters, I'd want you to kill me. I'd be beyond helping my brother, anyway."

"Your brother. You and he, your hearts are close to one another?"

Jason nodded. "I guess we weren't always close. In fact, I feel closer to him now, even being apart. I guess because I know what he's going through. I promised him that I'd find the creature that attacked us and kill it, and I haven't found a damn thing in three years. I haven't seen him, either."

Tala wet her lips, bringing them to his attention.

She had a great mouth. "You have managed to stay alive, to keep the beast from taking complete control. I imagine he has done the same."

"I hope so." Jason ran a hand through his hair. "Why haven't you asked how it happened?"

Her dark eyes darted away from him again. "How it happened is not so important, only that it did happen and what the consequences were. I imagine you were in the wilderness. Maybe hunting."

"Are you sure that you don't read minds, too?" he asked with a laugh. "That's exactly what happened."

"I am sorry for you," she said. "For you and your brother. I understand your pain. I miss my sister."

He ran his fingers along her hand. "Why did your sister leave?"

Tala pulled away from his touch. "She could not follow our ways. She wanted things from the outside world."

"Can't say as I blame her. Can you?"

She twisted her fingers together. "We all have our duties, our places. My sister was raised in the way that would keep her safe, but she did not want to be safe. She did not want to take her place, but to create a place for herself outside."

"Ah, the black sheep of family."

"What does that mean?"

"Trouble-maker. Someone who marches to the beat of their own drum and to hell with everyone else."

"Yes, she is like that," Tala agreed.

Jason couldn't resist reaching out and snatching a piece of her long hair. He liked the way it felt between his fingers. "But not you. You have accepted your duty."

"My duty to the tribe is my life. My powers are a gift. I am not allowed to want or need more."

"Seems like a lot to sacrifice for the privilege of watching out for everyone else, or making a fire grow at your command."

His hand suddenly flew away from her hair, but not by his own doing. She narrowed her gaze. "You belittle my powers?"

Still trying to figure out what had just happened, Jason said, "No. I'm only saying it doesn't seem fair. I'm saying the payoff might not be worth what the powers have cost you."

"There are no choices," she explained. "It is foolish to envy what one cannot have."

"I'm just surprised you aren't curious. I know I would be."

She rose and put distance between them. "I am not curious, Jason Donavon. I am happy with my life."

He didn't think so. He didn't know why. Jason had never been what he considered the sensitive type. Hell, he'd been flat out told he wasn't by too many women to remember. There was something, though . . . a sadness about her, a vulnerability that surfaced only at times, very rare times like a moment before when she'd talked about her sister.

"My hand? Did you do that a minute ago, or have I become spastic?"

Her brows rose. "Did I do what?"

His gaze fused with hers. He saw something in her eyes, a spark of mischief. "You did," he answered and felt a chill race up his back. "That was denying me my free will."

"That was protecting myself," she corrected. "It is

allowed. Protecting myself or my people."

Things in her world got weirder by the minute. As if they weren't weird enough in his! "So you can move things with your mind?" He wanted verification.

"I can repel. It is a survival instinct."

Intrigued despite his wariness of her, Jason stepped closer to her. "Can you *com*pel? Make things or people come to you?"

She shrugged. "If I need something, my feet will take me to get it. If I cannot draw one close without using my powers to do so, I am not a good person, or I need a bath."

"But you could use the power to lure a creature to you," Jason pointed out, ignoring her small joke.

"*I* find *them*," she argued. "I have no wish for them to find me."

She was right about not needing powers to draw another close to her. The fact that Jason now stood before her proved that. "The chanting I've heard you do. Isn't that some type of control over another person's will?"

Glancing behind her, she took a step back. "They are spells, and yes, I suppose they do control another to some degree, but only if it is for my safety or the safety of my tribe do I use these."

"Sounds convenient," he said dryly. "Have you used them on me?"

"Yes," she answered. "To make you sleep those first nights. For my protection. I needed rest."

He couldn't take his eyes off her mouth. He swore he'd tasted her lips before. "Are you using one on me now?"

She tried to back away another step, but he saw that

there was nowhere for her to go. She said, "I do not understand why you would ask. Why you would believe so."

And he didn't understand why he couldn't resist her. "I want to kiss you. Why would I? You've taken me prisoner. You've slashed me with your knife. You've given me a black eye, poisoned me. It must be some kind of spell."

"I have cast no spell," she whispered. "It makes no sense that I would wish for you to touch your mouth to mine."

Her eyes hypnotized him. He couldn't look away from her. "Not unless despite what you say, you *are* curious about what you might be missing."

"You are wrong."

Her voice sounded breathless. She didn't try to move around him or break the contact of their eyes. Jason took that as sign. He leaned forward, only pausing long enough to see her lashes flutter downward in total surrender.

His lips were warm as they brushed against Tala's. She knew she should push him away, but the emotions he stirred within her were new, exciting. His arms went around her and pulled her closer. He turned his head and slanted his mouth against hers. She opened to him, as he'd instructed her to do the night she had cast the spell over him.

Their tongues touched; his kiss deepened. What began as sweetness, a soft merging of mouths, became something else. Her heart began to pound. She had trouble breathing. The heat of Jason's body penetrated her clothing. Her arms crept up around his neck.

"Do you know how long it's been since I've held a woman?" he asked against her lips. "Kissed a woman? Felt like a whole man?"

Tala did not want to hear about him kissing or holding other women. She understood his craving for contact now. The need to feel human. They were emotions denied to her all of her life. Bravely, she ran her hands down his bare chest. She had borrowed a shirt for him. It would be better if he were wearing it. His skin felt hot, smooth and muscled.

"Can I touch you? The way you're touching me?"

His question, deep and low, made her ache. Ache for the unknown. It was wrong to allow him so close. Wrong to want the feel of his hands moving over her skin. Tala craved the contact that had been forever denied to her. She wanted to be held. To feel emotions that were forbidden to her.

"Yes," she whispered.

He untied the thin straps that held her dress in place and eased the buckskin from her shoulders. His mouth touched her throat, sending a shiver up her spine. She felt the night air touch her breasts, then the warmth of his hands as he cupped her, his thumbs brushing her nipples until they stood erect. His lips dipped lower until his mouth settled over her hardened nipple. He sucked gently. She gasped, her fingers digging into his scalp.

A strange coiling in her belly began. A tightening that seemed connected to the pull of his mouth against her breasts. The feeling frightened her. Tala pushed him away, and although his mouth traveled back up to her lips, he did not release her. She had wondered about the feel of his bare skin against hers. It was not something she could have imagined. The sensation was much like a fire leaping to life between them. She burned, she ached, she feared what he made her feel.

"You must stop," she said, but her voice did not sound convincing, even to her own ears. "What we are doing is forbidden. It is wrong."

He caught her earlobe between his teeth. "It doesn't feel wrong. It feels very right."

Another shiver raced up her spine. What he did to her felt right, but that did not change who and what she was . . . who and what *he* was. She pushed him away. "You must stop. Do not force me to protect myself from you."

Her words made him draw back. "I would never force you to do anything that you didn't want to do. At least, I don't think I would. I know the man inside of me wouldn't, but I'm not sure about the beast . . . and you definitely bring that out in me."

Suddenly embarrassed, she moved away from him, fumbling to pull her dress back up around her neck. "We must forget this happened between us. It must not happen again."

He snorted. "Unless you can cast some type of spell over me to make me forget, I'm not going to. But you're right. It shouldn't have happened. Shouldn't happen again. It would be different if . . ."

"If what?" she asked.

"If I were a normal man, and you were a normal woman. And I've never been with a woman who hadn't been with someone else before me. I'm not into deflowering virgins."

His response to her purity confused her. "Among my people, women remain pure until they find their mate. Then they mate for life. Why is this wrong in your world?"

He shrugged, then walked over and seated himself on her furs. "My world and yours are different. People who marry seldom stayed married. Women are allowed as much sexual freedom as men. Being intimate doesn't have to include any commitment other than the one two people make at the moment. For most, it's just sex and nothing more."

Tala could not understand. Jason Donavon had already taught her about desire, but it seemed wrong to want him for no other reason than the purpose of mating. "Those are ways of an animal, not the ways of humans. And even some animals mate for life. I would not fit into your world."

"No, you wouldn't," he agreed. Shaking his head, he changed the topic. "These powers you have. I'd like to know more about them."

"My powers are secret, known only to my people." She settled across the fire from him. "I have shown you too much already. I only did so because you must believe in me. You must believe in what you do not understand. You must open your mind."

"Why can't you just use your powers to find the wolf that bit me, tell me where it is and send me on my way? It sounds a lot simpler."

She shook her head. "I told you, they only appear to me when they represent a threat to my people, or to someone I care about. The only chance you have to survive among my tribe is to hide what you are from them. The only choice you have to survive in your world is to learn to control the beast within. I cannot set you free until you have. And if you fail, I must do my duty and rid the world of your threat. I have gone against the laws of my people by bringing you among us. I cannot go against all of them."

Scrubbing a hand over his face, he said, "I'd like to see these people you're protecting. So far, I've only met your brother and your uncle."

Tala reached behind her and snatched the shirt she'd borrowed for him. "If you do not wear this, we must continue to reopen your wounds. The Elders of my tribe have decided that you are to mix among us. I cannot keep them convinced for long that you are too ill to see the others. We must make plans."

He took the shirt, studied it for a moment, then slid it over his head. "I'm supposed to act sick when I do meet them, right? Too weak to make it on my own?"

"If you do not, there is no reason for you to be among us, and they will make you leave."

A lopsided grin spread over his face. "That doesn't sound like a bad option."

"It is better than a knife in your heart," she reminded.

Her words sobered him. He sighed. "I'm trying to take all this seriously. I keep thinking I must be dreaming. I keep hoping that the last three years have only been a nightmare and that I'll wake up."

Tala felt tempted to touch his face, to offer him comfort, but she held her wayward emotions inside. "To wake, you must first sleep. The hour grows late." She rose, grabbed a colorful blanket, wrapped it around herself, and took up her position by the cave's main exit. She was gratified that Jason was unaware there was another way out: a secret door along the rocks lining the far wall of her cave that led into the tunnels. It would be an impossible task she set herself if he knew; powers or no, Tala could not guard both exits and entrances.

"You're sure you don't want to share the bed? We both have a lot of catching up to do," he asked. He lay stretched out against the furs, his long, muscled frame relaxed, his head propped up on one hand. He was tempting, with his sky-colored eyes fringed by thick dark lashes. Firelight glinted off his long hair.

"You know that I do not wish to share the bed with you. You have asked me before."

"You can't blame a guy for trying." He rolled onto his back, staring upward. "I've always been a night person. I haven't had much exercise in the past couple of days. A lack of activity has made me restless."

Although she felt restless, too, and wasn't used to being confined as much as she lately had been, Tala said nothing. She closed her eyes and imagined herself outside, running wild through the moonlight. A strange noise made her open her eyes again. Jason now lay on his stomach. He lifted himself with his arms, then lowered himself to where it looked as if he meant to kiss the fur pelts he rested upon.

"What are you doing?"

"Exercising," he answered. "Pushups."

"Why?" The noise kept her awake, although she wasn't sleepy.

"Burning energy so I'll be tired and can get to sleep."

Up and down he went. Again and again. His arms strained, the muscles bulging. After watching him for a while, she decided what he did looked vulgar. Tala closed her eyes. She could still hear him. He made an animal sound each time he lifted himself.

"Are you not finished yet?" she snapped. "You are keeping me awake."

He did not stop the vulgar movements. "You're keeping me awake, too."

"I am doing nothing to you," she defended.

"Yes, you are." He continued to pump his body up and down. "There's something about you. Something about the way you smell."

Tala sniffed at herself. "You saw that I took a bath."

"Yes," he admitted. "I saw you naked."

She clutched her blanket closer around her. "I was in the water."

"Still naked. And I saw you."

Now the blanket felt like it smothered her. Tala shoved it off of her. "I have seen you naked before, too. I was not impressed."

He paused almost to the furs beneath him and turned to look at her. "I've never had any complaints before. And you sure have a beautiful body, Tala." He pumped up and down some more.

She had never discussed her body with a man, or his with him, though she had watched her own ripening self with some degree of curiosity as she grew into a young woman. And she had lied. His body *was* beautiful to her.

"You find me pleasing?"

His breathing sounding ragged, but he continued the strange movements. "I find the way you look pleasing. I find your body very pleasing. It's the whole Wonder Woman, anything-you-can-do-I-can-do-better, stab-me, jab-me, poison-me, keep-threatening-to-kill-me thing I have a problem with. Other than that, you're great. Just the kind of girl Mom would love for me to bring home to meet the family."

The tone of his voice she did not believe to be sincere. And his words again confused her. "Your mother wishes to meet me? Why would she? She knows nothing—"

He collapsed with an exasperated sigh and covered his head with his arms, cutting her off. "Never mind. My mother wouldn't even like to meet me these days. She thinks I'm dead. Except for my brother, everyone I once knew and loved thinks I'm dead."

She had nothing to say. Neither did he. Tala listened to his breathing become regular again. It had been a long time since the days she would lie awake at night and talk to her sister. She had been lonely these past three years, as had Jason Donavon. They were not so different from each other . . . not as different as he might believe.

Some longed to be special. Tala did not. She longed to be normal, to have what other women had. A lodge with a husband and noisy children to watch after. She had learned long ago that to be soft inside was to be soft outside. A killer could not have a kind heart. The one chosen must understand the necessity of killing— find honor in the duty when done for the cause of good. Tala had never liked killing, had not asked for the responsibility. Sometimes, she wondered whether she was any different from the beasts she hunted.

"You can relax. I'm not going anywhere. Not tonight."

Jason sensed her turmoil, but he could not know her thoughts. "Sleep well," she found herself whispering.

He did not answer. She closed her eyes, but sleep would not come. Like him, she should have done something to work off the restless energy she felt. Now she must lie awake and think of him. Think of their mouths joined, his fingers dancing over her skin, the woman's feelings he had stirred inside of her. She owed him a debt for helping her fight the Unma Kin Sica in the city, but she had owed him a life long before then. What would he think if he knew her secrets? What would he do? Tala knew what he would do. He would kill her.

Chapter Six

Tala stood arguing with the old man she'd said was her uncle. Jason sat huddled beneath a blanket in one corner of her cave, trying to appear sick. He couldn't understand their words, but they both kept pointing at him, which he considered a bad sign. He had a feeling it was time for him to go outside and face the music. Hell, he was ready to do something besides sit around trying to figure out if he should escape, or if Tala Soaringbird could really help him. His gaze traveled the length of her long legs.

He shouldn't be having the thoughts he had about her. Not under his circumstances. Certainly not under hers. But Tala's scent, it got to him on some primal level. The natural fragrance her body emitted had to be loaded with pheromones. He couldn't seem to fight his attraction to her, regardless of what she'd done to him, or might plan to do.

The old man suddenly turned and walked toward the exit. He glanced back, said something, and left. Tala stood staring after the old man. Her lips were pursed.

"Problem?"

She sighed and faced him. "The Elders request your presence at the meeting lodge. They want to see you."

"Do I look that bad?"

Her gaze flitted over him. "You look too well."

He cussed under his breath. "You're not carving on me."

"What if they ask to see the wounds?" she demanded, pacing back and forth in front of him.

"Ever heard of bandages?"

She stopped. Her face flushed. "Yes, I have heard of bandages. I know what to do."

Tala riffled through a basket. He'd never met a woman who could keep all of her clothes in a few small baskets stacked along one wall. But then, he'd never met a woman like Tala. Period. She grabbed a wad of white cloth and tossed it to him.

"Tear that into long strips."

Snatching up a water skin, she headed toward the exit, paused, then turned back toward him. He thought she meant to walk right through the wall, which would definitely impress him, but instead, she pushed against a rock and it swung open. Jason blinked.

"I did not intend to show you this, but the time I have is short before we must join the others. I must leave for a time. Do not go outside."

"Where does that lead?"

She cast him an irritated glance. "Down through

the tunnels and out the other side of the mountain. Do not follow me. Do not go outside. I will be back before you can tear the cloth into strips."

There she went, ordering him around again, and seemingly right at home in the role. "Down the tunnels?"

"One who does not know the way would become lost," she assured him. "You would wander from tunnel to tunnel and never find your way out."

It wasn't an appealing thought. He knew she told the truth. Without her guidance down the tunnels to the hot spring below, he would have never found his way. Besides, he was curious about her people. How many men in their lifetime got a chance to meet a secret tribe of Native Americans who hunted werewolves and lived as if time hadn't passed?

"Hurry back," he said sarcastically, and went about the task she'd set him. He tried to concentrate on tearing the cloth into long strips, but holding it to his face Jason realized the fabric smelled like Tala. After a moment of indulgence, he went back to work. True to her word, Tala was back a moment before he finished.

"Look what I have," she said, kneeling before him.

Jason glanced into the small opening of her water skin. "Berry juice?"

"Blood."

He drew back. "Blood? Where did you get it?"

She laughed. "Do not tell me the sight of blood makes you queasy?"

Jason straightened. "Of course not. I just wondered how and where you got it so quickly."

Shoving her long hair over one shoulder, she

81

shrugged. "I caught a rabbit. I buried him beneath some leaves and will go back later. He will be our dinner tonight."

"You caught a rabbit? With what?"

"I am an excellent hunter," she answered, which to him, was no answer at all.

She hadn't carried any weapons with her but her small knife. If she'd thrown it and killed the rabbit, that would have been an amazing feat; he would have liked to have seen it.

"We will smear blood on the bandages to make it appear as if your wounds are still seeping."

"Lovely," he drawled.

"Remove your shirt."

Jason tugged the garment over his head.

"Be still and let me bandage you."

He was being still, but found it difficult to stay that way when she touched him. Her fingers brushed his bare skin, her face bent close to his as she concentrated on wrapping a long bandage over one shoulder and across his chest. He noticed the marks upon her arm again.

"What are those crescent-shaped scars on your arm?"

"They are a mark of passage. All my people have them, except the children who have not yet reached the age to wear them."

"Some type of puberty ritual?" he guessed.

"Yes," she answered and glanced into his eyes. Their faces were close, lips only a hairsbreath apart. She shook her head as if to clear it and said, "Remember to act weak and sick, while you are in the presence of the other tribesmen. Do not speak. Lean on me to walk, and groan as if it hurts for you to move."

"I'll try."

Light sparked to life in her eyes. "You must more than try. Never forget that as long as you are among us, your life is in danger."

When she poured the blood across his bandage, Jason felt his nostrils flare. The blood smelled sweet to him. He unconsciously licked his lips.

"You must resist," she said, her voice soft. "The human side of you would not desire the taste of blood, but the wolf that stirs beneath your skin is attracted to the scent. You are stronger than he is. If you were not, he would have taken you already."

Jason tried to ignore the tempting scent. He fought himself to keep from snatching the water skin from her hand and drinking the contents. "Hurry up," he said gruffly. "I need some fresh air."

Tala quickly bandaged his arm where she had once made the cuts her uncle and brother saw. Again, she doused the bandage with blood from the water skin. Jason felt a sweat break out on his forehead.

"Put your shirt back on," she instructed. "The bloody bandages are only a precaution if they ask to see how you are healing. We must go now. They wait for us."

Relieved for any distraction, Jason drew his shirt over his head. He rose. Tala poured water from a bowl into the skin, rinsed the receptacle and used the water to extinguish her cooking fire. She grabbed a blanket and wrapped it around him.

"Remember to shuffle your steps and move slowly. Place one arm around my shoulders as if you need support."

"I think I can manage to play sick," he said. Her fussing only made him more nervous. What if he couldn't fool her people? What if something happened? What if the strong smell of animal blood that soaked his bandages made him change? What if he went on a murdering rampage and killed everyone? Horrible visions took shape in his mind.

What if they killed *him*?

"You will do fine," she said, and touched his arm. "Come. It is time to go."

Odd, but her voice, the feel of her touch, soothed him. Considering all that she'd done to him, and all that she'd threatened to do, he didn't think he should find himself too comfortable in her company. Jason slung his arm across her slender shoulders. He supposed they looked ridiculous: a woman of her delicate stature trying to hold up a man twice her size. She was strong though; she'd proven that to him. They moved outside, where he welcomed the cool, crisp smell of fresh air and pine.

Slowly, they made their way down the embankment. Jason figured they were being watched and stumbled a couple of times for good measure. The sunshine felt wonderful against his skin. The scent of his bloodstained bandages still distracted him, but he tried to concentrate on other things. A hawk circled overhead, calling down to them. Needles snapped beneath his bare feet. He wondered if his shoes were still lying in the alley where he'd changed form and they'd torn off him.

An odd thought occurred to him about shoes. It seemed there was always an abandoned one lying in the middle of the road, a ditch, an alleyway. Maybe all those shoes belonged to werewolves. A sharp jab to the ribs made him grunt in surprise.

"Do not smile. You do not look sick when you smile."

"I thought of something funny," he defended.

"Do not think," she snapped. "There is nothing humorous about your situation."

She was right. There was nothing funny about being a werewolf trapped in a secret society of werewolf hunters. Jason imagined there weren't many werewolf activists, either. He pictured a group lobbying outside of Washington wearing "Save the Werewolves" T-shirts and received another jab in the ribs for doing so.

He sobered considerably a few minutes later and shuffled to a stop. Beneath a thatched enclosure he saw a group of women working together, tanning a deer hide. A handful of children ran from one place to another, laughing and squealing. Younger men sharpened knives against rocks. All that was missing was a herd of horses in the background, maybe a few buffalo roaming about. And of course, there were no teepees.

"This doesn't seem real," he said. "It looks like a reenactment scene."

"What is a reenactment?" Tala whispered.

"People who like to dress up and relive history. You know, pretend they're from another time?"

"We do not pretend," she snapped and moved on, forcing him forward. A woman's laugh died. Children ran across their path, skidded to a halt and backed away with large frightened eyes. The younger men left their sharpening rocks behind, but kept their knives in hand as they moved toward Tala and Jason. Tala guided him around rocks, through the trees, past other thatched open enclosures, gaining a following as they went.

Jason tried to remember to move slowly, to shuffle as if he could barely get along. It was difficult not to turn and look behind him. He felt curious eyes on his back. He was curious, too. How could these people live this way when modern society stretched just beyond their fingertips? Why would they want to? Even the children wore clothing fashioned of deer hide. And there was something different about the boys and girls. Innocence in its purest form radiated from them. He supposed maybe because movies, or video games, or the nightly news hadn't touched them.

When they looked at him with their wide, dark eyes, it was as if they saw something they had never seen before. An outsider, he realized. A white man, no less. The boogie man. Well, they weren't far off the mark on that one. A larger thatched enclosure came into view. A few old men sat in a circle outside. Jason recognized one of them as Tala's uncle. He wondered where her brother was and glanced around. The leader stood not far away, arms crossed over his chest, a scowl etched across his features.

Their gazes locked. The big man could look fierce, he'd give him that, but Jason wouldn't cower before him. He knew the smartest thing would be to lower his gaze and shuffle along. He didn't, not even when he felt Tala's subtle jab against his ribs.

Tala said something in her language. Jason stared at Haidar a moment longer, then turned his attention toward the older men. With the motion of his hand,

Tala's uncle indicated that they should sit.

For the sake of pretense, Jason threw in a couple of groans and flinches on the way down, allowing Tala to help him settle on the ground. She sat beside him. The old men stared at him. Slowly, the others crept forward. They stared at him, too.

"What name are you called?" one man asked.

Jason started to respond, but Tala beat him to the punch. "The man is called Jason Donavon."

"What does he do in his world?"

That was one she didn't know. He liked the little lines that appeared between her eyes when she concentrated. "He lives there," she answered.

"I'm an accountant," Jason said. "Or was. I worked with numbers."

His answer drew blank stares from all present. "The green paper," he explained. "I figure how much of it another man has and how much of it he has to give the government. It's really very fascinating," he added dryly when all stares remained blank.

"How are you feeling?" The question came from Haidar, Tala's brother. "Well, I hope."

Jason tried to move so he could look up at the big man, purposely bringing a hand to his chest as if the movement pained him. He pressed hard against the soaked bandages, rewarded by the wet sticky feel of blood soaking into his shirt. "Not very well, as you can see."

"You have started the bleeding again," Tala fussed. She jumped to her feet. "I must take him back so he can rest."

No one protested, but Jason wanted to. He wasn't ready to go back to the small cave. The sunshine felt good against his skin, the air smelled fresh, the people intrigued him.

"Maybe I could rest beneath a tree," he said. "I think the fresh air might help me."

His suggestion received a dark glance from Tala. Her brother stepped closer.

"It would be good to have the man out in the open, where we can watch him."

The fact that Haidar spoke English when he didn't have to told Jason that the leader wanted him to understand his words, and the insinuation behind them.

"I will watch him," Tala said. "The outsider is my responsibility."

Tala waited for Haidar to argue, but it was her uncle who interfered.

"The man has kept you from us too long already," he stated. "You need the sunshine upon your face. A short amount of time outside will not make the man worse, but might improve his health. And it will be good for you to mix with the others, with those of your own kind," he stressed.

Her uncle was right, although having Jason outside among her people made Tala nervous. She had spent too much time with the white man. He had tempted her. She had tempted him. They needed space between them.

"I must move him to the shade." She turned to help Jason rise, but found Haidar already reaching for the white man. She saw her brother's fingers dig into Jason's arm, and at the very place where he knew he'd been cut. Blood from the bandages seeped through the buckskin. When the white man groaned as if in pain, Tala released a sigh of relief.

"You are too rough with him," she scolded her brother and nudged him aside. "You will only make him worse. I will help him."

The two men exchanged looks. Tala hoped she was the only one who noticed the tension between them. Haidar moved off, but she saw him turn, glance at her, then down at the blood that stained his fingers. He looked at Jason, who she'd helped to rise from the ground. Deliberately, her brother brought one finger to his lips and licked the blood from it, and then he turned and marched away.

"Sorry, but your brother is just plain creepy," Jason said softly.

Tala's blood had turned to ice. Her heart started to pound. "He knows."

"What?"

Feeling curious eyes upon them, Tala shook off her fears. She guided her patient to a stand of trees and helped him ease his weight to the ground. He sat with his back propped against a tree. Children immediately gathered around them.

"Hey, give me five," the white man said, and held out his hand. The children screamed and ran away.

"Do not try to take anything," she warned. "You have frightened them. Sit still and say nothing. I will mix with the others for a short time, and then you must appear very tired so that I can take you back."

"Do you know how amazing this is to me?"

"Shhh," she cautioned. "Excitement dances in your eyes. You must appear sick, weak."

He glanced around then lowered his gaze. "Your

people don't look dangerous to me. They seem more afraid of me than anything."

She bent low, pretending to straighten the bloody sleeve of his shirt. Her lips nearly brushed his ear. "What the eyes see is not always the true image. Watch, listen, learn."

Then, as much as she hated leaving him alone, Tala rose and walked away. She felt his gaze on her back, then lower. The man had no sense, no fear, but soon he would understand. It was almost the time of day the boys and young men practiced.

She joined a group of women who tanned the hide of a deer. Tala pulled her knife from the top of her moccasin. The low hum of conversation when she'd joined the women died away. Some did not look at her; some looked at her from the corner of their eyes, as if she would not see them staring.

"Noshi is growing into a man," she said to the woman on her left. Her name was Chandee, and she was the boy's mother.

"Yes," Chandee agreed. "Soon, he must face the call of the moon."

Tala touched the woman's shoulder. "He is strong. He knows the way of the *ba'cho*. You have taught him well."

The woman shrugged from Tala's touch. "My son knows our ways better I think than you do. Certainly better than your sister did."

It was not Tala's imagination. The women were acting strangely toward her. "I have been raised the same as you, Chandee. The same as all of you."

"Not the same," Annesha, the woman on her left, said. "You were the one chosen. Always, you were treated differently. You were not trained to guard your young, to teach them, to prepare yourself to be a good wife and mother. You were trained as a warrior, given special treatment. Now you go against the law, and the Elders allow it. Had one of us brought a stranger into our midst, it would not have been so. We would have been punished, the intruder killed to silence his tongue."

Tala was shocked. She had resented being different all of her life; she had not realized others resented her for it as well. "I obeyed the old ways," she said. "A life for a life. The man fought by my side against two evil ones, when I had only been prepared for one. I must restore him to health and repay my debt to him."

"It is not right," Chandee argued. "Allowing a strange man to stay in your lodge. You are the one chosen, Tala, but you are still a woman."

Until she'd brought the white man among them, no one had seemed to notice that Tala was a woman. Her tribe had treated her as if she had no particular sex. None had worried over the danger she placed herself in when she hunted their enemies. None had complained of the meat she provided, the skins, or the work she did alongside them. None had hesitated to bring a sick child to her for healing or ask for her guidance when choosing a mate.

"Do you fear for me? Do you believe I cannot protect myself against one white man? Do you think so little of my powers?"

Chandee lowered her gaze. "What we fear, Tala, is that our world is changing. That we must change with it and that we are not prepared. You are allowed outside, beyond the smallness of our lives. A chosen few have gone with you, but never a woman. The man you bring among us is a reminder that life goes on beyond this secret place. He is a reminder that we are not safe, that our children are not safe. We focus on one enemy, but he is proof that our enemies do not only hide behind a mask of glowing eyes and bloody fangs. The enemy is everywhere."

A shudder wracked Tala's slender frame. Chandee did not know the truth of her words. The enemy was everywhere; the enemy was among them.

"Women are left to guard because no man is as fierce as a female defending her young," Tala reminded. "Our world is small, but that does not mean our minds must be small. Fear is quick to fill a little mind. I would not allow the white man to harm one of you. I would give my life for you, Chandee, for your Noshi, and for you, Annesha. I owe the outsider a debt by law, but I have pledged my life to my people. Am I to be shunned for my actions?"

All women present bowed their heads submissively.

"We are wrong to doubt your powers and your wisdom because of our own fears," Chandee said. "Maybe we are wrong to judge the outsider simply because he is different and not of our world."

But they should not trust Jason Donavon, Tala knew. The people should not trust her, either. She felt a deep shame that she had deceived her people. She could not look the women in the eyes. It was true, she would allow no harm to come to those she had guardianship over, even if it meant she must kill to do so. But it did not change the fact that she had placed them in danger by bringing Jason among them, and by not fulfilling her duty of killing the evil ones she had fought in the city. Those beasts had the instincts of animals. They could track her more easily than a human, and they were much more of a threat to her tribe than the outside world.

"Let us talk no more of it," she said. "I have missed your companionship."

Chandee glanced toward the white man who sat beneath the trees. "My husband has been with you to the outside on a hunt. He told me that all outsider men were ugly."

"He lied," Annesha said, and the women laughed.

The tension had been broken, but Tala could not relax. All she could think was that Jason Donavon should not be among them. It would be different were he a normal man who had helped her, one she could heal, cast the sacred spells upon, and send back to his world. It would be different if she did not look at him and feel the forbidden.

"Practice begins," Chandee said. "Come, let us watch."

The women rushed from the enclosure as their young boys and men gathered in a clearing a short distance away. Tala walked slowly behind them. She glanced at Jason as she passed. He raised a brow in question, but she turned her gaze from him and kept walking. He would understand that her people were not harmless soon enough.

Chapter Seven

Pretending to be ill when his heart beat fast inside of his chest and excitement churned his blood proved difficult for Jason. How could a race of people truly look as if time hadn't touched them? He was fascinated by everything he saw, felt as if he'd been reborn and the world was new. Tala's tribe was gathered a short distance away. A young boy ran past, paused, smiled slightly, and kept moving.

Jason smiled too, but the boy had gone. He didn't want the children to be frightened of him. He liked kids. He'd always thought that he'd have a few of his own someday. Of course, that was out the question now unless he could break the curse. Even if Tala could teach him to control the beast within, that wouldn't change his DNA. He had no idea what type of creature he might spawn.

Those gathered spread out, and Tala came into

view. Of all the women present, she was the most beautiful. He liked the proud way she stood. She was petite, but despite her slight build, she still managed to look tall. She had presence. And grace when she moved. Spears were handed out, and although Tala had been given one, he noticed the other women present hung back, as if they wouldn't participate in what was about to take place.

The young male members of the tribe lined up, Tala in place among them. The first man balanced his lance, ran a few feet and threw it. A cheer rose from those watching. Jason struggled to see the target, but the trees and the members blocked his view. The man had evidently hit the mark. Two more followed, and again the tribespeople cheered over their obvious skill. Tala took her turn and the cheers seemed louder to him. By the satisfied expression on her face, she had mastered whatever game they played.

Jason grew tired of straining his neck after a while. He wondered if he dared stand so that he could see better. Tala would be angry if he didn't keep up his pretense of being too weak to move. The men finished, and the younger boys who'd been running to some distant point and retrieving the lances began to line up. The boy who'd smiled at him glanced his direction and huffed proudly. Going to show off, Jason thought, suppressing a smile.

A group of the men marched toward the target. At first Jason thought they did so to be able to retrieve the lances once the children had thrown. A few minutes later, he realized that was the not the case.

They were pulling something closer; the target, he assumed—which made sense because the children couldn't throw as far as the older people. At first Jason couldn't tell what it was. Once he got a better look, he felt the color drain from his face. The figure was carved out of wood. Tall and pocked with spear marks, it was a huge beast with the head of a wolf, mouth open, fangs bared, and the body of a man. He knew what it was. *Him.*

The boy ran a few steps, threw his spear and hit the target in the chest, right where the heart would be. He strutted back to the group, turned and grinned at Jason again. Jason could not smile back. His stomach churned. He truly felt sick now. Judging by their excitement and pats on the back, all considered hitting the mark a great accomplishment.

He glanced away from the boy, from the sight of the horrible wooden creature. Tala had wanted him to see this. She'd wanted to make sure he understood that she hadn't exaggerated the danger engulfing him. These people trained from an early age to hunt, to kill, to destroy the unnatural creatures like himself that roamed the earth. Jason had a feeling they wouldn't care if he had nothing to do with what he'd become, if he were only a victim. Tala probably wouldn't care either, if he hadn't helped her that night in the alley—if she didn't feel as if she owed him some type of debt.

"Are you ready to return to my lodge?"

He glanced up. Tala stood above him. "Yeah, I've seen all I care to see for one day."

She bent and helped him up. Jason would have liked to end the pretense at that point. He felt tempted to take off into the woods, to run and keep running.

"Do not follow the path of your thoughts," she said

softly. "You cannot outrun so many who know the forest better than you. You would not get far, and the trouble you would bring upon both us would be great."

"I think mine would be worse," he pointed out. "I'm sure they'd enjoy having a live target for practice."

Tala placed his arm around her neck. She glanced behind her and kept her voice low. "They . . . my people, know only the laws, the ways taught to them throughout the centuries. We hunt and destroy those who have let the beast rule their lives, but we know little about the others, those like you who are trapped in the outside world. Trapped between the call of the moon and humanity. Now you understand why I want to see, need to see, if your heart is pure enough to save you. Maybe to save others."

"I think *I* need to know more than you do." He shuffled forward, still tempted to take his chances at running. "I want out of here."

"It is time to do more than talk," she agreed. "Tonight, I will call the beast within you forth. Our journey together will begin."

Jason wanted more action and less talk, but he wasn't sure this kind of action was what he wanted. He feared for Tala. She might be some type of warrior woman, and she did seem to have special gifts, but would either be enough to save her from him if he couldn't control the monster inside? Or maybe he'd be the one who needed to be rescued, from her and her knives. Either way, the evening could prove fatal for one of them.

* * *

Tala breathed deeply of the crisp night air. She crept through the dark forest, aware of the scurrying creatures beneath the brush, the owl's hoot, the way the forest came alive around her. The white man followed, his footsteps nearly as quiet as her own. She heard the slight labor of his breath as they moved farther from her camp. If she could call the beast in him forth, she would not do it close to her encampment and place her people in danger. She had her knives for protection, and hoped she would not be forced to use them.

Killing Jason Donavon would prove difficult for her. He was not the same as those she had killed in the past. Those creatures had not been human to her. She had not spoken to them. She had not looked upon them and found them beautiful. She had not been tempted to touch her mouth to theirs, or hungered for the feel of their fingertips brushing her skin. Of course Jason was different. The man still ruled him more than the beast. But for how long?

"How much farther?"

"We are almost there," she answered. Tala had chosen a special place to take him. One she had visited often in her childhood. A place to think. A place to hide. A place where she could pretend she was someone else.

Tall trees surrounded the clearing and kissed the night sky. It was a fortress of sorts. In the center, a fire pit she had dug remained. A stack of firewood, old but usable, still sat stacked nearby.

"When I was very young, I would sneak from my uncle's lodge and come here," she told him. "I would light a fire and dance around it, singing to the night spirits. I would ask them . . ."

"What did you ask?" he prodded.

She rubbed her arms against the chill. "I would ask them to take away my powers. I would ask them to make me a normal girl. But the night spirits did not hear me."

"Well, if it's any comfort, no one has been listening to my prayers for the past three years either." His arms went around her from behind. "It's cold out here. Couldn't we have done this inside your nice warm cave?"

Tala pulled away, liking the feel of his arms around her too much. "I will not place my people in danger for you. No more than I have already done. I will light a fire to keep us warm."

Using the old cut wood, Tala built a fire and had it blazing in a short time. It helped that she could control a small flame, turning it into a larger one. Doing so made the white man shiver in the night air, but he said nothing.

"Be seated." She indicated the opposite side of the fire. "To become of one mind with the wolf within, you must understand him."

"Embracing your inner wolf, story at eleven."

She did not comprehend his meaning, but understood his tone. He made a joke. "You must take my words seriously, Jason. What we do tonight will be dangerous . . . for both of us."

He ran a hand through his hair. "I know. I crack jokes when I'm nervous." His gaze met hers across the fire. "I'm listening."

Tala drew a deep breath and began, "The wolf is

one of the most revered of all creatures to my people. Known for his cunning, he is an excellent hunter. One wolf does not hunt for himself, but for the pack. The wolves feed the old ones among them as well as the young, both being too slow to hunt for themselves. The wolf accepts his place among the pack. He understands his duties whether he is the leader, second in rank, or the lowliest one. Breeding is selective. Some are forbidden to mate. The wolves understand this and accept it because it is for the good of their pack. The wolf is a noble creature. It is when man and beast do battle to inhabit the same form that the darkest evil can be born."

Jason had once loved a good scary story told around a campfire. But all things considered, he no longer did. "Today the hierarchy of a wolf pack is called alpha, beta, and omega. I learned that on the Discovery Channel," he teased, then realized he was falling into his old habit of making jokes at inappropriate times. He sobered. "But the difference between the Sica and me is a pure heart? Right? I mean, that's what you said separates me from the evil ones."

"It is what separates you at this moment," she agreed. "But you must understand, temptation will weaken you as time passes. Without the ability to cleanse your spirit, to maintain balance, you will become lost along the path of good and evil. Bitterness will creep into your heart. Vengeance will burn there for those of a pure race who would crucify you. In your shame, you will seek to make others like you so you are not alone. It is your nature to run with the pack, both as man and beast. But you will not be allowed. Yet it is wrong to spread your misery. It is a selfish heart that turns others to their fate. You must learn the way of the wolf to survive, to keep your heart pure. The journey will be difficult."

"But if I do what you say, learn what you intend to teach me, then I have a shot at being fairly normal, right? If I learn to control the change, I can keep what I am hidden from others."

"Will that be enough for you?" she asked. "The deception will wear. You will want to mate, but like what you call the beta and omega wolves, you will be denied the right. You will have no place in the order of your world, no duty but to control the evil that might rise up to rule you. Can you accept that?"

His stomach twisted. She didn't paint a rosy picture for his future. Without an end to the curse, he wasn't really much better off than before. He still couldn't live a normal life. He couldn't marry and have children. But at least he'd be able to control the killer within. He wouldn't have to wonder during a full moon where he'd gone or what he'd done.

"Hiding a secret is not much of a life," he said. "Being denied the rights of my fellow man isn't either. I want my old life back. I want my brother to have his back, too. What good is this so-called gift you are giving me if it really doesn't change anything?"

"It can change the way you feel about yourself," she explained. "To control the beast inside, you must learn to accept him. You must become the leader— the alpha male of your spirit, and he, the lowest. The lowly one, the omega, is the least important member of a pack. You must learn to keep him in his place."

Jason rose and turned away from her. "I've never been good at accepting the short end of the stick." He wheeled to face her across the fire. "If you want to do something for me, seek a vision. Use these powers you claim to find the one that bit me so I can kill it!"

"I have told you, it is not that simple," she reminded him. "The creatures only come to me if they represent some future harm to my people, or to someone I care about."

"So you're telling me the best option I have is to learn to control myself and live out the rest of my days as a hermit?"

He thought her answer was yes when her gaze lowered, but then she said, "There may be another way to reclaim all that you have lost."

Grappling with his anger, he took his seat across from her again. "And what would that be?"

Her dark eyes lifted and met his. "A purely selfless act of love. I have heard stories where this has saved a human from the bite of the beast."

Jason didn't catch her drift. "What do you mean? What is 'a purely selfless act'?"

"A sacrifice," she answered. "Your life for the life of another. Or the surrender of something that you value above all else. That is the truest test of a pure heart."

Mumbo jumbo. He'd heard Native Americans had their superstitions, their legends, their stories. Now she was trying to use them to pacify him. Jason got to his feet again. "What if I run? What if I run right now?"

She rose, too, facing him across the fire. "Is that what you want? To go back to the life you were living? Stalking the forest, small towns, city streets like an animal? At the mercy of the moon? I can give you dignity, acceptance of all that you are."

The night called to him, whispered: *run—leave this place—leave her*. A wolf howled in the distance. It was a lonely sound. A sound that brought Jason's own solitude and alienation to light. He didn't *want* to return to the life he'd been living for the past three years. What Tala offered him might not be the solution he sought, but it was better than nothing.

"Tell me what to do."

Tala visibly relaxed. She drew a deep breath. "We must tempt the beast to come out. You must learn to control him at your will not the will of the moon, or the flare of your temper."

"But I can't control it," he reminded. "And I'm afraid I—he might hurt you."

She paced across from him, the fire throwing her shadow around the clearing. "You did not hurt me before. One thing that you must do is trust in my abilities, trust in yourself."

Jason wasn't sure he could trust Tala. After all that had happened to him, he didn't trust anyone. His trust in himself had been put through the wringer, too. And if he failed, she would kill him. But, then again, if he didn't try she might eventually kill him, too. Or one of her people would. "Okay. I'll do my best. What happens now?"

The shadows she cast became still. She returned to the fire and took her place across from him, nodding for him to sit as well. "I will chant the old words to bring the beast inside of you forth. When you feel him beneath your skin, you must fight. But first, you must remember the days of your youth, the days of your innocence, a time long before the moon first called to you. This is who you are, not who the beast wants you to be. Close your eyes, and remember."

He closed his eyes. Her voice, low and husky, began to chant. Jason didn't understand the words, but he tried to do as she'd told him. He remembered a tricycle; shiny red paint and rubber wheels. Rick, his older brother, helped him climb onto it. His feet found the pedals. Rick showed him how to make it go. Sailing down the sidewalk, the wind ruffling his hair, Rick pushing him faster than he could pedal. Laughter. Children's laughter. A birthday cake. His mother, looking younger than he remembered, smiling down at him. His father, also young, a camera at one eye.

There were seven candles. Rick blew them out before he had a chance. Jason cried. His mother lit them again for him, but it wasn't the same. A bike now. Racing Rick down the street toward the park. Football. Playing in the snow. The music from the ice-cream truck two streets over. Hunting with his father. These memories soothed his soul, made him remember other things he'd forgotten. The joy of youth. The bliss of innocence.

The voice inside of his head changed, and so did his memories. The chanting grew louder. The memories flashed through his mind at a speed too fast to grasp them. Darker days. Understanding death. Crying at his grandmother's funeral, watching his grandfather lose his memory. Fast cars, fast women. Drinking. Rick leaving. Loneliness. Heartbreak over a girl. Waving goodbye to his parents as he set out for college. The tears in his mother's eyes. Pressure. Tests. Passing the CPA exam. A job. An empty apartment. The hunting trip. He squeezed his eyes shut tighter. He didn't want to remember, but the voice commanded him.

Drinking beer with Rick. Bragging about women. The fire crackling. Stumbling toward the bushes. A sound. A growl. The pain. Darkness. Such emptiness. Staggering along the streets, bloody, confused, people screaming and moving from his path. What was wrong with them? What was wrong with him? He had to get back, back to the campsite. Rick would wonder what had happened to him . . .

Suddenly, nothing. Waking in the forest, naked, whole again, though he knew in his heart he'd been badly wounded by the wolf . . . knew in his heart, he'd been dead. He was weak from the loss of blood, dazed, roaming until he became lost. It took him a month to even understand that time had passed . . . time that had slipped through his fingers. Then the moon rose again. It called to him. It seduced him. Howling his pain, his confusion, he suddenly understood that his life would never be the same. That life as he knew it had ceased to exist. That Jason Donavon had also ceased to exist.

Rick again, a few months later. The shock on his face at seeing his brother alive, the disbelief when he'd told them what they had both become. Cursed by the moon. He'd made him a promise. But so much time had passed since then, and he still had not fulfilled his obligations. He was still cursed. They were both cursed. Cursed forever.

"No!" he shouted, forcing his eyes open.

Tala continued to chant, but now she stood before the fire, naked, her body moving in an uncanny, sensuous rhythm to a drum that only pounded inside his head. Her nudity surprised but delighted him. Her legs were long and slender, her hips those of a woman. The triangle of hair at the apex of her thighs was black as night. She had full breasts, small nipples standing erect in the night air. Her eyes were closed. Her hair swirled around her, lengthened until it became like a dark twister, cloaking them both in its inky darkness. His eyes burned, his skin itched, his gums hurt. Her scent, so womanly, so tempting in its blend of sweetness and primal allure, called forth the beast. The one that lived in all men. He wanted her.

He stood, no, crouched at the fire's edge. His fingertips began to pulse. The bright light kept him from her. He didn't like the flames. He swiped at the fire, then drew back when he felt the burn. He stared at his hand, saw the long nails protruding from his fingertips. This wasn't right. Suddenly, another image flashed through his mind. A young boy watching his father roast marshmallows over an open flame.

Jason shook his head. Tried to clear his thoughts. The memories slipped away from him; he slipped away. He fought it—summoned back the boy he was, the man he had become. Not a monster. A man. He rose and howled his anger at the sky. The chanting stopped. He stared across the fire at the woman. She stood, breathing heavily, her dark gaze trained upon him. He knew her. *Tala*.

"It's gone," he said, and fell to the ground on trembling legs.

"No," she breathed. "I sense a presence. It is—"

Suddenly a dark figure stepped into the circle of light. Jason knew him, too. And he wasn't surprised to see him.

Chapter Eight

"Haidar," Tala whispered. She reached down and snatched her dress from the ground, holding it against her nakedness.

"What are you doing?" her brother demanded. "Why have you brought this man out here in the darkness? Why are you standing before him naked and unashamed?"

Words would not come to her. There were no lies she could quickly form in her mind to explain what her brother had witnessed. But how much had he seen? Had he seen Jason's eyes glowing red in the dark? Had he seen the claws tear from his fingertips? Did he know what Jason was?

"Tala?" Haidar commanded. "Explain."

"A strengthening ceremony," she whispered. "I danced for the night spirits to return his strength to him."

"I have not heard of this ceremony," Haidar scoffed. "And today, I know it was not human blood that seeped through his shirt. Why are you deceiving your people for this man? Why are you deceiving me?"

She had feared her brother knew the blood was a trick. He was too wise to fool. Still, she could not tell him the truth. If she did, he would pull his knife and slice Jason's throat without batting a lash. The laws of her people were simple for her brother to follow; they left no room for mistakes to be made. And Haidar allowed no mistakes . . . except maybe with their youngest sister. The traitor.

"Get dressed, Tala," Jason said in the silence. "And you, Goon, speak English so I can understand what you're drilling her about."

Her brother strode toward the white man. "You do not order Tala or me! You do not know your place here!" He whipped a long knife from the sheath strapped to his thigh. "I should cut out your tongue for your insolence. If Tala's sacred spells do not erase the memory of your time among us, you cannot speak of it."

"Brother," Tala warned. "He does not know our ways, our laws. He—"

Suddenly she was knocked to the ground. A foul smell, the hiss of hot breath above her, identified her attacker. It was Unma Kin Sica. A bad one. Her knives lay on the ground, beyond her reach. Haidar was no longer fixated upon the white man, nor was Jason interested in her brother. Both stared, their mouths gaping open.

"Get away from her!" Jason shouted. He made a move toward them.

The Sica's sharp teeth went for her neck. She dodged and called out to Jason, cautioning him: "No! Do not come closer."

Haidar still gripped his knife. Her eyes met his in silent communication, then she rolled suddenly to the side. The beast's long claws whooshed by, close to the bare skin of her back. Haidar lunged forward, placing himself between her and the beast.

"You dare enter my territory," he baited the Sica, jabbing his knife at the monster. "I will have your head."

The evil one roared and lunged forward, knocking him to the ground. Haidar's knife flew from his hand and landed in the fire. Tala could still not reach her own weapons; they lay beneath Haidar where he fought. The creature opened its large jaws and went for his throat.

Tala jumped on the Sica's back. It howled and knocked her off. She scrambled up from the dirt, but Jason got between them. He had snatched up a piece of burning firewood, and he struck the creature with the lit end.

"Do your thing!" he yelled at her.

She did not understand for a moment; then she knew what he asked. Narrowing her gaze, she willed the flame to grow. The beast burst into flames. It howled, jumped up, clawing at his raging inferno of a body, then ran into the forest. Tala started after it.

"No!" Jason took hold of her arm, nodding toward Haidar. "Your brother, he's bleeding bad. I don't know what to do for him."

109

Tala rushed to her brother's side. She bent before him. His throat gaped open, blood gushing forth. She grabbed her dress from off of the ground and pressed it against the horrible wound, hoping to stanch the flow.

"Help me carry him to my cave."

Jason lifted the injured man, hefting him over his shoulder. He had great strength. More than he knew, and Tala felt thankful for that. She walked behind Jason, holding the cloth of her dress tight around Haidar's neck. She did not remember she was naked until they had placed her brother on the furs inside her cave. Jason reminded her. He'd obviously gone to her baskets, for he handed her a dress.

His eyes moved over her, but then he glanced away.

"Keep the pressure against his neck," she instructed, and when Jason did as she asked, Tala hurried to dress. She headed for the cave exit.

"Hey, wait a minute," Jason called. "Where are you going?"

She glanced over her shoulder. "I must warn my people. Guards must be stationed around the camp for our safety."

"That creature's toast," he argued. "Burned up."

"Maybe," she agreed. "Maybe not. I will seek a vision as soon as I have returned. But first I must act for the good of all."

"What about him?" He glanced down at her brother's pale features. "You can't just leave him here to die. I sure as hell don't know what to do for him."

She sighed and ran a hand through her hair, fighting back tears. "He will not die. You know this."

Jason's dark brows drew together. He glanced back down at the man lying before him and her meaning suddenly registered. He shook his head sadly.

"Welcome to my world, big guy."

Chapter Nine

Haidar looked remarkably well for someone who'd had his throat ripped out two days before. Jason stirred the stew Tala had left for him to tend, watching her brother. Haidar lay on his back, staring up at the rock ceiling.

"Your sister says you need to eat," Jason said. "It will help you get your strength back."

"Do not speak to me," the man growled. "I will not be told what to do by you, or by my sister."

"I wouldn't let her hear you say that." Jason laughed. "She'd probably kick your ass from here to next Sunday."

He received the pleasure of watching the other man's brow wrinkle, no doubt trying to figure out what he meant. He liked that; payback for when Haidar and Tala spoke in their strange language to deliberately exclude him. He didn't at all like being left alone with the big guy, though. There was a mutual animosity that neither man could disguise . . . nor wanted to.

Tala entered, and Jason was relieved to see her. Her brother immediately spoke. She responded. The man tensed, so Jason guessed that she told him more bad news. He'd watched her seek her vision two nights before, going into some kind of a trance—and she hadn't looked happy when she'd come out of it. The beast was not dead. The big guy was cursed.

Regardless of his feelings toward Haidar, Jason wouldn't wish his troubles on anyone. Still, he found it a little difficult to feel *too* sorry for the guy. "He refuses to eat," Jason told Tala. "I'll be damned if I'm going to force feed him."

"Leave us," she suggested. "Go and sit outside in the sunshine. The fresh air will be good for you."

"He must not leave," her brother argued. "We cannot trust him to stay in our camp. He might run away."

Jason gave him a dirty look. "I could leave," he agreed. "I could run. But I'd rather stick around and hunt the bastard that bit you."

Haidar raised a brow. "What difference does it make to you?"

Tala gave Jason a warning glance, but he ignored her. "I know what's going to happen to you. I don't like you, but I wouldn't wish that on any human being."

"How do you know these things?"

He shrugged. "I helped Tala fight that thing in the city, remember? I wanted to know about them. She told me."

The leader's dark gaze moved to his sister. "We should talk alone. Go," he added to Jason.

"I like being bossed around by you about as much as I like being bossed around by your sister."

"Jason," Tala said softly. "It is time he knew."

Their gazes met, locked. The fine hairs on the back of his neck prickled. "I don't think telling him is such a good idea. You're the one who said so, remember?"

Making a pacifying gesture at Haidar, she walked over, took Jason's arm and guided him outside. As they moved down the incline to the meadow below, she said, "My brother already knows something is not right. He knew the blood I soaked your bandages with was not human."

"How in the hell would he know that?" Jason demanded. He felt nervous about Tala telling her brother the truth. The big guy was just looking for an excuse to get rid of him, and if she told him, he'd have a good one.

"I do not know how he knew," she said. "Only that he did. You fought for him when the Sica attacked. That will work in your favor. You must trust me to sway my brother to let you stay until I have helped you learn the way, helped you to control the beast within."

"And what if he wants me dead?"

She glanced away. Jason took her chin and gently forced her to look at him. "What then, Tala?"

"I do not know," she answered. "I will be torn."

"Yeah, me too," he said. "My head will be torn from my shoulders." He rubbed the back of his neck. "But maybe he will listen to you. Hell, he has the same problem I have now, right? It'd be like the pot calling the kettle black."

"His problem is not the same," she argued. "The creature still lurks within the forest. We will find and kill it. Then Haidar will be spared."

A sudden jolt of hope shot through Jason. "Maybe that werewolf is the same one that bit me and my brother. If we find it and kill it, not only your brother will be spared, but also my curse would be broken. My curse and Rick's."

She surprised him by touching his cheek tenderly. "Do not believe in this too strongly. The chances—"

"But there is a chance, right?" he interrupted, and he couldn't contain the excitement he felt.

Tala sighed. "Yes, I suppose there is a chance, but it would seem unlikely."

"There are a lot of unlikely coincidences that happen in the world. Take you and me meeting for instance. Sometimes people just happen to be in the right place at the right time, or the right place at the wrong time. This could be the one, Tala. Admit it."

Her dark eyes searched his. "Do not expect too much," she said.

He felt annoyed. She could at least show a little enthusiasm. Instead, she turned away and headed back up the incline.

"Stay close. If you see my brother come out of the cave searching for you and holding his big knife, run."

The white man had been nothing but trouble for her since Tala first set eyes upon him. She climbed the incline, her stomach twisted into knots over what she must tell her brother. Maybe she should no longer bother with Jason. Let him go, let him become one of the creatures he detested. But she could not.

There were no chance meetings in life. She had found Jason for a reason, and she knew her duty. She owed him a debt. One she would fulfill as best she could, then what happened to him would no longer be her concern.

Tala sucked in a deep breath before reentering her cave. Telling Haidar the truth would be difficult. She must face punishment for her own misdeeds.

Her brother sat before the small fire, eating the food she had prepared for him. At her approach, he glanced up.

"What is the man to you?" he asked. "Why do you lie for him? Deceive your own people for him? He is not sick. I saw that with my own eyes the night the beast attacked us. A sick man could not move as fast as he did. A sick man—"

"He is not ill," she interrupted. Tala walked to where her brother sat. "I have deceived you and our people for him. I knew that you would not allow his kind among us. I did not lie when I said he fought by my side in the city against two beasts. I did lie when I allowed you to believe that I had killed the beasts."

"The one that came here, it was one you fought?"

Shame consumed her and she nodded. "It must have tracked my scent. I believe that I killed his female, and he came for revenge."

Haidar shook his head. "And you did not tell me we were in danger? This is not like you, Tala. This man has cast a spell over you."

Maybe Haidar was right, but Tala felt moved to defend the white man. "He may have saved my life,

116

and he fought for yours when the beast attacked. Can you fault his courage?"

"Even a foolish man can show bravery," Haidar scoffed, shoveling food into his mouth. "You had no right to bring him here. You will cast your sacred spells, erase us from his mind and send him away."

She pressed her dry lips together. Her knees shook. "I cannot send him away. It would be the same as letting an enemy go free. I might have to hunt him one day."

Her brother's head snapped up. "What are you saying?"

Tala sat to hide her trembling legs. "The night I fought the beasts, they were attacking him. Then the male creature knocked me backward and stunned me. The white man changed. He became one of them, but in pure form. He fought against them for my safety."

"He is one of them?" Haidar asked, his expression one of disbelief. "You brought the enemy among us?"

"I owed him a debt," she reminded. "And he has not allowed the beast to rule him . . . not yet."

Her brother set his food aside. "What do you think to do for this man? He is lost. An outsider cannot overcome the call of the moon, the call of the beast. He is doomed to die by your knife . . . or by mine."

She drew a shaky breath. "I believe that I can save him. His heart is still pure. He is strong. He does not want to become the beast. I can teach him the ways, teach him to control the beast and keep it hidden."

Haidar pinched his lips together, then blew air from his mouth. "This is madness, Tala. You seek to make a wild animal into a pet. He has not been raised in the way. He cannot fight the evil within himself. His

117

kind is born to fail. Greed. Lust. Self gratification. These they learn at a young age. It is no wonder they so easily turn when bitten. They do not know how to control themselves when they are men, much less when they become something else."

What her brother said was true. Most she hunted and killed, she suspected, had not been in their altered state for long. But Jason was different. She knew it, felt it in her heart. Or maybe she wanted to believe in him. "When I see this man fighting what he has become, it makes me think of our sister, and her battle with the darkness."

Her brother sighed. "Meka is lost, Tala. We must forget her."

"She is our blood."

"She has become our enemy!"

Her temper rose. "I have not seen her in my visions. She is like the white man, still between phases. He could be her salvation!"

"And both could be our deaths!" Haidar slammed his fist against the bowl from which he'd been eating, spilling the contents. "Have you not suffered enough for her sins? You could have both been lost to me because of her."

Tala straightened. She would not be cowed by her brother. "But we learned the truth. One pure act of sacrifice can save one from the beast."

He snorted. "Where was her sacrifice? You spared her for a time, Tala. But out there, on the outside, she will listen to dark whispers once more. Listen and succumb to them."

Tala did not want to believe her brother. She would not. It was time to tell him the truth. "He is the one."

Haidar cocked a dark brow. "The one?"

Before she lost her nerve, she rushed on, "It was by her doing that he became what he is."

Her brother's face paled. "Are you certain?"

"I was there, Haidar. I am certain."

He ran a hand through his long hair, then rubbed his forehead. "You should have told me this from the beginning."

"You have made no secret to me or to The People that Meka is dead to us. She is outcast. I was not certain that knowing the white man was her victim would matter to you, but it mattered to me."

His dark gaze pinned her. "This man, is it only duty that binds you to him? He was our sister's downfall . . . I will not allow him to become yours."

"I know who I am, Haidar," she said, hating the bitterness in her voice. "I have been told since I was a little girl. I owe the man a debt, as do you now. That is all."

He glanced away. "He has been wronged, and he did fight to save me, just as he fought to save you, but I do not trust him. It is dangerous to have him among us, for him and for our tribe. If he turns . . ."

"He knows if he cannot learn the ways, learn to control the beast, that I must kill him," Tala said softly. "He wishes it to be so."

"I should find him now and cut off his head," Haidar growled.

Tala held her breath. Her brother was a hard man to sway where duty was concerned.

Finally, he said, "But he did fight for me, and there are no good feelings between us. He must keep his memory of us or lose all that you would teach him.

You know this goes against our ways. To let one who has been among us leave with so much knowledge is dangerous."

"We cannot keep him here," she argued. "Not against his will. He wishes to return to his world. Why would he speak of something that would set him apart from those he wishes to blend with? The outsiders would think him crazy."

"You ask too much, Tala."

"A life for a life," she reminded him. "The life he had was no life at all. Can your gift to him not be an opportunity to win his battle against the beast? He knows if he cannot, he is to die. What sacrifice is there in giving him a chance?"

"I do owe him a debt," Haidar admitted. "We must find the beast that bit me and kill it."

"We will," she assured him. "And what of the white man?"

When Haidar took a long time to answer, Tala feared he might hear the loud pounding of her heart.

"He will stay for now. You will teach him the ways, but if he cannot control the beast, he must die. I will keep a close watch on him since he is a threat to us. We will not tell The People what he is. Not yet." His gaze hardened. "You should be punished for deceiving us, though."

Tala accepted his words as truth and bowed her head submissively. "Yes." The gentle touch of his hand upon her hair made her glance up.

"Maybe it will be punishment enough to see him die if he fails . . . or to see him leave if he does not."

She tried to keep her expression blank. "I owe him

a debt. What happens to him after I have repaid it is of no concern to me."

Haidar rubbed his chin, his expression thoughtful. "The man will train with you, but he will not sleep in your lodge. He will sleep in mine."

Her brother's sudden decision did not please Tala, although in truth, she had no right to complain. "W-What will the people think?" She felt certain she knew what Jason Donavon would think: He would not like the arrangement.

He shrugged. "Less than they are thinking now. We will tell them the outsider is better, but not fully healed. We will say that we thought it wise to send him to a man's lodge to continue his recovery."

Without looking suspicious, she could not argue. Tala knew it was best if Jason slept in her brother's lodge, but what was best did not always please a person. "I will tell him."

Haidar rose. "It is time I returned to my lodge. Give the white man herbs to make him sleep. We will leave him in your home tonight while we hunt."

Tala started to respond, but a strange yet familiar feeling washed over her. Her eyes rolled back into her head. She smelled burnt hair, burnt flesh, and the stench she associated with a beast, one who was rotten on the inside. The vision came to her, but she already knew what was happening. The creature had come among them. It was here, waiting somewhere along the perimeters of their camp.

Jason walked slowly, shuffling his steps. He knew he shouldn't have ventured far from the incline leading to Tala's cave, but curiosity had gotten the better of him. He wanted to see her people again. They fascinated him. He almost envied them in their own little world and couldn't imagine living the way they did. But, then again, maybe it wouldn't be so bad. Far from traffic jams and city smog, crime, the everyday pressures of trying to make ends meet . . .

They made good with what they had, what the forest provided. They followed their laws, prepared from an early age to fight one foe. It sounded a hell of a lot less complicated than most people's lives. But, then, his own hadn't been all that complicated up until three years ago. He'd thought it was, but becoming a werewolf had changed his perspective. His mother used to tell him: No matter how bad things got, they could always be worse.

"Got that right, Mom," he muttered, then shuffled along around the outskirts of camp. He knew there were guards posted and wondered if any would be watching him. Probably not, he decided, as their eyes would be peeled for an intruder trying to make it into their camp. Regardless of the high alert he imagined blanketed the camp, Jason heard the sound of children at play.

Drawn by the noises, he moved in the direction of the voices. A minute later, he spotted the children. Jason allowed the trees to hide him as he watched their play. Their mothers were close by, and he noticed more than one woman glance nervously toward the kids, then scan the area.

The boys and girls played some type of game. They all carried long sticks and were batting a makeshift ball around on the ground. The game reminded Jason of soccer, only instead of kicking the ball and passing it to each other, they whacked the round hide-covered ball along the ground. He noticed the boy who'd smiled at him, the one who'd been such a good marksman. The kid was a natural athlete. He easily got in front of the other children and gave the ball a good whack that sent it flying into the trees. The kid raced to get it. He didn't come back.

"Noshi!" A woman called.

When the boy didn't appear, Jason felt the hair on the back of his neck prickle. Suddenly, mothers raced to grab their children. The woman who'd called, and who Jason assumed was the missing boy's mother, ran into the trees. A moment later, he heard her scream.

Jason took off. Although barefoot, he hardly felt the sharp pine needles and jagged rocks that cut his feet. He came across the woman and drew up short. Something hideous lay upon the ground before him. It wasn't the boy, but one of the guards who had been posted. The man had a hole in his chest. His heart was gone.

The woman shrieked words at him he couldn't understand. In the distance, the wail of a child rose up. Jason turned from the distraught mother and raced toward the boy's cries. As he ran, jumping over fallen logs like a deer, the wind blowing in his hair, he felt the wolf inside him. Not the beast, but the animal. The hunter.

He lengthened his strides, the trees moving past him in a blur. Then he saw them. Ahead, a large dark shape carried a small pale one over one shoulder. The boy still clutched the stick he'd been using to bat the ball. He beat his abductor's back, tears streaming down his young face. Jason gathered more speed.

From the corner of his eyes, he saw something—dark shapes that seemed to be running with him.

He smelled the beast now, the burnt hair and flesh that hung off its body like strips of dried meat. He was close enough to see the terror reflected in the boy's eyes. Another burst of speed and Jason sprang. All three of them went tumbling to the ground.

The beast roared and scrambled up. The boy scurried from reach. Jason rolled and gained his feet. The creature, more hideous than before, bared its yellow fangs and growled at him. They circled one another. Suddenly sure he couldn't win against this creature as only a man, Jason found himself with no choice: He willed the beast in him to come forth. Nothing happened. His foe lunged forward and swiped at him with long claws. Jason jumped back, an inch away from having his stomach torn open.

"Run!" he yelled to the boy, who stood wide-eyed and probably in shock. The kid didn't move. Jason needed a weapon. He couldn't take more than a second to glance around while the beast circled him. In that second, he didn't see anything useful. Panic started to choke him. If he didn't kill the thing, it would take the kid and he didn't want to imagine what it would do.

His panic brought the desired results he'd hoped for earlier. Fury coiled inside of him. His eyes started to burn. His skin itched. His gums ached.

"Outsider!"

The boy's voice distracted him, and he glanced over. A stick came hurling through the air toward him. Jason reached up and snatched it. The werewolf roared, charged, and knocked Jason to the ground—

but he brought the stick up just in time. The creature lunged, then screamed as its full weight came crashing down on his makeshift lance. The juicy sound of wood impaling burnt flesh was a sickening one. The creature jerked. It drooled over Jason's face. Disgusted, he shoved the thing off him.

The beast rolled onto its back, the stick jutting up from its chest. Before his eyes, Jason saw the creature reclaim the shape of the pimp he'd seen in the alley the night he met Tala. Only, the man's skin was still burned and falling off his body.

He was dead.

With the sleeve of his shirt, Jason wiped the creature's spittle from his face. When he glanced up again, he was surrounded. Tala's tribe stood in a circle around him and the fallen beast, an "evil one" as Tala called them. The members looked shocked. He supposed for a wounded man, he'd run pretty fast and fought pretty hard.

He felt a light touch upon his shoulder and nearly jumped from his skin. The boy stood before him. Although the kid's face was streaked with tears and his bottom lip trembled, he smiled bravely. Jason ruffled his hair. Whoops went up from the gathered crowd.

Haidar appeared from nowhere. He walked forward, bent, took out his knife. "I told the evil one I would take his head," he announced. "Without it, he cannot return to harm us again." With a great swipe, he beheaded the creature.

Jason glanced away from the gruesome sight. The mother of the boy he'd saved knelt before Jason. She smiled at him, tears of gratitude streaming down her cheeks. He smiled back. It was a moment. Jason

125

looked for Tala among the others. She stood proud and stone-faced like all good warrior princesses, but when her eyes met his, a twitch pulled at the corner of her mouth, and he knew she wanted to smile.

Jason didn't feel like smiling. He'd killed the beast, Haidar would be spared from his curse, but inside, Jason didn't feel any different. He stared at Tala, the question he hoped to relay screaming through his mind. She didn't say anything, but lowered her gaze, which was answer enough. The beast was not the one that had bitten him and his brother.

Chapter Ten

Jason attended the funeral of the fallen guard. He wore a blanket around his shoulders and tried to appear sicklier than he had the day before. A woman wept, he assumed the dead man's wife. Tala explained that her people did not bury their dead beneath the ground where scavengers could dig them up, or lift them toward the sky where birds could pick at their flesh. All who died were burned. Ashes to ashes. Dust to dust.

They had traveled into the forest earlier, away from the camp, and they had walked in single file. He'd taken up the rear so he could pretend to hobble. Tala walked in front of him; her brother, behind. The big man was not happy. That fact alone helped lift Jason's spirits, but not much. His life might have suddenly changed had the beast he killed been the one that had bitten him. Maybe Tala had been right, and it was too much to hope for—but he *had* hoped, and now that hope was gone.

Last evening, while he brooded inside Tala's cave, she had told him that she'd spoken to her brother about him, had in fact revealed all to him. Haidar had agreed to let him stay, but only long enough to learn the ways she would teach him, only long enough to either control the beast inside or die trying.

There seemed to be more she had wanted to tell him, but she left him alone to stew about his bad luck. He'd fallen asleep and later heard her arguing with her brother. This morning she'd told him they must see the fallen guard to the spirit world. Jason had asked his name, but she said it was now forbidden to speak it.

Although Jason didn't know the unfortunate guard, he felt bad for him. Bad for his family and those who loved him. He didn't feel bad for the pimp. Tala was right. There had been nothing human about the man.

The burnt color of the soil beneath his feet spoke of other passages to the spirit world. The dead man had been wrapped in buckskin and laid upon a stack of kindling and wood. Words were spoken, but Jason didn't understand them. A few tribesmen with torches went forward and lit the wood. They all stood in a circle and watched as the flame caught and the fire grew higher. They chanted and sang. Jason felt out of place, but at the same time, he felt he had the right to be among them. He had earned it yesterday.

Before the fire burned out, the members turned toward camp. A few men stayed, no doubt to make sure the fire burned the body but not the forest. Jason followed the group. They walked in silence, heads bowed, single file. Once they reached the camp perimeters, they went about their business. Jason followed Tala to the incline below her cave. Haidar went, too. He and Tala broke into an argument a few minutes later. They didn't speak English, but seemed to reach some type of compromise before Haidar stomped away.

"Come," Tala said to Jason. "We will eat."

She led the way up the embankment toward her cave. Jason wondered what she'd do if he refused to follow her commands. Come, sit, stay—he felt like a dog. But he was hungry. They ate rabbit, left over from a meal the night before. Too bad there wasn't a McDonald's around the corner. Jason didn't want to think about all the "what ifs" he had let plague him throughout the night. The beast he'd killed wasn't the one that bit him. It didn't mean he wouldn't eventually find the right one and kill it, ending the curse.

"What you did yesterday was brave." Tala broke into his thoughts. "You have won my people's respect."

He glanced up at her. "Well, I know one who doesn't think much of me. Your brother didn't even thank me for saving him from this hell."

She touched his hand. "Haidar is . . . he keeps his feelings inside. I am certain he is grateful."

Jason snorted. "Yeah. He's an asshole is what he is. I'd appreciate it if you'd try to make sure our paths don't cross all that often while I'm here."

Tala took her hand away and ran it through her long hair. "That will be a problem." She shifted her weight upon the furs where she sat. "There is something that I have not told you."

He lifted a brow.

She wet her lips, and he wished she hadn't brought them to his attention. "My brother insists that you stay with him during your time among us."

Jason was glad he wasn't eating or he would have choked. "Please tell me you're joking."

"I do not joke."

He couldn't argue that fact. Tala didn't have much of a sense of humor. "Why?"

"He believes that it is not right for us to be alone in my lodge. And now that he knows about you, he wishes to guard our people."

Jason snorted. "So now instead of being your prisoner, I become his? At least I don't mind waking up to your face. His is a different story."

What closely resembled a blush settled in her cheeks. "He says the people will talk less if you stay in his home."

"Afraid I'll deflower the warrior princess, are they?"

She cast him a blank look.

"Steal your precious virginity," he clarified.

The blush in her cheeks darkened. "Yes. That along with my powers."

"Well, there's no chance of that happening . . . is there?"

Despite her tough outer shell, she became flustered easily when the subject turned to sex. He enjoyed that. Then she said, "No."

He sighed. "Didn't think so. What about our training?"

"We will continue," she assured him. "The other night was a good start. I called the beast within you forth, and you controlled him and sent him back into hiding."

"I remember." He realized that was something in itself. "And I remember you dancing . . . naked."

She shrugged. "The beast inside you is no different than the man. He is tempted by lust."

"I did lust," he agreed. "I lust now. Does that mean the beast is getting stronger?"

Lust was both a human and an animal trait. Tala could not answer his question, so she tried to steer his thoughts from the subject. "The People will give you a celebration ceremony. They will allow a short time for mourning our brother's passing to the spirit world, but then they will have a feast for you. They will honor your bravery."

"A party?" he asked, then smiled, although it was not one that reached his eyes. "I guess I could use some cheering up."

Tala felt bad for him. She wished the Sica he had killed could have released him from his curse, but she had known that was not possible.

"What do you think of my people?" she asked.

He stretched his arms overhead, making his muscles bulge in an attractive manner. "I find them interesting. Most of them anyway," he added, then frowned, and she knew he did not find one of them to his liking.

"You must go to his lodge. I have let you stay too long already. Haidar is expecting you."

Jason rose, but continued stretching. He glanced down at her. "Will you miss me?"

His question, along with the sound of his soft, deep voice, made her quiver in places he could not see. "I will have my bed again," she said, which she knew was not an answer. "It is better this way," she tried to convince both herself and him.

A moment later, he bent beside her. "Why can't you just say that you'll miss me? Where's the harm in that?"

She glanced up at him. She would miss him inside her cave, but she could not say the words he wanted to hear. What burned between them was not harmless. Jason was not harmless. She, herself, was not harmless. Danger came in many forms. Sometimes, in something as small as a word.

"You must go," she whispered.

His face lowered to hers. "No goodbye kiss even?"

"Jason," she warned, but his name sounded like a caress upon her lips.

The touch of his fingers sliding along her cheek sent tongues of flame dancing along her skin. He cupped her chin, turning her face up to his.

"I'll miss you, Tala. I'm not afraid to say the words."

"You have less to lose."

"I have nothing to give," he agreed. "But at least my words are mine and not what someone else has told me to think or say."

"You still do not understand," she breathed, and his lips kept inching closer to hers.

"I understand that there is something between us. I understand that it's been there from the beginning. I understand that you're not happy in the role you've been given. In my world, people change what they're unhappy about if they can. They dare to reach for what they want, and don't settle for only what they've been given."

"Our worlds are not the same," Tala said, and she believed that, but she allowed her lips to seek his because at the moment, that would make her happy. Just the touch of his mouth against hers.

"Tala!"

She jumped at the sound of her brother's call. Tala jerked her face from Jason's hand and quickly scooted away from him. Her brother appeared a moment later. Jason rose.

"You said you would send the white man. He has had enough time to eat."

"He was leaving."

Tala hoped Haidar did not notice the trouble she had catching a normal breath. She hoped he could not see the fire she felt burning within her, the ache for the forbidden, one kiss, a lingering touch.

"Come, White Man. We will go," her brother commanded.

For a moment, she feared Jason would refuse. His gaze, filled with the same heat she knew burned in her own eyes, would not turn away. It was good that her brother had come for him. Jason made her question what was not right to question, desire what was not hers to desire.

His gaze lowered, and he retrieved the tattered sack that held his few belongings.

"Thank you for breakfast, Tala."

"You are welcome," she whispered and cleared the huskiness from her voice.

Haidar glanced from her to Jason, as if he felt the current that crackled and sizzled between them like a lightning storm. He frowned and shoved Jason ahead of him.

"I said we go."

"Watch it, big man," Jason growled. "I've taken down larger guys than you."

"You should learn respect," Haidar snapped. "Maybe that will be the lesson *I* teach you."

Tala heard Jason mumble something else as he departed her cave and a lower threat returned by her brother. They would kill each other, her brother and this man from the outside world. This man who did not follow the way of the *ba'cho*, but his own heart. She was not brave enough to do the same.

"I will miss you in my home, Jason Donavon," she said, now that it was safe to do so.

Haidar's lodge was a cave much like Tala's. It lacked something, that feminine touch—no, it lacked a hell of a lot more than that. It lacked Tala. Something was happening between them, something that shouldn't, but it was something Jason couldn't stop. How could he learn to tame the beast within, when he couldn't even control the feelings developing for a woman forbidden to him?

Of course, all women were forbidden to Jason . . . it was just that other women he might meet weren't chosen for some divine purpose in life. The others wouldn't have special powers or live among a secret society of Native Americans where getting involved with a white man, much less a werewolf, ranked right up there with the rest of the seven deadly sins.

"My sister," Haidar grumbled, bending to add more

wood to his fire. "I do not like the way that you look at her."

Jason sat on the hard floor of the cave. "I look at her like a man looks at a woman."

"She is not a woman," the huge man said, his voice low, threatening. "Not to you. Not to any man. She is the one chosen. Her destiny has been decided. It cannot be changed."

Jason scoffed at the notion. "If I didn't believe destiny could be changed, I wouldn't still be here. Did it ever occur to you that your sister might not like being the one chosen? That she might want to make her own choices about what she wants and doesn't want?"

They were obviously not good questions to ask her overprotective brother, whose face turned red. "Our destinies, our ways, are not to be questioned. Not by us and not by a fool who knows nothing of our world, a fool who looks at my sister the way no man has the right to look at her. You are a *wapiskisiw* and would not be accepted even if Tala were not forbidden, even if you did not have a wolf beneath your skin."

Jason got the distinct impression Haidar had a race issue. "You don't just dislike me because of what I am. You don't like me because my skin is a different color than yours."

The big man glanced up at him, then shrugged. "I will not say otherwise."

Shaking his head, Jason said, "If you want to learn more modern ways, at least learn to pretend you aren't prejudiced. That's what bigots do in the outside world."

"What is a bigot?" Haidar demanded.

"You," Jason answered. "A man who thinks he's

better than someone else because of the color of his skin."

"I *am* better than you," the man said with a snort. "I will not pretend I feel different than I do. Your kind, the White Eyes, have long committed wrongs against my people."

"That's true," Jason admitted, thinking his ass would go to sleep sitting on the hard rock floor of Haidar's sparsely furnished cave. "But your bunch hasn't been so nice to us either."

"In the past, my race fought for what was ours by right. We fought for our way of life."

"And we fought for a chance at a new beginning, a better life," Jason countered. "Everyone fought for something back in those days, and I guess they still are. I envy your people," he admitted. "This simple way of life they lead."

"Simple," Haidar snorted. "You have not lived out a winter here. Our life is hard, but we accept that to be free. To live the way we need to live, the way we want to live, we must endure the struggles. Tala is invaluable to us. It is not her place to think of her own wants and needs, above the destiny she has been given. I think you try to confuse her upon these issues. I think if you continue to try, I will kill you."

Haidar couldn't be faulted for his directness. Jason knew to continue the argument would lead nowhere. At least not with this man. They sat in silence for a time; then Haidar threw a piece of wood on the fire.

"Can you make it grow higher like your sister can?" Jason asked.

"Can you never stay quiet?" the man snapped. "No.

I do not have the powers my sister has, powers she should not have shown you."

She'd shown him more than her powers. Jason didn't think saying so was a good idea, though. And he was getting a whiff of what he suspected might be a case of good old-fashioned sibling jealousy. "You think you should have been the one. The one chosen. Not your sister."

Haidar's dark eyes cut toward him. "It is a great honor. It is also a great responsibility. A woman . . ."

"A woman what?" Jason goaded.

The big man straightened. He brushed his long hair back over his shoulders. "A woman is weaker than a man. Her heart is softer. The path of the one chosen would be simpler for a man to follow."

"A bigot and chauvinist pig," Jason muttered under his breath, and he figured he might as well save it. The conversation did nothing to bridge the gap that yawned ever widening between himself and Tala's brother. They were too different . . . or maybe too much alike. He balked at that thought. He wasn't like Haidar. The man was right out of the Stone Age.

"I'm tired," Jason said. "I'd like to go to sleep."

Haidar shrugged. "Then do so."

Jason only saw one mat on the floor. "Where should I sleep?"

"Wherever you wish." Haidar rose, grabbed the edge of his sleeping mat and positioned it between Jason and the cave's exit.

A muscle jumped in Jason's jaw, but he'd be damned if he would ask Tala's brother for anything. He laid on the cold, hard, rocky surface of the cave floor and shoved his tattered plastic bag beneath his head. If Tala still didn't have possession of his razor, he felt sure he'd slit her brother's throat.

He rolled over and went to sleep.

Chapter Eleven

"Why do you move like an old man?" Tala asked.

Jason rubbed his shoulder. "Ask your brother."

Tala glanced at her stone-faced sibling. She'd brought the men breakfast, using it as an excuse to make certain both were still alive this morning. Haidar only shrugged.

"The floor is hard," Jason answered what her brother would not. "And cold," he added, his voice an indication that his mood was no better than her brother's.

"You did not give him pelts?" she asked Haidar. "Blankets?"

Haidar finally spoke. "He did not ask."

Her gaze strayed back to Jason. "Why did you not ask?"

His neck made a loud popping noise when he moved his head to the side. "In my society, a guest shouldn't have to ask for the basic necessities while staying in another's home. All that is needed should be thoughtfully provided without having to grovel."

"Grovel?" she repeated.

"Beg," he explained.

She rolled her eyes and set the food in front of the men. "Our society is different from yours," she said to Jason. Then to her brother she added, "But not that different. It was rude not to offer a—"

"He is not a guest," Haidar interrupted. "Why should he be treated as one?"

While her brother's words were true in that Jason was more of a prisoner than a guest in their camp, even an enemy should be given basic considerations. Of course, they had never had either a guest or a prisoner in their camp before.

"I will bring him what he requires to sleep," Tala decided. "Now, eat. I have prepared this meal for you."

Haidar did not need further prompting. He dug his fingers into the food she had prepared. The white man, she knew, preferred eating utensils. She moved to her brother's belongings and found Jason a wooden bowl and a spoon Haidar had fashioned from the horn of a deer.

"Here," she said, handing him the items.

"I'd like the food better without your brother slurping over there," he muttered. "He should learn some manners."

Haidar slammed the pan down. "All this man does is complain! Nothing pleases him!"

Her brother's temper surprised Tala. Haidar usually controlled his emotions well. This was not good, two dominant males sharing the same den.

"I think the white man needs fresh air," Tala said. "And you, Brother, need time alone."

"Do not take him past the perimeters of camp," Haidar warned. "Keep him from the others."

"If I take him outside and not past the perimeters of camp, how do I keep him from the others, Haidar?"

"I do not know," her brother admitted.

"The people will want to mix with him," she argued. "He saved Noshi's life. He risked his own to do so. You know that they plan a ceremony to honor him."

"Excuse me," Jason cut in. "Talking about someone as if they aren't present is also rude."

Tala wished Jason would stay silent. He only angered her brother with his bold attitude and his careless remarks. She cast him a warning glance.

"They would not honor him if they knew the truth," Haidar said. "But by our agreement, I will not tell them. Not unless it becomes necessary."

Her brother scowled at the white man; Jason scowled back. Tala thought both were being childish and wanted to end their play before it erupted into violence.

"Come with me, Jason . . . Donavon," she added because the use of his first name sounded too intimate in her brother's company. "We will walk outside."

"Anything to get away from him," he muttered, and rose, stretching his back before he followed her from the cave.

"You must try harder to get along with Haidar while you are among us," she said. "You test his temper too often."

141

"Me?" he asked. "He's the one with the problem."

She stopped when they reached the bottom of the incline and faced him. "*You* are the one with a problem, remember? The full moon fast approaches. You are not ready to face the call and remain in control. We must prepare."

Jason knew that the wolf still lived inside him, but being with Tala, being part of a society, even if it wasn't his own, had made him feel more human than he had felt in three years. At times, he almost forgot he was cursed.

"What do we need to do?"

"Tonight, when the camp is quiet, we will slip away into the forest. You will try to become the wolf and try to keep your human thoughts."

The idea still daunted Jason. He'd almost done it last time, but he also knew the power of the beast within. Could he contain it, hold it back? "What if I run away while in the form of a wolf?"

"You will return," she answered. "The animal will remember there is food here, a den where it has slept."

A mate, he thought—but didn't speak it aloud. He didn't even like the thought. Tala might be accepting of him, at least more accepting than his own race would be, but unless he could break the curse, he had no right to want her. He had no right anyway, not according to her brother . . . and not even according to Tala. His brain, along with other parts of his body, obviously didn't get the message.

She looked beautiful to him this morning. He liked her long, dark hair, would love to run his fingers through it, feel it brush against his bare skin. Jason glanced away from her, afraid if she looked at him she'd see his thoughts reflected in his eyes.

"How long do I have?" he asked.

She glanced at him. "What do you ask?"

"I know your brother won't let me stay here indefinitely. How long do I have to master the wolf? How long before I either succeed or you kill me?"

In a gesture that surprised him, she placed her fingertips against his lips. "You must succeed," she whispered. "You *will* master the wolf," she added, her voice stronger.

Jason wrapped his fingers around hers and removed them from his lips. He didn't release her hand. "How long?"

Her dark eyes lowered. "Not long. Until the full moon cycle."

"Then we'd better get busy."

"Niece!"

The call had Tala quickly wresting her hand from his. Jason watched her uncle approach. The old man's hair hung past his shoulders, snowy white. His face was wreathed in wrinkles, his body stooped from old age—and arthritis, Jason suspected, by the slow way the man moved.

"Uncle," Tala said, then moved forward so the old man didn't have to walk so far to reach them. Jason followed, moving as if he were sore, which wasn't a pretense. He knew his body would recover quickly, however, which was not the case for the old man.

"You look well this morning," Tala said upon reaching her uncle.

"If only these old bones did not swell and ache inside my skin," he complained. "And my bowels either do not move or they move too quickly. It is one way or the other."

Jason fought a smile when Tala's cheeks darkened a shade. "I will pick you some berries to help. Just don't eat too many at once."

"You are a good niece," he said. Then his gaze fell upon Jason.

"How are you, outsider? You must be healing to have attacked and killed an evil one. Already, the people are telling stories about your courage."

Stories? About him? Jason's face grew hot. "I didn't think about my injuries. When I heard the woman scream and discovered that beast had taken her son, my response was automatic . . . without thought," he clarified.

"The people wish to honor you with a ceremony," the old man said. "See, the men prepare now to hunt for game to ready a feast praising your courage."

Jason took note of the men preparing to leave. Haidar was among them, and he didn't look pleased that he'd spend his day hunting for Jason's food. Once the men were ready, they moved single file from the camp. Jason turned back to Tala's uncle.

"I don't know your name," he said.

"Nayati," the old man provided.

"Jason Donavon." He stuck his hand out. "In my culture, when men meet, they shake hands."

Tala's uncle stared at his outstretched hand, then slowly clasped his palm. They shook. Jason released his hand and the old man smiled at him.

"It is a strange custom," he observed.

Jason supposed it was if one thought about it. Two

men touching hands. A hearty slap on the back seemed manlier.

"Do you toss bones?" Nayati asked.

Although Jason had seen the old men tossing them, he really didn't understand the game. He didn't have to answer. Tala answered for him.

"Gambling is a bad way to spend your days, Uncle," she scolded. "Soon, your lodge will be empty with all that you have lost to the other old men."

"There is little an old man finds pleasurable when his back is stooped and his feet move slowly," he defended. "Besides, you will replace all that I have lost. You always do."

"Give the guy a break," Jason cut in, then turned to Tala's uncle. "I'd like to learn to play bones when I'm feeling better."

The man did not smile back at him. His white brows furrowed. "Why do you ask my niece to break something of mine?"

Jason kept forgetting he wasn't in his world anymore, and it was astounding how literal this tribe of people could be. "It's just an expression. It means to cut you some slack, uh, to leave you alone about what you like to do."

"Ahhh." Nayati shook his head. He glanced at Tala. "You heard him. Give me a break."

Instead, she gave both of them a dirty look and prodded Jason forward. "He does not need to learn to speak back to me; he does that fine already."

"I like him," Jason decided as they walked away.

"He is hard to dislike," Tala agreed, and she smiled. "When we were young, he used to tickle me and my

145

sister until we screamed for him to stop. He made us laugh even when we were feeling sad."

"I bet he didn't tickle your brother," Jason muttered.

"No. Haidar did not like to be touched."

They walked in silence for a few minutes. Jason could tell Tala's thoughts had drifted to the past. "Do you think your sister will return someday?"

She shook her head. "Meka broke a sacred law by leaving the tribe. She is cast out now. She must make her way alone."

"Maybe she isn't alone," he said. "Maybe she's found someone. Maybe she's happy with her new life."

"I would like to believe so," Tala said. "But I do not think so. She is . . . different, like the rest of us. She will not fit into your world, no matter how hard she tries."

He didn't know what to say. Tala had lost the slight smile that had brightened her face. Now she looked somber. "What are those women doing?" he asked to distract her.

Beneath one of the lodges, sat a big boiling pot. The women took turns stirring.

"They are making glue," she answered. "They take the brains, gums, eyeballs—different parts of a deer that cannot be eaten—and boil it until it becomes sticky."

He was sorry he asked. "Interesting," he said. "Do you make your own clothes?"

"Of course we do," she answered with a laugh. "Do you think we buy them in the stores like I see when I travel to the city?"

"I guess not. Those leggings and . . . what are they called?" He indicated the long cloth the men wore that covered their front and back, hooked to a thin belt.

"Breechclouts," she provided.

"Yeah, anyway, their clothes look comfortable."

She glanced at his jeans, which now had a hole in both knees. "Would you like a pair?"

"Yes," he admitted. "And some moccasins. The knee-high kind like your brother wears."

"I will see what I can do," she said, and the half smile had returned to her lips.

His attention turned to her lips, too. They were full, inviting, petal soft, very kissable. She laughed at some of the antics of the children in the distance. Her face took on an inner glow as she watched the children.

"You like children, don't you?" he asked.

She nodded. "They are the center of our world. We love and protect them as if they are our own, even when they are not. As you can see, we do not have many."

Jason had noticed that. "Why not? It seems for a tribe dying, you'd want to produce as many children as possible to strengthen your numbers."

"We are ever mindful of who we can provide for. At times the winters are harsh and game is scarce. We will not have our children starving. Those who are mated must seek permission from the Council before they conceive a child. And for most of the women, conception is difficult."

"I'd think you'd have the opposite problem," he said. "Unless your tribe has managed to discover birth

147

control, I don't see how conception can be controlled."

"What is birth control?"

"Pills, condoms . . . ways to prevent pregnancy when two people are intimate with each other."

"There are other ways," she said. "Abstinence is one of them."

He laughed. "You're kidding? You expect married people to abstain from having sex? This might be a nice place to visit, but I wouldn't want to live here."

"That is because you come from a world where all only think of their own needs and not the needs of the society in which they live. We cannot do that here. We must always do what is best for the tribe."

"You didn't," he reminded her. "You brought me here."

She frowned. "My shame is great for what I have done."

He hadn't wanted to make her feel bad. "You're only trying to help me," he said. "I'll try not to let you down."

"I am not standing on anything," she puzzled.

Jason knew when he laughed at her, it made her feel ignorant. "I mean, I'll try not to disappoint you."

"Yes, I believe that."

Their eyes met, held for a moment. A young boy suddenly appeared from nowhere, touched Jason and ran away. Tala laughed.

"What was that about?"

"He has counted coup on you. You are now a great warrior in The People's eyes. It is a show of his bravery to touch you."

Jason wasn't totally ignorant of Native American

ways. Television and world history had given him an advantage over Tala. He felt a sudden sense of pride rush through him. He'd been called a considerate lover, a good son, a clever accountant, but never a great warrior. He liked it. He liked walking outside with Tala next to him, the sun filtering through the trees. People worked around him, going about their lives, even if their lives were different from the rest of the world. Only one thing dampened his spirits.

Tonight, he would face the wolf within once more. Tonight, he'd be forced to let go of the human, to put Tala in danger.

Chapter Twelve

Haidar had trudged back into camp with the other hunters late in the evening. The men carried two large deer, gutted and stretched out on long poles, the hooves tied together so the men could easily manage the haul by balancing the poles upon their shoulders. Jason was glad the leader was too tired to do more than scowl at him and find his mat once he entered his lodge.

He watched the big man until his breathing grew heavy, until he started to snore softly. Jason rose from the pelts Tala had given him to use as bedding. He crept past the sleeping man, expecting him to suddenly wake and grab his ankle, but Haidar didn't stir.

His soles had toughened from not wearing shoes, and when he made his way down the incline, he hardly felt the rocks. Tala waited below. She glanced behind him.

"Where is my brother?"

"Asleep. I made it past him without waking him up."

She frowned. "I told you to tell him that we were going out into the forest tonight. He would have wanted to come with us."

"I know." He smiled at her in the darkness. "That's why I didn't tell him."

Her expression didn't soften, but a smile almost tugged at the corner of her lips. "He will be angry if he finds out we were alone together . . . that you called the beast forth and he was not there to watch over me."

Jason shrugged. "He wasn't along to watch over you in the city when you fought the evil ones. You said you didn't need a man to protect you."

"I do not, or I did not when I told you that. Now, things are different between us."

He knew things had changed, but he was surprised she would admit it.

"Now it would be harder for me to kill you if you attacked me. If the beast within desired the taste of my blood, stabbing you in the heart with my knife would be difficult."

His teasing mood vanished. "You must. Promise me if I ever come at you, you'll kill me." When she didn't respond, he took her shoulders between his hands. "Promise me, Tala."

"I promise," she whispered.

She turned from him and lifted her face to the night breeze. "Hahnee guards our camp tonight. He has chosen a good place to watch the perimeters. We cannot slip past him. We must use the tunnels."

Jason wondered how anyone could watch in the dark. Tala had already started back up the incline leading to her lodge. He quickly followed. Once inside her cave, he saw her push the rock that opened the secret passageway. He followed her into the narrow tunnel and watched again as she pushed a rock that made the door swing closed. He noted that the rock was smoother than the ones surrounding it, probably due to the frequent press of her hand against the secret latch. He might have to escape at some point. A secret route might come in handy.

The darkness was almost suffocating, even for him. He didn't know how Tala could see so well, but he assumed she knew her way from traveling the tunnels often. Again, he wondered how he'd ever find his way down the tunnels without her. The passageways twisted and turned, some leading off in other directions.

"Where do the other passageways lead?"

"Be quiet," Tala whispered. "The sound of our voices travel these tunnels easily. Some lead nowhere. Some lead to other lodges. There is not a lodge occupied by a tribal family that does not have two escape routes."

"That's amazing. It must have taken—"

"Centuries," she agreed. "It took many years to carve our world from these bluffs."

It still seemed inconceivable to Jason that Tala's tribe had managed to survive in secret for so long. They came to an opening and were outside a moment later, beneath the stars. He liked the night. The cover of darkness made the world hidden for most, but his superior eyesight allowed him to see almost as well as he did during the day. That would be lost to him if he managed to break the curse. A small price, Jason supposed, to win back his humanity. His night vision, his keen sense of hearing and smell, all would return to normal. He would adjust to the loss, just as he had adjusted to the changes when he first became a werewolf.

"How will I call the beast forth?" he asked Tala now that they had moved a short distance from camp.

"I will tell you when we reach the place I have chosen," she answered. "It must be something you learn to control yourself. Not something that controls you."

Excitement rushed through his veins with even the possibility that he could control the change. "But you're not sure that it can really be done?"

She didn't answer for a moment. He stared at the back of her head, watching the sway of her long hair and wondering why he followed behind her, single file, his footprints covering hers.

"I told you, I have only heard stories, legends. But I believe all things are possible for one who is determined. You must become determined, Jason. You must call on all that is good in you to give you strength, and ignore the dark whispers in your mind that cause you doubt. You must accept what you are."

That might be a problem. Jason had been fighting what he'd become for three years, and now he was supposed to accept the curse, his fate, and the loss of a normal life? He understood now when she'd said the trials before him would be great. Accepting himself even when he'd been human hadn't always been easy.

"Is there a good side to being a beast?"

"You are not yet a beast," she snapped. "You are only a man who has the potential to become one. I believe the evil ones turn because they are lost. They let fear overpower them, change them, fill their hearts with loathing for what they have become. They see no good in themselves. They soon see no good in others. They cannot control their bloodlust, or think with human thought once the change is complete. They are like wounded animals, cornered, growling and snapping at any who stumble upon them."

"So they can't rationalize like a human once the change takes them?"

"No," she answered, glancing over her shoulder at him. "But they can be as cunning as a wolf."

"That night in the city. The woman purposely stalked me."

"Once the evil ones have tasted blood, they cannot resist it. Even in human form they crave the sweet taste."

"Why didn't she know? Why didn't they both know what I am?"

Tala stopped, turning to face him. "Your scent attracted her, but in her human form, she did not understand why. The human mind only accepts what can be seen at first glance."

"Can you see him now, while you're looking at me? Can you see the wolf?"

Tala did see the wolf staring down at her, but Jason did not understand how the sight affected her. The animal in him was not ugly, but beautiful, the same as he was beautiful to look at as a man. "Yes, I see him," she answered. "But I do not fear him."

He gently touched her cheek. "I would never want to harm you, hurt anyone. Help me, Tala."

Her heart twisted, felt as if he'd ripped it from her chest. To see this man, tall and strong, begging for her help nearly destroyed her. Shame such she had never known washed over her. Tala must help him. She had taken upon her sister's sins, and now the guilt, the fault, lay within her. She must help him accept what had been done to him. Either that, or make another sacrifice. The ultimate one.

"Can I kiss you, Tala? If you're not afraid of me, and if you don't find the beast within me ugly, can I have this moment to only be a man in your eyes?"

She should resist. The woman within her wanted what Jason wanted. Human contact. A moment to know the brush of lips, the touch of hands, to feel as if they were both part of a normal world, and not the one fate had given to them. In his arms, she was not Tala Soaringbird, the chosen one of a tribe that had kept itself shut off from the rest of civilization for centuries. In his arms, she was only a woman.

"We should not," she whispered.

"I didn't ask if we should. I asked if I could."

The stars shone in his eyes. She felt the strength in him, but she also felt the gentleness. If she told him no, he would not use force. Her body spoke what her lips would not say. She moved closer to him, tilted her face up to receive a reprieve from a lifetime of loneliness. For only a moment, she could pretend he was her mate. Pretend the laws by which she lived allowed her to have a man, to live as normal women lived.

He took her mouth with less gentleness than she

155

expected. His feelings for her were raw, new, as were hers for him. His passion did not frighten her, but fueled her desires. His lips were firm, warm, demanding against hers. She opened to him and his tongue crept inside her mouth, swirled around hers, and swept all rational thought away.

Tala's arms went around his neck. He pressed his hard body against hers. She liked the feel of him, the smell of him. He needed to shave again. The thought drifted through her mind as his rough whiskers rubbed against her sensitive cheeks. He ran his hands down her back, and she did not think of anything but the heat building between them.

Deep inside, she knew she wanted to feel his touch against her bare flesh—to lay with him, naked, unashamed, limbs entangled. He had given her pleasure with his kisses, with his touch, but she sensed there was much more she did not understand, would not and could not ever experience. It brought resentful feelings to the surface, feelings she had told him did not exist.

Lies. So many lies lay between them. She broke from him. The truth brought logic that his lips easily stole from her. He groaned softly, but he did not reach for her again. Tala turned and started walking. She wondered for a moment if he would follow. Maybe he would run away . . . and maybe she would let him. He could not escape, reason reminded her. Not until he had learned the ways.

"It is not much farther," she said, and noticed that her voice sounded deeper, breathless. He did not respond, but she knew he followed her. Tala led him deep into the forest. Tonight, she was much more aware of the man than the night sounds or the animals scurrying for cover as they approached. Her lips still tingled from his kisses. Her cheeks still stung from the friction of his coarse whiskers against her skin. Tomorrow night, he would be given his ceremony. She would see that he shaved and dressed properly for the occasion.

They reached the place she had chosen. It was a hot spring, like the underground Sacred Waters of her cliffs but much smaller. Hot springs were numerous in her forest. The heat from the bubbling water created a thin mist that cloaked the area. It also provided a moist heat that would allow them a measure of comfort.

"You must remove your clothing," she said, turning to face him.

"Do what?"

She tried to pretend his nakedness would not affect her. "You must be naked to take your pure human form, to summon your pure wolf form."

Jason didn't have a problem with getting naked, but he'd have less of one if she agreed to strip down with him. Her kisses were no longer inexperienced, and he had trouble remembering that she was forbidden to him—to all men. His mind easily provided doubts to assuage his guilt. He didn't think Tala wanted the life she'd been given. It sounded like a hell of a responsibility for anyone who didn't care to be the one chosen of her people.

To him, it was like being born into poverty or to parents who were cruel. Or turning into a werewolf. Sometimes life dealt you a bad hand, but that didn't mean a person couldn't draw a few new cards. Tala wanted to teach him acceptance, but deep down, he didn't think she accepted who she was or the duties she'd been given. The sorrow he saw in her eyes at times told him that she was not happy with her life or with her choices. Maybe he could teach her to change what made her unhappy and reach for what would. It was the way of *his* people.

She turned away from him, and he stripped off his clothes. The warmth from the hot spring made the night chill bearable. "What now?" he asked.

"I—I must face you."

Her sudden shyness made him smile. "I don't think anything I have has changed since the last time you saw me naked."

"Understand that I will not be looking at you the way a woman looks at a man, but as your spiritual guide, who is focused on nothing more than the merging of our minds."

"Fine," he said. "At least we can merge something."

Slowly, she turned to face him. She kept her gaze locked with his. "You will close your eyes, and my mind will send yours a picture of what you have not yet seen. The hidden part of you. The wolf. You will summon him, but you will fight to keep your thoughts those of a man, even as you command your body to shift, to become what you fear the most about yourself."

He took a deep breath and closed his eyes. "Okay, show me."

Nothing happened for a moment. He thought he felt her eyes moving over him and tried to ignore the possibility that she might have lied—that she might in fact be staring at him as a woman would stare at a naked man. Then something did happen. A form took shape in his mind. At first, it was hazy. Like a reflection in a rippling pool of water. Gradually the ripples became larger. Then the water stilled.

The shape became clearer. A wolf—large, black, with blue eyes. Jason didn't find the creature horrifying. The animal was just that, not a monster. It didn't stand on two legs. Its head wasn't grotesquely larger than its body. It didn't have red glowing eyes or yellow fangs that dripped saliva.

"Is that me?" he asked.

"Only a part of who you are. Call him to you."

Jason willed the image to come closer. The wolf moved with a grace only something wild and untamed possessed.

"Look into his eyes," Tala said. "You must make him recognize you."

Concentrating, he stared into the wolf's eyes, into a reflection of his own gaze. The animal curled back its lips and growled. Jason's first instinct was to withdraw from the confrontation.

"No," Tala cautioned, recognizing his fear. "You must show him that you do not fear him. You must subject him to your will, not be subjected by him."

Jason clenched his fists at his sides. He stared the animal down, even though he heard a growl rise from his own throat.

"Join your mind with his," she said softly. "Know what he knows, *be* what he is."

He sought the wolf's thoughts, imagined the two of them merging as one. A burst of adrenaline shot through him. Then Jason was running. The night rushed past him in a blur of distorted colors. He caught the scent of prey, the scent of disease, the scent of the weak. His long legs picked up speed. The diseased animal came within his vision. It hung back from the others, the rest of the herd quickly outdistancing him.

His heart pounded in rhythm with the animal's hoofbeats. His prey stumbled, went to its knees. He lunged, sank his teeth deep into the soft flesh of its rump. The sweet taste of blood filled his mouth. The animal squealed in pain. Jason tried to break the contact between his mind the wolf's.

"No," Tala said again. "You must accept him. You must understand him."

The ravenous hunger in his belly registered—a need to eat, to gorge himself because tomorrow, there might not be food. He ate until he could eat no more; then he left the rest for scavengers. The night air ruffled his fur. So many scents on the air. So many sounds echoed around him.

He moved like a shadow through the night. Ahead, a flash of movement raced across his path. He stopped, sniffed the air. This smell was one he knew, yet one unfamiliar to him. He howled, called to someone or something. Then he waited. It came a moment later, an answering call.

Darkness enveloped him, swirled and danced around him until he became lost, until there was only the darkness, only the wolf, and the man slipped away.

Chapter Thirteen

"You must wake, Jason."

A gentle nudge against his shoulder. He snuggled deeper into the furs.

"Jason, it is morning. You must wake before my brother comes looking for you."

Another nudge, this time not so gentle. "Okay, okay," he grumbled. Jason suddenly wondered what he was doing in Tala's lodge if it was morning? What he was doing in her bed? He bolted up, knocking his head against something. When he opened his eyes and saw Tala rubbing her forehead, he knew what he'd bumped.

"Sorry. Are you all right?"

"Yes," she answered, but kept rubbing her head.

Jason glanced around. He lifted the furs and noticed he was naked beneath them. "What am I doing here?" He remembered last night . . . parts of it anyway.

"And . . ." Suddenly he noticed his hands. They were covered in blood. "Oh my God, what did I do?"

"Calm yourself," Tala said. The sound of her voice soothed him somewhat. "Do you remember becoming the wolf?"

He did, but he didn't. "I remember sharing his thoughts, killing an animal, the taste of blood. Then I saw something, another wolf or something, and I don't remember anything after that."

"You must have hunted," she said. "That is why there is blood on you." She set a bowl of water beside him. "Quickly, wash it away and get dressed. Here are your garments from last night."

"Did you see me change?"

"We will speak of it later," she insisted. "You returned here as the sun rose. You climbed into my mats. Haidar will be here any moment looking for you. You must pretend that you were hungry and came here for food." Tala scrambled to her place before the fire.

Jason had no idea about what he ate—where it came from, or what in the hell it might be. He also realized with a sick feeling he wasn't at all hungry.

"What are you making?" he asked when he finished, sliding on his worn jeans. He slipped his shirt over his head.

"It is a mixture of roots and worms, boiled into a paste."

His stomach lurched again. "One of these days, I'm going to have to teach you to cook."

"I am a good cook," she insisted.

Jason bent, cupped his bloody hands into the bowl of water she provided. He rinsed his face. "I'll reword that. One of these days, I'm going to have to teach you to cook food that is edible." He picked up a piece of cloth she provided, and wiped his face and hands.

"Throw the water outside," she instructed.

"I feel like I've acquired a bossy wife," he muttered, but did as she instructed. Jason tried not to look at the blood-tinged water as he carried the bowl to the cave exit. He stepped outside and tossed the water right into Haidar's face.

It might have been comical, had he drenched anyone else. This was hysterical. He fought his laughter. "Oops," he said, then shrugged. "Just following orders like a good captive."

The man scrubbed a hand across his dripping face. "What are you doing in my sister's lodge?"

Again, Jason shrugged. "What else? Begging for scraps. I knew I couldn't count on you to get up and prepare me something this morning. I was starved, so I came here."

Haidar marched past him. Jason sighed and followed him inside Tala's lodge. Brother and sister immediately broke into conversation. Whatever explanation Tala provided for Jason's presence in her lodge so early seemed to satisfy her brother. She motioned for him to sit. He did so with a grunt. Tala dished Haidar a bowl of her mixture of roots and worms. Jason's stomach twisted when she dished up another bowl and motioned for him to join them.

Seating arrangements were a problem. Jason didn't think Haidar would approve if he snuggled up next to Tala, but he sure as hell didn't want to sit next to the tree man. He found a place a short distance from both. He took the bowl Tala offered, careful to avoid looking at the contents. His stomach felt queasy enough.

Watching Haidar's less than perfect table manners didn't help. The man ate with his fingers again, and he still wasn't quiet about his chewing. Jason stirred the spoon Tala had given him around in the mixture, hoping to appear as if he were eating. His thoughts turned to the previous night. He had failed Tala's test.

The wolf had taken control. Jason could only remember up until he'd spotted the other wolf, if in fact it had been a wolf. His spirits sank. Was Tala disappointed in him as well? He glanced at her. She also used a spoon, one fashioned from the hoof of something, but at least it was an eating utensil. She seemed to be doing more stirring than eating, too. He willed her to look at him.

She must have felt his regard because Jason felt relatively sure he couldn't will her to do anything. Their gazes met, touched, then she looked away. He had a hundred questions rolling around in his head to ask her. Instead, he had to sit in silence and listen to her brother's annoying smacking noises.

Tala knew Jason had questions. She also knew he felt disappointment that he had not maintained control of his thoughts while in wolf form. He expected too much too soon from himself. It might take several attempts to teach him—it might take longer than she would be allowed.

"Why do you not eat?" Haidar asked the white man. "You said that you were starving."

She thought Jason's color turned a shade lighter. He brought the spoon to his mouth, then threw it back into the bowl. He clamped a hand over his mouth, rose, and hurried outside. Haidar glanced at Tala and lifted a brow.

"He is not used to the things we eat. I should not have told him about the worms."

Haidar grunted. "The man is soft."

"He is not soft," Tala argued, but quietly so her brother would not find her defense of the white man passionate and therefore suspicious. "He is different, as are all outsiders. But you know he is not weak, Brother. He has proven his courage twice in the short time he has been among us. Tonight The People celebrate his courage. You can rule our people, Haidar, but it is wrong to believe that all should feel the way you do about everything in life. Who we are makes us all the same, but our minds are free."

Haidar grunted again and set his bowl aside. "It is my duty to make certain our clan is safe. And my right to distrust and dislike this man."

"You do not give him a chance because his skin is white, because he is from the outside. You know that we owe him a debt. And you also know that we owe him more than our lives. We owe him his."

"How can I forget when you remind me at every opportunity, Sister?" Haidar snarled. He drew a deep breath, as if to calm himself. "I will try to dislike him less, but I will never trust him."

His words were at least a beginning. Her brother was a stubborn man at times, but she had always known him to be fair.

"He needs clothes," she said. "He admires the dress of our people. Tonight, I think it would be fitting for him to wear what we wear."

"He is not one of us," Haidar warned softly. "See that you do not forget that, Tala."

She lowered her gaze, but being submissive had always proven difficult for her. "The man has no moccasins for his feet. He has only one shirt, and it is one I borrowed. There are holes in both knees of the—"

"All right," Haidar interrupted. "I will see that the man has something to wear."

"He needs a bath, and his face needs to be shaved." She handed Haidar the object that Jason called his razor. "He uses this to remove the hair from his face."

Her brother took the object, stared at it, ran his finger along the edge and jerked his hand back. A drop of blood oozed from his fingertip.

"It is sharp. A weapon."

"That is why I kept it from him," she said. "Give it back, but be certain to take it away once—"

"I do not have time to watch this man like he is a child," Haidar growled. "You see that he is groomed. I will find him clothes." He rose and tossed his long hair behind his back. "Keep watch over the man. I have duties to attend."

Haidar swept from her lodge as Jason reentered. Neither man acknowledged the other with more than a growl.

"Are you feeling better?" Tala asked.

He settled across from her where her brother sat only a moment before. "A little." He glanced behind him as if to make certain Haidar had left. "What happened last night?"

Tala gathered the bowls, scrapping Jason's uneaten portion back into the pan. She would take it to her uncle later. Maybe she would send Jason. She felt he needed tasks to perform to make him feel useful.

"You became the wolf, and then you ran off into the night. I told you that I believed you would return. Since I could not keep up with you, I came back to camp."

"I failed."

She glanced up at him. "You have only begun your journey. It is too soon to fail."

He ran a hand through his tangled hair. "At least I remember some of what happened. That's good, isn't it?"

"It is very good," she agreed, sensing he needed her encouragement. "Next time, you will remember more."

"When can we try again?"

His determination pleased her. She also liked that his spirits did not stay low for long. "Not tonight. We must attend the ceremony." Tala handed the pan of food to him. "Will you take this to my uncle?"

Jason accepted the pan, but he did not glance at the contents. "You mean take it to him without you?"

"Are you afraid to move around the camp alone?" she teased.

"No. I just didn't think captives were supposed to move around freely. At least they didn't in any of the movies I've seen or in the books I've read."

"Do you still think of yourself as a captive?" Tala asked. "Are you not here now by your own decision?"

His answer was slow to come. Tala's feelings for the white man had changed. She'd seen him as a prisoner at first, but she did not see him that way any longer. Did not the touch of their lips, the warmth that spread through them when their bodies touched, mean his feelings for her had changed as well?

She was naïve about his world, about the feelings men and women shared. Maybe Jason Donavon kissed all women he met. Maybe he touched them, made them all hunger for the forbidden. The thought did not please her.

"I'm here because this is where I want to be," he finally answered. "For the time being."

For the time being was all they had—all they would ever have. Tala had no right to be jealous of women he had held, or women he might someday hold. She had no claim on him. But he had one on her. She must make right the wrong committed against him . . . at least as right as she could make it.

Jason rose. He stood tall. She liked feeling small next to him. She might even like feeling helpless, but of course she was not, would never be.

"Where will I find your uncle?"

"Outside throwing bones with his friends. Do not let him talk you into joining them," she warned. "It is a silly way to pass the time. I will gather what you need for a bath and meet you outside."

"A bath?" His dark brows lifted. "Will you join me again? Maybe your brother won't interrupt us this time."

The thought made her heart beat faster, the breath inside of her chest lodge in her throat. "No," she managed to answer. "You know that it would be wrong for me . . . for us . . . that is . . . what I mean—"

"I'm only teasing," he said, stopping her. "I enjoy watching you become flustered. You're always so serious."

Her face burned. "You are making fun of me

**PLEASE RUSH
MY TWO FREE
BOOKS TO ME
RIGHT AWAY!**

Enclose this card with $2.00
in an envelope and send to:

Love Spell Romance Book Club
20 Academy Street
Norwalk, CT 06850-4032

again." That, she did not like about him. "I am a serious person because my responsibilities do not allow me to make a joke of everything. I—"

He stepped forward and placed a finger against her lips. "I didn't mean to put you on the defensive. Your smile lights up even this dingy cave. I just wanted to see it again."

His eyes were his best defense and her greatest weakness. She could not stop the smile from forming upon her lips. "There," she said. "Are you happy, now?"

"Almost." His finger traced the shape of her bottom lip. His hand moved down and cupped her chin, tilting her face up to his. "I'd be happier if I could kiss you. If I had the right and if you weren't promised to your destiny."

For a traitorous moment, she agreed that she would be happier as well, but Tala pulled away before she gave the thought voice. "We are what we are, Jason. We are separated by more than worlds."

"It doesn't seem like it at times, though, does it?"

If she continued to agree with him, she feared they would kiss again. This time, they might more than kiss, more than touch. "My uncle will be hungry. Please take him his breakfast."

She held her breath, fearful he would continue to tempt her. Tala had never been tempted before . . . but she had taken on her sister's sins, and they had weakened her. She could not blame the man. He had done nothing wrong. Nothing except happen along at the wrong time, in the wrong place.

"I'll see you below, then," he said. "Don't take too

long or your uncle will probably corrupt me. I'm easily lured into sinful practices."

The teasing tone had returned to his voice. He meant to ease the tension between them, but his tactic did not work. The tension remained—a force nearly as strong as her powers. "I will join you in a short time. I will bring your razor and soap so you can remove the hair from your face again."

"Out of curiosity, how do the men in your tribe remove the hair from their faces and bodies?"

"They pluck them out from an early age, when they first begin to appear."

"Ouch. My way is less painful."

Tala busied herself as if she were making preparations for his bath. She wanted him to go so she could breathe again, think again. He went. She sensed his absence more than heard his departure. Slowly, she let the air escape her lungs in a deep breath. A realization made her muscles tighten again. Haidar had said she must watch over the man. Her brother would not sit with Jason like a woman watching over a child. Jason was not a child, and she must watch him while he bathed. Torture. Why did the man torture her so?

Chapter Fourteen

Jason had enjoyed watching the older men toss bones. He especially liked Nayati. Tala's uncle was a light-hearted man, very different from his serious niece and nephew. The game had been interesting. The men split up into two teams. Each team had two bones, one marked and one unmarked. In the center of where they sat, they placed ten sticks. The captain, so to speak, of each team would mix up the bones and quickly place them behind his back. Members from the other team would try to guess which hand held the marked bone and which held the unmarked bone. If they were right, they got a stick.

Jason had the feeling the sticks represented something else—whatever the men chose to gamble. After a guess had been made by the opposing team and re-vealed to be correct or incorrect, the opposing team's captain would then snatch up the bones and throw

171

them again, then quickly hide a marked and an un-marked bone behind his back. Tala had appeared before Jason had gotten too far into the game, which he supposed was just as well since he had nothing to trade if he lost. Even the shirt on his back was borrowed,

As Jason bathed in the Sacred Waters, he realized that for man who'd once had money to burn, his current financial situation was a joke. Still, he had never valued money over happiness. He thought a man should at least be given one or the other. If he learned to control the change, he supposed he could get some type of job—one better than the short stints he'd taken just to put food in his belly.

There was one problem concerning a serious job, though. Jason had no identity. According to his social security card, all his forms of ID, he was dead. Killed in a hunting accident. Attacked by a wild wolf.

"Your mind is far away."

He squinted through the steam, barely able to distinguish Tala sitting upon the rocks. "Thinking about my past and I guess my future, if I'm going have one."

"Do you miss your world?" she asked.

Jason waded toward her. She'd brought soap, but he hadn't been allowed to use it in the water. Instead, she'd told him to use the sand on the bottom of the lake to scrub his skin and scalp. The reason her people had kept the lake so clean through the centuries was because they didn't pollute it with toxins or chemicals. She'd brought along a bowl, his razor, and the soap for shaving.

"I miss some things about the outside, but not enough to count for much. Of course I miss my family, but I can't return to them now. Not the way that I am."

"They have accepted your passing. They hope that you have found a better place."

Her hazy image became clearer as he approached. "How do you know?"

"It is what all wish when one they love departs this world."

She was right, but not everyone thought he was dead. "My brother knows I'm still alive. He'll be worried about me, wondering if I'll ever be able to keep my promise to him."

He was close enough to see Tala lower her gaze and chew on her bottom lip. She looked as if she would say something for a moment, but she remained silent. Picking up his shaving items and her bowl, she rose and moved down to the water.

"Your brother's fate should not be your responsibility. It was not by your doing that you both became cursed by the moon."

Jason had entered the water in a place where the drop-off from the rocks nearly reached his shoulders. He moved toward where Tala now seated herself. She hiked up her dress and dangled her legs over the edge into the water. Her dress, leggings, and moccasins usually covered her legs. A shame, Jason thought. Even if she didn't stand tall compared to him, her legs were long. They were also smooth and brown; her calves nicely muscled like the legs of an athlete. The water receded to his waist before he reached her. Tala stared at his chest before she glanced down, fingering the items she held in her lap.

"I do feel as if what happened to Rick is my fault,"

he resumed their earlier conversation. "He wasn't really a hunter, but I kept after him to go with me. We hadn't spent much time together since he left home. I thought it would do us both good to get away. I hoped we'd become closer, like we were when we were young. You know, before life got in the way?"

"I do not know," Tala said. "Life only moves from one sunrise to the next here. We are never too busy to spend time together. All we have is each other."

All Tala's people had were the basic necessities in life. Jason realized how easy it was in his world to lose sight of what mattered most. He'd done it. Rick had done it. Maybe that's why they'd been cursed. Tala scooped water from the lake into her bowl, then sat his razor, her homemade soap, and a cloth next to the bowl.

"I'm not used to shaving without some type of mirror. I'll probably cut my face."

"I have seen these objects that capture one's image," Tala said. "I brought back a small piece of one I once found in a city where I went to hunt. Some people of the tribe became so taken with their own reflections that they soon began to fight over the piece of glass. Haidar took it away and destroyed it. He said it was evil."

Jason laughed. "I guess in a way it is. Vanity can make a beautiful person ugly. We're not supposed to judge people or ourselves by the way we look. What's inside should matter the most, although very few really follow that teaching."

He dipped the soap the bowl, then lathered the bar against his face. "I never worried too much about my inner self until three years ago. Now what's on the inside is all I think about."

"The outside is nice," Tala said, her gaze still lowered. "But I believe the inside is also good. I have told you to ignore the whispers in your mind that cause you doubt." She glanced up at him. "If you do not believe in your goodness, you cannot do battle with the moon. Inside all of us, there is a black hole—a place where our darkest secrets, our greatest fears, hide. They lay in wait to rise up and strike against us when self-pity weakens the spirit. If you accept all that you are, what you fear will no longer control you. If it cannot control you, it can no longer harm you."

Jason brought the razor to his throat. "What you're telling me is the same thing you've told me before, right? I have to accept who I am? Accept the beast and all that is now a part of me?"

She reached out and took the razor from his hand. "Yes. To find happiness, you must make peace with your demons. At the same time, you must let them know that they will not rule your life."

Tala seemed wise beyond her years. Certainly more mature than most women her age. Jason found that maturity an attractive trait. The outside package was impressive, too. Soulful dark eyes, full tempting mouth, womanly curves. But he was attracted to more than her physical appearance. They were connected in a way he'd never been connected with a woman before. She knew what he was, and she still treated him like a human being.

"If you give me back my razor, I promise not to slit my wrists," he teased.

"I—I will shave you," she stuttered. "I do not want

175

you to cut yourself because you cannot see what you are doing."

Not long ago, the thought of Tala and a sharp object doing anything to him would have made Jason very uncomfortable. Now, he trusted her.

"You can't reach me from where you're sitting." He moved closer. There was an awkward moment, before he parted her knees and wedged his body between them. A side of him, the darker one, whispered that this was where he'd wanted to be from the moment he first saw her. Between her legs. He tilted his face up to her.

"Is that better?" he asked.

Tala was too stunned to answer. She imagined her eyes were round, and her heart made a strange leap the moment he spread her knees and moved between them. Their position felt intimate, dangerous, stimulating. She drew a deep breath and tried to concentrate on removing the whiskers from his face.

She placed the razor against his throat. His pulse beat there, strong and fast. She had never used such an object, but knew not to press the sharp edge too hard against his skin. Slowly, she brought the razor up his neck. It came away with soap and whiskers. She swirled the object in her bowl and began again.

He swallowed and she nearly cut him. She jerked the razor away.

"Sorry."

His voice sounded husky. She glanced down at him. Again, she marveled at how such cool-colored eyes could send out such heat. Her clothing clung to her. The steam from the water swirled around them. She leaned closer and tried to focus on the task before her. His breath touched her cheeks. It smelled like mint.

Her people often chewed the plant to sweeten their breath, but his came from the paste he carried in his sack, along with the small brush he used to wash his teeth. He had let Tala try it once. It was much better than scrubbing teeth with a cloth. There were things from the outside world that could greatly benefit her people, but they did not have the green money the outsiders used to purchase goods.

Suddenly, she became aware of his hands balanced upon her knees. His touch felt warm. Tala tried to ignore the heat of his hands burning into her skin. She had finished his neck and now drew the razor down the side of his cheek. His features were chiseled. He had grooves around his mouth. She liked the way they deepened when he smiled. His lashes were dark and thick. They were too pretty to be masculine. His jaw was strong, though, his nose short and straight, his forehead wide but not too high.

"If you keep staring at me like that, I won't be able to stand here and remain passive."

She had been staring. In her distraction, Tala was surprised she hadn't cut his face. An excuse for her behavior did not come to her on the steamy air. Tala said nothing, but returned to shaving him. She had nearly finished when he spoke again.

"It doesn't seem to matter if you stare at me or not. I still respond to you."

His hands, she noted, slid farther up her legs and now rested upon her thighs. She liked the feel of them against her skin. "You should not," she warned. "It is wrong to think of me as a woman." She lifted the cloth she'd brought and wiped what remained of the soap from his face.

"It's impossible not to think of you as a woman." His hands slid higher. "You look like a woman. You smell like a woman. You feel like a woman."

As if they did not belong to her and she could not control them, her fingers moved over his now smooth face. "You make me aware of being a woman. It is wrong to want what I cannot have. It is wrong for you to want what you cannot have. The path our minds have taken is a foolish one. One that will only lead to suffering."

"Would you suffer for me?" he asked softly. "I would suffer for you. I'm suffering right now."

He did not appear to be in pain, but his eyes were bright, as if a fever burned inside him. Moisture clung to his face, his broad shoulders, and his muscular chest. Again, as if she could not command her will, her hands slid down to his shoulders.

"What would ease your suffering?" she whispered.

His first response was a groan. He glanced away from her, then as if he, too, had no control, back up at her. "It would ease my suffering . . . if you would leave."

They were not the words she expected. They were words that slashed at her, made her feel the first sting of rejection. "You do not want me." It was not a question, only a realization that left her lips before she could stop it. She did not like the feeling of being unwanted, so unlike the other emotions he stirred within her.

"No, Tala." He grabbed her arms as she started to pull away from him. "I do want you. I'm in agony with the pain of wanting you, but sometimes I forget who you are, who I am. Sometimes, all I can think of is having you. Touching you. Bringing you pleasure and taking my own. I won't force myself on you, or try to seduce you because you're innocent. I wouldn't have done either of those things three years ago, and I won't do them now."

The sting of his earlier rejection faded. Tala felt the wall she'd built around her heart teeter. "Release me," she said. He did so immediately. "Now, you are not forcing me to do anything. I stay, even though you have warned me to go. Our bodies cannot join in the way of men and women. In the way of all creatures. But your touch alone gives me pleasure." She slid her fingertips down his chest. "Does mine not do the same for you?"

Chapter Fifteen

Jason knew they were headed for dangerous waters. He could drown in the depths of her eyes, never draw another breath and feel as alive as he felt in that instant. She was the forest, the sunset, all things pure and good about the world, and he was not worthy of her. It didn't stop him from allowing the light brush of her lips against his. Or from capturing her mouth when she teased him the second time.

She opened to him, and not only her sweet mouth. Her legs widened enough to send him a signal—one that made words unnecessary. His hands slid up her smooth thighs as her tongue danced with his. He thought she trembled, but realized it was his hands that shook. It had been years since he'd touched a woman the way he touched Tala, since he'd even kissed a woman. His senses were pounded by the sensations running through him. He knew touching, kissing—giving her pleasure were his only options. And Jason also knew that the man in him would abide by her rules. But would the beast?

Doubt almost overpowered passion. Then Jason remembered what Tala had told him earlier. He had to face his fears, fight his demons, and this was a test he would not fail. He found her, the core of her physical sensation. She was already wet for him. He moaned against her mouth and stroked her velvet warmth. Soon, her breathing grew ragged and she moved against his fingers. He bent to nip at her nipples through her dress. A moan rose up in her throat and she threw her head back, her long raven hair falling past her hips.

He wanted to put his mouth against her bare breasts, wanted to taste her everywhere. Reaching up, he fumbled with the straps that held her dress in place. Her fingers pushed his aside a moment later. She almost had the strap untied, but she writhed and gasped against him until he thought she would climax before he could add to her pleasure.

"Tala? Are you here?"

Her knees clamped together. Her head jerked up. She quickly scooted away from him. Jason groaned and pressed his forehead against the smooth rocks that surrounded the lake. Her brother had interfered again.

"I am here," Tala called, her voice breathless.

Jason glanced up, watching her tie her strap back and smooth the sleeves of her dress down in what would probably be a record time, if there were competitions for getting dressed. Her breasts still heaved beneath her dress, a reminder of what he'd been denied. Of course, what she had been denied was much worse.

Haidar appeared. Jason stifled the urge to growl at the man. Tala's brother carried a bundle in his arms. "I have found him clothes," he said. The man glanced from his sister, who still tried to catch her breath, her cheeks flushed, to Jason, then back at Tala. "Is something wrong?"

"No," she managed. "I gave Jason ... the white man his things for shaving, and I tripped climbing back up onto the rocks. It only knocked the breath from me."

So now he had corrupted her? She lied with the ease of a practiced sinner. Jason made it a point to keep his expression blank when Haidar glanced suspiciously back at him.

"He removed the hair from his face very quickly if you only now gave him the items."

"It's a gift," Jason said dryly. Then, to change the subject, he nodded toward the bundle in Haidar's arms. "Did you say that you brought me clothes?"

Haidar grunted. "Tala said that you need them. The one departed from us has no further use for them. His woman gave them to me."

Jason supposed a dead man's clothes were better than the rags he'd been wearing. "I'll thank her for them."

"You cannot speak with her. She is in mourning and will not attend the ceremony tonight. Come." He motioned him out. "We will see if they fit."

Considering what he had going on beneath the water's surface, Jason didn't think climbing out was a good idea. He glanced at Tala. "Your sister is present."

"You may leave, Tala," Haidar said.

Her dark eyes met Jason's. Tala rose, snatched up her moccasins and walked away. Once she made it past her brother, she turned and walked backward, staring at Jason until the steam swallowed her.

"She is gone now."

The big man stood there, waiting, and by the slight tapping of his moccasin against the rock floor, not very patiently.

"I, ah, I'm shy," Jason said. "You could just leave the clothes and go off so I can change."

"Only men who have little . . . confidence are modest in the presence of other men."

Jason wouldn't allow a challenge to overrule common sense. He'd like to hop out and let Haidar see that his confidence wasn't at all small. Instead, he shrugged. "It's the way I was raised. And I get uncomfortable around men who want to measure my masculinity. In my world, any man caught gawking at another man's equipment is considered suspect."

Haidar's dark brows drew together. "Suspect of what?"

"What some consider a perversion. You know, a man who desires another man?"

Color flooded Haidar's face. "I have heard of this. I am not such a man."

The conversation had given Jason time to get rid of most of his problem. He had a feeling he didn't have to worry about the part it hadn't gotten rid of. He climbed from the water. Haidar quickly turned his back and laid the clothing on the ground.

"I will wait for you at the entrance into the cave. It is time to prepare for the ceremony."

Once Haidar left, Jason moved to the bundle. He bent and examined the contents. A new shirt, a nicer one than Tala had borrowed for him. A breechclout and leggings, even a pair of knee-high moccasins. He touched the garments reverently. The clothes were not made at a factory or in a sweatshop overseas. They were made by a woman's hands—lovingly prepared for her husband. He felt guilty for having the clothes. He was an outsider, a white man—a man at the mercy at the moon. Maybe he should return them to Haidar.

One glance at the faded, holey jeans he'd shed before his bath, and Jason sighed. Maybe it would be rude to refuse them anyway. The buckskin shirt was well tanned and comfortable. The sleeves were trimmed with long fringe. The neck was open but a lacing of rawhide kept it from gaping open at the chest. The breechclout was also long and fringed around the bottom. It took Jason a while to figure out how to put the garments on, but he managed.

He picked up his discarded clothing, the blanket he had used to dry, and moved to the water's edge to retrieve the shaving items Tala had left behind. A picture of her, head thrown back, full lips parted, writhing against him, floated through his memory. Damn Haidar for interrupting them. Another minute and Tala would have experienced the pleasure of release. He didn't want to think about what might have happened after that. He'd been impassioned, hard with need for her; maybe he wouldn't have left it at pleasing her. Maybe it was just as well that Haidar had interrupted.

Part of him knew that he had no business becoming involved with Tala Soaringbird in a physical sense, or an emotional one; the other part, the man, maybe the beast, maybe a combination of both, whispered that it was already too late. Jason shook his head as if the action would scatter the thoughts from his mind. He was still more man than wolf. He could change his path. If he won his battle against the call of the moon, he could change his fate, at least to a degree.

Tala had made it clear that he had no place in her life. Because of his curse, she had no place in his. Why couldn't he resist her? Why couldn't he ignore the fact she was a woman, like she'd told him to do, and concentrate on what she taught him, the gift she wanted to give him? Freedom. Control. Some semblance of a normal life?

Women had come and gone in his life when he'd lived a normal one. He'd never been in love. He didn't remember being particularly upset when one of his former lovers left him, claiming he would never commit to a serious relationship. He had known they were right. And they'd known the type of man he was from the beginning. Deep inside, he'd always felt there would be one he couldn't walk away from someday. One he couldn't let walk away. One special enough to win his heart for all eternity.

Tala was special. But she wasn't the one. Fate had already dealt him a bad hand. Surely it wasn't cruel enough to send her to him when neither of them were free to love—not while he was trapped in a nightmare and she was trapped in another world. She had started the love play between them earlier. Now he would end it.

*   *   *

Tala donned a special dress for the ceremony. The doeskin had been tanned until it almost appeared white. There were beads sewn into the yoke. Beads also decorated the fringe that hung from the sleeves and the bottom of the dress. The beads had come from a dress that once belonged to her great-grandmother. She did not braid her hair, as had long been the fashion with her people, but she wore it loose, a beaded band around her head.

She received several curious glances from those gathered within the lower chamber when she joined her people. All knew that her mother had fashioned the dress Tala wore tonight. All knew that her mother had made the dress for Meka, the only daughter she bore who would someday be allowed to join with a man. Life was hard among them. The two male children eligible for Meka had both died before reaching manhood. Her sister had not accepted her fate, and her bitterness had led to her downfall.

"The dress is beautiful," Chandee remarked as Tala joined the women to lay out the feast.

There was no point in making pretenses. "No woman in my family will wear it for the purpose intended, so I wear it tonight. In memory of my mother . . . and of my sister."

A woman gasped softly. No one had spoken of Meka since she disappeared. A deserter was as bad as an evil one in the tribe's eyes. Tala raised her chin and continued to work. She felt different tonight. Changed. Empowered by more than fate, but by feelings new and exciting to her. When she thought about what had taken place between her and Jason, her face flushed and other parts of her body grew warm. He had taken her to a place she had never been, left her poised upon the brink of some wonderful discovery, and she was angry that her brother had intruded.

Guilt argued that it was good her brother had interrupted. She had no right to experience the forbidden pleasures Jason gave her with his hands and his mouth. But she had experienced them . . . and not as fully as she suspected she would have had Haidar not called out to her. Tala wanted to know what she had missed.

The air changed around her. Voices rose in pitch. She did not have to glance at the entrance of the lower chamber to know Jason had arrived among them. She knew his scent, knew that the way her heart sped whenever he was close would always alert her to his presence. Subtly, she turned her head. The sight of him nearly stole her breath. He brought life to the clothes of the dead, filled them with his height, his muscular build, the power he held as a man. His hair had been tied back with a leather strip, showing off his now smooth features in a way that pleased her. He smiled at one of the younger boys, a flash of white teeth against his tan skin, then mussed the boy's hair.

Slowly, his gaze moved around the large cavern. She knew he looked for her, waited for him to find her. When he did, a fire leapt to life in his azure eyes and she felt a warm tingling beneath her skin. Then he abruptly glanced away—turned his back and began speaking with her uncle.

The warm tingling faded. Tala felt as if someone had taken her heart and twisted it inside of her chest. Why did he look away from her so quickly? Why did he not come and speak to her? Why did he stand with his broad back to her as if she were no one of importance to him? She kept staring, willing him to look at her again, but he did not. Instead, she drew another man's regard.

Haidar frowned at her. His gaze swept down the dress she wore, and his face turned red. For a moment, she feared he would storm to her side and demand that she change. She would be humiliated if he did such a thing in front of The People. The pain of Jason's rejection made her brave. She had always used her courage to conquer her fears, or at least to pretend to do so. She lifted her chin and stared him straight in the eyes.

The tactic worked. Haidar turned his attention to the conversation between her uncle and Jason. Tala knew she could join them and none would think it odd. Her brother, her uncle, she should speak to them. But pride would not allow her to do what her heart wanted most; be beside Jason. To feel the heat of his body touch hers. To pretend she was his woman, if only within the safe confines of her mind. She might be ignorant of the ways between men and women, but Tala knew enough to understand that Jason purposely ignored her.

Did he think less of her now because she had allowed him to touch her where no man had touched her before? How could his eyes burn with fire for her one moment, then act as if she did not share the same space with him the next? Tala threw herself into helping arrange the food on a long table erected from stone; confused, hurt, and angry that he could make her feel these new emotions—emotions that were sometimes more pleasurable than she could stand and sometimes more painful.

Maybe she had not been missing so much before she met him. Her mind immediately argued the opposite. Jason had made her feel alive, human, and she knew to be human, one must accept the joys and the sorrows of life, the good and the bad. The drums started, capturing everyone's attention.

Her brother lifted his arms so that all would quiet and listen to him. "Tonight, we pay honor to the outsider who has come among us and shown his courage."

Voices lifted in whoops of approval. Tala did not join hers with the others. She glanced at Jason from beneath the cover of her lashes. He looked embarrassed by the attention but also pleased, she thought.

"We will feast," Haidar continued. "We will dance. We will tell the stories of our ancestors. We will celebrate a life spared among us, and we will feel sorrow in our hearts for one who is gone. But first, I will give Jason Donavon a gift."

A gift? Tala wondered what her brother would give the white man. She stretched her neck to see as The People gathered closer around the two men. Haidar motioned to Noshi. The boy came forward, smiling as he held a long object wrapped in buckskin. Haidar nodded at the boy and he handed the object to Jason.

Jason returned Noshi's smile. Once he unwrapped the buckskin, his face lost most of its color. She could not see what her brother had given to him and tried standing on her tiptoes. A moment later, Jason cast her brother a dark look, then raised the object in the air. Whoops bounced off the cavern walls, causing Tala to flinch over the noise. What Jason held also made her wince. It was a lance, decorated with the severed human head of the Sica Jason had killed.

Chapter Sixteen

He would not puke. Jason wouldn't give Tala's brother the satisfaction. Instead, he held the lance high, as if it were a treasured gift. But he knew it wasn't a gift. It was a reminder of what he might become, of the fact that he was different from those who might welcome him in their midst. A wolf among sheep. The sight of the grotesque human head, burnt human flesh, and blank staring eyes was enough to turn his stomach, and add to it the guilt he felt over ignoring Tala.

This was not his idea of a good time. In the back of his mind, Jason admitted that he'd been thinking he might belong here, if nowhere else. He thought if he could control the beast, he might stay. Maybe Tala would someday have a vision of the beast that had cursed him and his brother. He couldn't just give up on the hope of becoming completely human again. Not for himself or for Rick.

But he'd been fooling himself to believe that he could stay, become part of even an abnormal community again. Tala might accept him, curse and all, but these people wouldn't. Jason couldn't take her away from them, knew she wouldn't go, and he wouldn't ask. He had no right. The expression of hurt she tried to hide from him, even now as his gaze scanned the faces whooping and smiling at him, made him feel like the worst kind of jerk. He didn't want to teach her about this part of a relationship between a man and a woman. The part where one must disappoint the other.

Her uncle slapped Jason on the back and steered him toward a group of older men, the men who made up the Council, he recalled. He sat with them. The woman whose son he'd rescued from the beast brought him a large tray loaded with food. She sat it before him and smiled shyly before hurrying away.

Jason wondered what he should do with his "gift" while he ate, and he didn't have much of an appetite now, thanks to Haidar. He guessed he couldn't really blame the man for putting him in his place; the leader only wanted to protect his people . . . his sister. Jason had to at least respect him for that, though he still didn't have to like him. Tala's uncle nudged him, nodding toward the food.

"You will insult everyone if you do not eat. All are waiting for you to begin so they can fill their own bellies."

The tribal members were all staring at him. His gaze snagged on the boy he'd saved from the beast.

Noshi looked reverently at the lance he held. Jason motioned for the boy to join him. When Noshi stood before him, Jason handed him the lance.

"It was your stick that killed the beast. You should have this fine lance."

Noshi's gaze widened. He glanced behind him at Haidar, who stood, arms folded across his chest. Haidar's eyes met Jason's—dark, intimidating, but a slight gleam of what might be respect shown there. He nodded. The boy stepped forward and took the lance. As if dazed, Noshi joined the other children. Another boy tried to touch the lance, but Noshi snatched it from his reach. Jason had to laugh. All laughed with him. All but Haidar and his sister. Tala stood at the back of the group, doing a fine job of ignoring him.

"The food," her uncle reminded. "Will you eat?" The old man was always hungry.

"Only if you'll join me," Jason answered. "I cannot eat this much by myself."

Together, Jason and Nayati tore the shank of a deer in half and began eating. Soon, everyone dug into the food prepared. The drums started again. Some tribesmen and women began to dance. Tala stayed across the large cavern from him. She spoke with other women, smiled, laughed, gently touched a child who passed, and had seemingly forgotten he even existed. She could play the game as well as he could, and he'd had a hell of a lot more experience at it.

Questions about the outside were soon asked. Jason told them about the skyscrapers, the pollution, the crime, the museums, the mixture of beauty and filth that made up his world. His audience grew. But still, there was one missing: Tala hadn't joined those gathered around him. Instead, she busied herself cleaning up discarded trays of food.

Jason didn't realize how interested the tribe was in his stories until he grew silent. Tala's uncle nudged him.

"Tell us more."

They were sometimes like children, even the old. Jason wasn't sure it was a good idea to fill their heads with visions of the outside, but then, he wasn't sure it was right to keep these people secluded from all that modern life had to offer, either.

Haidar made the decision for him, stepping forward. "The outsider should hear *our* stories," he said, glancing across the cavern. "Tala, come and tell our guest the legend of the outcasts."

As if startled, Tala glanced up from her work at her sibling. Something passed between them, brother and sister. Jason couldn't tell if she was angry that Haidar had included her in the festivities when she obviously didn't care to be near the honored guest, or if something else made her eyes blaze and her cheeks darken. He figured if she didn't want to be included, she'd refuse, but she moved toward the group.

All became quiet. Tala stood in the center of the cavern. Flaming torches were mounted along the walls, and a fire burned in a pit at the room's center. The soft light silhouetted her slim form, cast her shadow long against one wall. God, she was beautiful, he thought. Her soft buckskin dress hugged her lush curves. Her hair hung down her shoulders like black silk. She was a mixture of innocence and sensuality. Irresistible.

Her head had been slightly bowed, but now she

glanced up, her gaze moving over the crowd before it came to rest upon him. "A time long ago, when The Tribes Of All People first roamed the land, Father Sun forsook his mate, Mother Earth, and left her for another. Without Father Sun's love, Mother Earth grew bitter and cold. All that sprang from her union with Father Sun began to disappear. The trees died, the rivers froze, and darkness fell over the land. The Tribes Of All People began to die as well. They could not stay warm against Mother Earth's chill. They could not find food to eat, or wood to burn for fires. They forgot about their petty wars with one another, and all joined together, appealing to Mother Earth for mercy."

Tala walked around the circle of those listening, pausing before Jason. "Mother Earth heard their wails of hunger, carried to her by the sacred North wind. She looked into her empty heart and found a small place that still lived. In her mercy, Mother Earth granted The Tribes Of All People a special wish to help them survive the destruction her broken heart had wrought upon the land. She told them to choose a few among them, and she would make them into whatever animal would most serve their needs."

The fringe on the bottom of Tala's dress made a soft swishing noise against the rock floor as she paced before her audience. "The Tribes Of All People thought long and hard about their decision. They argued among themselves. Some said the mighty mountain cat should be their choice; others, the deadly badger. But when the decision was made, all agreed that the wisest choice was the wolf. The wolf was a respected hunter. The wolf hunted for the pack and not for itself. The wolf taught and cared for its young. The wolf fed those in the pack too old to feed themselves. The wolf protected the pack from intruders. The wolf lived a life almost parallel to their own."

Jason felt a prickle of unease, but found himself enraptured by Tala's words, by the melody of her voice. He wondered if her people had trouble following along since she told the story in English for his benefit. Jason also felt that Haidar had chosen this particular legend for his benefit, as well. Tala's voice recaptured his attention.

"The Tribes Of All People then chose a group of its most seasoned warriors and the same number of its strongest women, and placed them inside a circle. The People chanted for Mother Earth to keep her promise and change those chosen into wolves. But they asked for more. Afraid the transformed warriors would not remember the human within them and recognize the tribe as their pack, their people asked Mother Earth to give those warriors the power to become both wolf and human. Mother Earth warned The People that no man or woman she changed could ever drink of human blood or eat of human flesh, or their human souls would be lost.

"Mother Earth said in order to give the rest of her creatures still living a chance at survival, the wolf warriors could only change by the light of a full moon. The Tribes Of All People agreed to Mother Earth's laws, and she granted them their wish. The ones picked were changed. By day, they were humans who helped with the duties of the tribe, but by night, beneath a full moon, they shed their human skins and became wolves. They hunted for the tribe, they protected them against other animals, and soon, they became the tribe's most valued members."

Tala paused, Jason assumed for effect, before she began her pacing again. "For many years, those who had been chosen provided food for the tribe, pelts from the animals they killed to keep The People warm, and protection against predators. They were treated like gods among the tribe, and all were happy to serve as Mother Earth intended. But then, one day, the world changed again."

Tala's gaze moved over every face. Jason supposed the tribespeople had heard this story many times, but when he glanced around him, they all looked as if they were hearing it anew. He waited, like the others, for her to continue.

"Father Sun came back to Mother Earth. He seduced her with the warmth of his touch, the brightness of his smile, and he melted her cold heart. Life returned to what it had once been. Trees shot from the soil, rivers formed from ice that covered the land. The Tribes Of All People could hunt again. They no longer needed the thick pelts that had kept them warm against Mother Earth's chill. Soon, they no longer needed the chosen among them."

Bowing her head, as if saddened by the turn of the events, Tala let her words sink in. Somewhere in the group, Jason heard a woman softly weep. When Tala glanced up, he saw tears shining in her dark eyes.

"Much returned to the way it had once been. The Tribes Of All People began to war among themselves. They split into bands, separate from one another. Few wanted the wolf warriors among them. They were different. They were outcasts.

"Given little choice, the outcasts formed their own band with those who did not hate them, but there were those among them who were angered by The Tribes Of All People. Angered by the sacrifices they had made on their people's behalf. The angry ones had wanted to be treated as if they were special, but instead they had been sneered at, laughed at, forced from contact with those whose lives they had saved. Some of the warriors' hearts turned bitter, and to punish The Tribes Of All People, they began to hunt human prey. They ate of human flesh, they drank of human blood, and they became the Unma Kin Sica that Mother Earth had once warned The Tribes Of All People against.

"The Tribes Of All People remembered their promise to Mother Earth, and they hunted these outcasts. But the evil ones had the cunning of the wolf inside them, and they spread their curse among those who hunted. The Tribes Of All People came together once more. They begged those they'd cast out, those wolf warriors whose hearts had remained pure, to help them kill the evil ones. The pure of heart agreed, and in exchange for their sacrifice, Mother Earth blessed several warriors with special powers. She gave them wings to fly and the ability to become anything their minds envisioned. These were the 'ones chosen.' "

Jason looked up at Tala, glanced around to see that everyone was staring at her in awed silence as well. He wasn't surprised; she had a hypnotic voice.

She continued: "But still the evil wolf warriors spread their curse and grew in numbers greater than those who hunted them. They lost their human souls and were no longer ruled only by the moon, but by the stars as well. Mother Earth lifted the moon's power from her pure-hearted warriors so that the evil ones did not hold an advantage. But it was not enough. Many were slain by the evil ones or turned to the dark side. Only a handful of the pure warriors remained true to their cause. Yet this must have been Mother Earth's design, for she had blessed her pure warriors with one thing greater than all their powers combined: She had not taken their human hearts or the trials that came with such a gift. She knew that some would falter upon their paths, and some would lose their way, but Mother Earth knew that few might triumph where many would fail. And it is the way of the world for good to conquer evil if you have but the strength to let it—for evil has no heart, no spirit, and no wings to fly."

There was a short silence; then Tala walked away. The tribal members began to whoop in appreciation of her story. Jason clapped his hands and whistled, although doing so received several baffled glances from those seated around him. Tala's uncle leaned close.

"She is not so good of a storyteller, my niece," he said under his breath. "She left out some parts of the story."

He wondered which parts. Jason also wondered why Tala left, for he saw her slip from the cavern. Although he had enjoyed the sound of Tala's voice more than the story, he understood the reason Haidar had chosen this particular legend. It was to remind him that he was an outcast. The leader didn't want him getting too comfortable among his people or too friendly with his younger sister.

Although Tala's story was only a legend, from what she'd told him, what he'd seen with his own eyes, it was one that followed the beliefs of her people closely. She called herself the one chosen. She said she had powers, and he had seen some of them. Because Tala had been born with some type of special abilities, had her tribe placed her in the role of an outcast? As a chosen one from their ancient legends?

The drums started again. Shadows moved against the rock walls of the cavern as the people took up their dancing. Someone snatched his hand and pulled him up into the circle of dancers. Jason wanted time alone. Time to think. Tala's story had started suspicions in his mind. He wanted to talk to her—to tell her he was sorry if he'd hurt her earlier. Maybe to discuss the injustices done to her by her own superstitious people.

As he was prodded into a circle of dancers, Jason decided that would have to wait for another time. Tonight, Tala's people honored him for his courage. Tonight, he felt accepted again for the first time in a long while. Tonight, he would dance—because tomorrow, he would still be an outsider. Tala was not the outcast. He was. She believed that she could save him because of the silly teachings of a legend made up long ago. A legend about the pure of heart. She couldn't help him. And if she couldn't help him, Jason realized it was time for him to leave. Before he did, however, he would talk some modern-day sense into her.

Chapter Seventeen

He came to her later. Tala lay awake in her furs, staring into the small flame that burned in her cooking pit. He made no sound—he had learned to move like a shadow across the night—but he could not hide his scent. The bold, masculine smell of him arrived before he did.

She closed her eyes, hoping he would think she slept and leave her alone. The night had been an emotional one, and earlier at the Sacred Waters, even more so. Tala feared he would see the hurt in her eyes, the confusion over his behavior during the ceremony. Only one who had the right to expect more from him should feel what she felt.

His body heat touched her first, then the feel of his gaze. A moment later, his fingertips traced the shape of her cheek.

"I would never want to hurt you, Tala," he said

softly. "I'm afraid of what you make me feel. It's my way to run from my emotions. To avoid them."

Slowly, she opened her eyes and looked up at him. "You should not be here."

"I know. I couldn't stay away. I couldn't sleep knowing that I might have hurt you this evening."

Just the sight of him stirred her senses, but she would not allow him to so easily see her feelings for him again. During her schooling from the Elders, she had often been called a fast learner.

"You are too sure of yourself," Tala scoffed, using the dry tone that often colored his words. "To have hurt me, I would have to care about you."

He frowned down at her. "Your tongue is sharper than your knife."

She turned, presenting her back as he had done during the ceremony. "Go away. I am tired, and you risk my brother's anger by being here."

Warmth spread through her when he touched her shoulder. "I would risk more if you would let me apologize. What happened between us today went unfinished. You have every right to experience pleasure with a man, but I have no right to be that man."

Tala sighed. Jason still did not understand her position among the tribal members, her duties to her people. "I had no right, really. I have told you this many times."

"I believe that you do have the right. I believe that you've been wronged by your people. Just because you can make a flame grow higher, do a few tricks, they've cast you in the role of a legend. Something that was made up to entertain your ancestors before a late evening campfire."

She had not wanted to tell the story. Her brother had suggested it as a reminder that she was different. As punishment for wearing the joining dress meant for her sister. Her destiny did not include a mate, and Haidar would not forget her duties, even if Tala sometimes did.

"You come among us for a few days and think that you know all there is to know about us?" She turned to face him, no longer content to hide her anger. "You think we are ignorant, backward, that we are savages who know no better, who must be led into the light by the superior white man?"

He lifted his hands. "Whoa. I never said that."

Throwing the heavy furs aside, she sat up. "You do not have to say it. As I told the story, you did not listen to my words, only to the sound of my voice. You do not believe such things are possible, even after all you have experienced, you walk around with the eyes of a blind man."

Jason settled in front of her. "I do believe in the supernatural. I'm saying, there are others in the world who can move things with their minds, Tala. Who have abilities most of us don't have. It doesn't mean those people can't live normal lives. It doesn't mean that you can't."

Only proof of her powers would convince him. "I am not like them," she said. "I am not like anyone you have ever known, or know of. I am—"

"A woman," he interrupted, and he touched her face again. "A beautiful woman who has been brain-washed into believing she can do miracles. You can't save me, Tala. I wish that you could, but now I realize

203

your beliefs are based on nothing more than a fairy tale."

"What is a fairy tale?" she demanded.

With a sigh, he ran a hand through his hair. "Stories that are made up to entertain children. Good versus evil. Mythical creatures that roam the earth. They aren't real, Tala. These chosen ones in your legend, they—"

"Do not speak to me of what you do not know about!" she interrupted. "My world is not yours. I thought you would have come to realize that during the time you have been among us."

His voice was softer when he responded. "I see that your world is different. But I don't feel as if it should be. This gift you have of finding the evil ones, it could only be your physical ability to sense what is unnatural in the world. Just because you can sense these creatures, see them at times, doesn't mean it's your sole responsibility to fight the evil ones. Your people have chosen your destiny for you. They've placed a burden upon your conscience because they can't let go of the past and move to the future. You've all been brainwashed from the time you were born to believe you have some sacred purpose in life."

His words stunned her. "We all have a purpose, Jason. Even you, though yours has not been fully revealed to you yet."

As she feared, she saw words would not sway him from the path of his thoughts. There was no acceptance or understanding in his eyes, only . . . pity.

"I'm leaving. You can't help me, Tala. If you want to believe in this superstitious nonsense, that's your right, but don't expect me to believe in it, too. I could take you away from here. Teach you my ways so that you can survive in the outside."

Did he mean that he wanted her with him? She did not think so. That was not a commitment he would make to her. Tala suspected it was not a commitment he had made to any woman. She wanted to make certain she understood his offer. "What will happen then?"

His gaze darted away from her. He rubbed one of his dark brows. "You can make a life for yourself there."

"Alone?"

He laughed, but he did not sound amused. "Believe me, with the way you look, you won't be alone for long."

Tala was not amused either. "I do not care to be with people who only judge me by what they see at first glance. There is more to me than that. Much more."

Jason rose. "I know. I'm sure someone else will see it, too. Are you coming with me?"

She shook her head, and her heart felt as if it would break, but beneath the robes, she reached for her knife. "I cannot let you leave. You have not faced the call of the moon and beaten back the beast. You knew from the beginning what I must do if you tried to escape."

"You can't kill me," he said, his ice-blue gaze locking with hers. "I'm not one of them, Tala. You know that."

"You are not one of them now, but—"

"I will *never* be one of them."

It would be easy to believe him. Much simpler than

to kill him. Tala could not kill him, she admitted. Her heart would not let her. The choices left to her were few. She must make him believe. Tala rose from her furs, the firelight glinting off of the knife she held.

"Look at me," she commanded softly. "Tell me what you see."

Jason saw a woman he didn't want to walk away from. She had thought to rescue him from the dark fate she felt certain awaited him, but now he wanted to rescue her. It wouldn't change anything for him, but it would change everything for Tala. Away from her people, she might see how foolish their beliefs were. She might come to accept that her destiny was not the one they had decreed for her. Jason supposed she would find a life, a man, have children. Although he felt a stab of jealousy over the fact, he cared enough for Tala to want those things for her.

"I see a beautiful woman, inside and out. One who is special, but not as different from other women as she's been led to believe. I see a woman who can choose her own destiny, if she's brave enough."

Tears welled up in Tala's dark eyes, but she blinked them away. "You see only what I have allowed you to see. Only what you wish to see. Look closer."

The knife fell from her hand, which was the first thing he noticed. He also noticed that she slept in a shift, doeskin, but tanned very thin. It was short, too. Her skin gleamed like a pretty polished rock. But her eyes, they were always what had mesmerized him about her the most—dark and revealing of her emotions one moment, mysterious and secretive the next. He stared into them, helpless to look away.

Did she think to cast some type of spell over him? Maybe she thought she could bend him to her will. He tried to look away, but couldn't. That bothered him. A moment later, something else bothered him. Tala grew hazy before his eyes. He tried to blink, but again, he couldn't. All he could do was stare at her and watch as her image became dimmer, then almost faded. Her eyes seemed smaller, her nose longer, sharper. She looked smaller ... much smaller. Her long hair became ruffled—like feathers.

His mind rejected what he saw. She was changing into someone, or something else. Tala continued to grow smaller, to take on features that were not human. One minute she had been a woman; the next, she was a bird. A hawk. Her beak opened and she screeched at him. Then she spread her wings and flew from the cave. Jason stood still, too shocked to move. This had to be some kind of trick. She'd cast some type of spell over him to make him think that she'd turned into a bird. He glanced around the cave, looking for her, but he was alone.

His heart pounded and his knees nearly gave way, but he ran from the cave, scrambling down the embankment. He glanced at the dark sky. A hawk circled above. *Come with me.* He heard Tala's voice in his mind. He raced after her, wondering if the guards would be a problem, as he'd wondered earlier when he planned his escape.

They will not see you. I have willed them to watch me instead.

There it was again, her voice inside of his head. He felt like he was losing his mind, but Jason did as she instructed. He raced through the trees, past the perimeters of camp where he spotted a guard; his head turned toward the night sky.

See yourself as the wolf. A creature of the night. One with nature. Hear your heart pound inside your chest. Feel your blood race through your veins. Call upon the wolf's strength, his swiftness, his cunning.

In his mind's eye, Jason saw the wolf. Large and black, eyes glowing in the darkness. He envisioned the change, saw his feet become paws, his skin become fur. He understood that he now ran on four legs instead of two. He understood that the shapes rising around him were trees, and that although he had taken the form of the wolf, the thoughts running through his head were human. A surge of adrenaline shot through him. He ran faster, his keen night vision allowing him to see the world around him as if it were daylight. Above, a hawk called down to him, but he knew her voice.

This is the gift I promised you. The freedom of a wolf. The mind of a man. The joy of acceptance. Will you take my gift? Or will you run away? Now is the time that you must decide, for I will not stop you. Find your own way, or accept mine.

Her voice echoed through his mind, sounding a long way off. . . . Jason came awake with a start. He sat abruptly, gasping for breath. He was in Haidar's cave. The man squatted before the fire, eating a greasy piece of meat.

"Bad dream?"

Jason glanced around the cave. His clothes lay folded neatly next to his sleeping mat, just as he had left them the night before. But he'd risen later when Haidar slept, dressing again to sneak away and visit

Tala. Hadn't he? Or *had* last night been a dream? His rational mind told him a woman could not change into a hawk and fly away. She couldn't speak to him through telepathic thoughts. He'd been dreaming. But the dream seemed real. The legend Tala had told spoke of Mother Earth giving the "ones chosen" wings to fly. That was why he'd dreamed Tala had changed into a hawk—wasn't it?

"There is food," Haidar grunted, motioning him toward the fire. "Left from last night. We do not waste what the forest provides."

Jason rose. He dressed and joined Tala's brother next to the fire. His head hurt, as if he hadn't had enough sleep. He needed a good, strong cup of coffee. Of course, the forest didn't have a Starbucks. Instead, he grabbed a water skin and drank. Haidar wasn't much of a cook. Tala would have taken the leftover venison and prepared a thick stew. Haidar had only slapped the slabs of meat upon a warming rack he'd placed over the fire. Jason lifted a piece of meat and started eating. He realized a moment later that both he and Haidar smacked and licked their greasy fingers like barbarians. When in Rome . . . he thought, and continued.

"Did you enjoy the ceremony last night?" Haidar asked.

Jason eyed him warily across the fire. The big man wasn't usually much for conversation first thing in the morning—well, anytime really. "I particularly liked your gift," he said dryly.

Haidar smiled. "I thought you would."

"You know"—Jason tore off another chunk of meat and popped it into his mouth, not caring if he spoke and chewed at the same time—"you'd probably be a lot easier to get along with if you had a woman."

Tala's brother paused while bringing a chunk of venison to his lips. "That is not possible. I am related by blood to all women in my tribe. In some cases, the blood is very distant, but it is still there."

"Bummer," Jason said.

Haidar lifted a brow. "Bummer?"

"Not a good thing," Jason supplied. "Why can't you find a wife from the outside?"

Haidar cast him a dark look. "You know that it is forbidden for my people to mix with those from the outside."

Jason shrugged. "I'd think in cases like yours, an exception would be made. I mean—hell, it's what your ancestors did, right? They raided other tribes and carried off women?"

"*My* ancestors did not," Haidar argued. "Our strain is pure and has been for centuries. We do not taint our blood with the blood of those different from us."

Jason couldn't shake the dream he'd had last night with idle conversation. Just how "different" was Tala? He'd been determined to leave last night, had planned on escape. Something had stopped him. Had he fallen into a deep sleep and couldn't rouse himself? Or had he done exactly what he'd planned, dressed and gone to visit Tala? He needed to see her now. Needed to run his hands through her long hair and look into her dark eyes. Needed to reassure himself that she was just who he thought she was: a woman with some physic abilities who'd been brainwashed by her tribe into believing that she was more.

"The moon will be full in five days."

Haidar's words brought his thoughts back to the conversation, only it wasn't the same conversation they'd been having. "I knew it wasn't long," Jason admitted.

"You understand, it will be the test for you. Tala would like to give you longer to prove yourself, but you have been among us too long already. If you cannot fight the call of the moon during each night of the cycle . . ."

"I become target practice," Jason finished.

He didn't plan on being around. Tala had given him hope in the beginning. Now, he was confused. She had helped him do things he hadn't been able to do before. But he was a long way from feeling as if he had control over the change. After hearing her story last night, he had lost faith in her—lost faith in himself. But then he'd had the dream. Maybe it was a sign for him to not give up. Maybe it hadn't been a dream at all.

"If you fail, I will do it," Haidar said softly. "And I will make it quick."

He curled his lip in an imitation of a smile. "Thanks, big guy. That makes me feel much better."

Haidar shrugged. "I do not like you, but I would not enjoy killing you. You must listen to my sister, follow her advice, and learn what she will teach you. The days are short, so I will allow you time in her company. Use it wisely."

The last statement Haidar said with a low growl of warning. In other words, Jason was to make certain he was the student and not the teacher. Of course, Haidar had no idea that his sister might be a willing pupil. Or maybe he did, and he meant for Jason to be the wise one concerning the matter. In that case, leaving also seemed to be the smartest move.

"Go," Haidar motioned him out. "Find her. She is below with the others by now."

Jason couldn't get away fast enough.

Chapter Eighteen

Tala was aware of the looks she received while she served her uncle his breakfast. All were thinking of the joining dress she'd worn the night before and wondering why she had left the ceremony. Let them think, let them wonder, she decided.

"The outsider," her uncle said. "I like him."

She smiled. "His name is Jason. And I like him, too. Most of the time," she added, then realized her uncle watched her closely. "He is different."

"Yes," the old man agreed. "But he fits among us well. It is good to see a new face inside our camp. Our numbers become smaller every year. I am thinking he might not wish to go away. The one we cannot speak of has left a widow. She will need a mate."

"No!" Tala immediately felt her face suffuse with heat. "He will not want to stay among us," she said,

213

her voice calmer. "He misses his world and wishes to return."

"He has told you this?"

She nodded. "Besides, you have forgotten that we are not his kind."

"We are only a little different," her uncle argued. "A small thing to overcome when a man and a woman have love between them."

Curious, Tala said, "You have never spoken to me of love, Uncle. You never took a mate. Why?"

He glanced down, rubbing the joint of a swollen finger. "The only woman my heart beat for was already taken . . . by my brother."

"My father?"

"Yes. So instead, I took his children, and I loved them as if they were my own."

She reached forward and touched his hand. "We love you, too, Uncle. All of us, although . . ." She did not finish.

"Meka will come home one day," he said.

Tala wished his words could be true. "She is an outcast. The tribe will not accept her."

He patted the hand she still held over his. "I have told you that our world is changing. We must change with it. I never spoke to you of love between a man and a woman because I knew you were one of the chosen, and that kind of love would not be a part of your life. Sometimes, the heart does not listen to destiny, to what has been decreed. Sometimes, the heart makes plans of its own." His gaze moved past her. "Your white man is looking for you."

Glancing over her shoulder, Tala saw Jason walking slowly through the trees. Her heart sped a measure to see him. Tall, dark, strong and so very handsome. "We have been taught that destiny cannot be changed." She took her hand from her uncle's and rose.

"It cannot," her uncle agreed. "But what we believe to be our destiny is not always our true course. We must wait and see."

There was no waiting for Tala. While some might stumble along blindly, like Jason, looking for their purpose, Tala's had been revealed to her from an early age. Wishing something was not so did not make it that way. If it did, she would have wished herself into becoming a normal girl years ago.

"Take care, uncle," she said. Then she went to join Jason.

When they met, he stood, staring intently at her. He stared so hard and long she felt her cheeks grow warm beneath the rising sun.

"Why do you stare at me as if you have never seen me before?" she asked.

He did not answer, but ran a hand down the side of her hair. Tala thought it best to get him away from the camp and curious eyes.

"Come with me," she said softly, then turned and walked away.

The guards posted around their camp did not stop them. Haidar had lifted the rule that the white man not be allowed outside of their camp perimeters. He had amended it, rather; the white man could only be allowed outside if he were accompanied by Tala or himself. She did notice a strange look from the guard as they passed. Wearing the joining dress to the ceremony the night before had been rebellious and a foolish act on her part. It was the first hint to her people that she wished her destiny had been chosen for another.

"You said that to me last night."

She glanced sideways at Jason. "Said what?"

"Come with me. Only . . ."

"Only what?"

Again, he did not answer. He glanced away from her. They walked farther into the forest. Tala lifted her face to the sky. She let the warm rays that fell between the trees beat down upon her. She would never choose to be anywhere else, only to be some*one* else.

"I had a dream." He laughed. "It was very weird."

"Dreams, like visions, are sometimes hard to understand."

"You were in it."

She lifted a brow. "What was I doing in your dream?"

Jason ran a hand through his long hair. She knew he did this when he was frustrated, or confused, sometimes when he was angry. "Flying."

"In the air? Flapping my arms?"

He shook his head. "No. I mean, it wasn't you, but it was you. You turned into a bird. I could hear you speak in my mind."

"That is strange," she agreed. "What did I say to you?"

"You told me to become the wolf."

"And did you obey?"

Silence.

"Did you obey me?" she repeated.

"Yes," he answered. "I ran through the forest, felt free, enjoyed who I was."

"But still, you have doubts that I can help you. Your thoughts are not upon what you must do, but upon running away."

He stopped and pulled her around to face him. "How do you know that?"

She could let him believe a lie, but that was not the purpose of what she had shown him the night before. "You told me when you came to me last night, remember?"

His face paled beneath his dark complexion. "That wasn't a dream?"

"You thought my people had made me believe that I was something I am not. I had to show you."

He stumbled to a fallen tree and sat. His face looked even paler, and he placed his head between his knees. He sat that way for a time.

Tala joined him. "Are you ill?"

"A little light-headed." He glanced up at her. "You . . . you're . . ."

"A 'freak'?" she provided. "One who is different. Different from you. Different from your people. Different from even my own tribe."

Jason placed his head between his knees again. Deep sadness washed over Tala. He would not look at her the same now. She had lost her humanity in his eyes—her womanhood. It was for the best, she told herself; her purpose was to save him from the beast, not to find love with him. She had been wrong to pretend there could be more between them than a debt owed. One she could never repay.

217

"I am Tala Soaringbird," she said softly. "I am the one chosen among my people."

Jason drew a shaky breath and stood. "I know I'm not supposed to be shocked by anything anymore, but I am. You turned into a bird and flew away, Tala. You spoke to me in my mind. Maybe I wasn't listening too close last night to your—can you turn into anything?"

She did not like the way he looked at her, as if the woman he knew was gone. As if she were suddenly a stranger to him. She walked away. "You did not listen to the story last night, only to the sound of my voice. I can become anything my mind envisions. I can even become whatever your mind envisions."

He fell into step beside her. "Have you? I mean, taken a form that I would find pleasing? Am I looking at *you*?"

His question made her draw up short. "Yes. You are looking at me. A human being. The form that I was born in. But you are no longer looking at me as you once did. You are looking at me as you fear your people will look at you if they knew the truth."

She thought to storm away, but he touched her arm, then as if she had burned him, removed it. "Tala. Give me a break. This is all just a little hard for me to comprehend, regardless of what I am. I thought—I knew you were different, but . . ."

"You thought a lie. I had to make you understand. You had lost faith in me, lost faith in yourself. You must believe in the impossible to fight the call of the moon. You must believe in my powers and in your own."

*   *   *

Jason felt as if his head might be spinning around on his neck. He'd been certain Tala had some degree of physic ability, but he'd had no idea of *this*. What she had shown him last night went way beyond controlling a fire with her mind or even repelling, although he'd thought those two abilities were impressive enough. What she could do . . . well, it was impossible, but yet, he'd seen her turn into a bird with his own eyes. Or had he?

"You've told me that you can cast spells. How do I know you didn't cast one on me last night? Make me believe I saw and heard things that I didn't?"

She rolled her eyes at him and started walking again. "Your mind is stubborn for a man who has lived for three years in a world with shadows. You can accept that you can change into another form, but not that I can? It has long been a gift among my people. A few of them, anyway."

He realized he lagged behind and hurried to catch up with her. "Can you change into a wolf?"

"A wolf, a bear, a rabbit, a bird, whatever I choose."

"That night in the city, that's how you got me to follow you," he realized. "You became a wolf."

"You had trouble keeping up with me." She laughed. "And me, having to carry your little bag in my mouth."

His knees felt weak again. Jason took deep breaths to combat his light-headedness. All things considered, he didn't know why he had so much trouble believing what she said, accepting that she could have such powers. His sane world had ceased to exist three years ago. Nothing should surprise him. Maybe he had so much trouble believing her because he considered himself part of the darkness, under a curse, and when he looked at Tala, all he saw was the light.

"I can see now where your people would consider you an asset to the tribe. Besides your ability to find the evil ones and destroy them, as a hawk, you can look below and find food they can't. Hell, you can do anything."

She paused, glancing up at him. "I cannot do everything, Jason. I can change who I am on the outside, but not who I am on the inside. I can change your destiny, but I cannot change my own."

Jason had been forced into being something he didn't want to be for three years. Tala had been forced into it her whole life. She had a gift all right—a tremendous gift, but she didn't want it.

"I'm sorry," he said. "Sorry for you."

Her chin shot up. "Do not pity me. Pity yourself. Run away now if you choose. You told me it is what you do when you fear what you cannot control. The full moon is almost upon us. Fighting its call is the greatest battle for one of your kind. My brother will not give you more time. Fight or flee."

She stood proud, tough on the outside, even if he knew a different woman lived inside. One who was vulnerable. One who craved what had been denied her. One who only wanted to be a woman—a normal one.

"You gave me that same choice last night," he said. "I'm still here. I want to fight."

The rigid set of her shoulders relaxed. "I knew you would. You are a warrior, Jason Donavon. You must never forget that."

Pride swelled inside him. He wanted to fight . . . for

her. "Your brother told me that I must listen to your advice, allow you to teach me. What will I learn today?"

She smiled, somewhat sadly he thought. "You will learn the beauty of what you are. Follow me."

They moved farther into the forest. Jason watched Tala's long hair swing back and forth as she walked. Her powers humbled him, made him aware of her importance. He'd been a fool. Just like him to think he knew what was best for her, probably because what he considered best for her, was also best for him. He thought she should experience what had been denied her. Believing that had served his own desires to become intimate with her.

"I'm sorry, Tala."

She glanced over her shoulder. "Sorry? For what?"

"For trying to convince you that your powers weren't worth what they cost you. I didn't understand."

Her dark eyes softened before she turned her attention upon the path they took. "You are the only one who understood. I thank you for showing me, even for a short time, how it feels to be . . . no one special."

He couldn't stop himself from reaching out to pull her up. Jason turned her to face him. "You could never be no one. Not to me. Even if you hadn't shown up that night in the alley with your knives and your courage, I would have known you were special from the moment I saw you."

She closed her eyes, and he noticed a tear drop clinging to her thick lashes. "When you leave us, will you remember me always?"

The urge to kiss her became overpowering, but he couldn't. He had to respect the gifts she'd been given, her importance to her people. He was a man with no place now in either his word, or in hers. Tala at least had her destiny.

"Always," he promised, then reluctantly released her.

She stood there, eyes closed for a moment longer, then seemed to rouse herself. Turning from him, she set off again. He had no idea where they were going. They walked in silence for a long time to get there. She moved to a fallen tree and sat. When he started forward, she held up a hand. "Stand very still. Do not speak."

Jason did as she asked. The day was beautiful. A light breeze played with the long strands of Tala's hair. Sunlight filtered down from the trees and surrounded her in an unnatural light. She looked like a wood nymph. A dark shape crept from the shadows and appeared next to her. First one, then another. Soon, she was surrounded. He stood still, but felt his body tense. Wolves.

She made crooning sounds as she reached out and ran her hand along the fur of a large wolf's back. Soon, they all vied for her attention. She laughed at their antics to push each other out of the way to get closer to her. Jason had watched wild wolves, his gaze always searching for one that seemed different. He'd viewed them in a dark light, just as he viewed what had happened to him because of a wolf as a curse.

Slowly, he began to relax. Tala glanced up at him, a serene smile upon her lips. She motioned him forward. He took cautious steps to reach her, the wolves moving aside to make room for him to sit next to her.

"Do not fear them," she said. "They do not fear you. Your scent is the same as their own to them. They are not like humans, who identify only by sight."

He reached out and touched a wolf, ran his fingers down its back as he had seen Tala do. When he stopped, the wolf nuzzled his hand as if to urge him to continue. He laughed. Tala laughed, too, and the sound of her voice tinkling on the warm breeze brought him a peace he hadn't felt in a long time.

They sat, watching the wolves play, smiling over their antics with one another. There was love between the animals, a special bond, and for a moment, a longing so fierce to belong somewhere rose up inside of Jason, that it almost stole the beauty of the afternoon.

The wolves raced away, still playfully snapping at and bumping against one another. Jason and Tala watched the pack until they moved out of vision.

"I'm glad that you did that for me," he said. "Showed them to me in another light."

"You did not see them as they truly are. The same as you could not see me as I truly am. For many years, my people have cherished the beauty of the wolf, but it is not the same with yours. Your people kill what they do not understand. They eliminate what they fear. The wolf once roamed the land in great numbers, like the buffalo. Now there are few of either."

It wasn't a heritage he could feel proud about. "Well, yeah, unfortunately it's not really something most people take the time to think about. Not my people, anyway. We have other worries. Survival of the fittest."

"Or those with the most weapons," she added, and

he noticed she now mimicked his own wry tone. "Your brother has come to see the beauty of the wolf."

Surprised, he glanced at her. "How do you know that?"

The pollen that had floated down from the trees and dusted their clothing suddenly seemed of interest to her. She brushed it from the fabric of her dress. "I would assume so. He heals animals. His connection would be much stronger than someone who has not come to know all creatures on a deeper level."

Jason was confused. "I don't remember telling you that my brother healed animals. A veterinarian is what we call that in my world."

She shrugged. "You must have at some time. I know this about him."

Bringing Rick into the conversation reminded him that his duty was not only to himself. "I don't know what I'm going to do about Rick. If I pass your test, and then later, you see something in the future that might help us, will you find me, tell me? Or if I don't pass your test, is there any way you can find him?"

"You must pass the test." She rose, turning her back to him. "In your mind, there can be no doubt."

"What will happen during the full moon? Besides the change?"

She didn't answer for a moment. "It is the change we do not want to happen. My brother and I will watch you. I will try to help you fight against what has now become natural for your body. During the cycle, we will be with you every night when the moon rises, until it sinks again."

"And if I make it through the cycle without changing, then what? Am I free to leave?"

"Yes. You will go."

As the fresh smell of pine filled his lungs and the sun continued to shine down upon them, Jason came to a startling realization. He wasn't sure he wanted to leave.

"I'll never see you again."

"That is what we will hope," she said softly.

He couldn't hope for that, even though he knew what she meant. She didn't want to see him in the outside because she'd have been forced to come looking for his head. "You told me that you only see the evil ones if they affect your tribe, or someone you care about." He stood and turned her to face him. "You care about me. If you didn't, you wouldn't be helping me."

She wouldn't look up into his eyes. "I owe you a debt."

"Tala." He tilted her face up to his. "There's something between us, there has been from the beginning. Even if that something can't go anywhere, it's still there. Tell me it isn't."

Her dark eyes fused with his. "Do you feel the same as before, Jason? When you realized who I am, you did not look at me as if you knew me. You had forgotten that I am a woman."

He liked the way she said his name. The emphasis she placed on certain letters made it sound different. He'd been shocked to find out the truth about her, angry with himself for trying to convince her that she was less important to her tribe than he now knew. But he'd never forgotten that she was a woman.

"No, what I feel hasn't changed. But the common sense of fighting my emotions has become stronger. It was futile before, now it's . . . impossible."

"Do you not see that we are alike?"

"We're not the same," he argued. "Your powers stem from goodness, my curse stems from evil. You're from one world, and I'm from another. We have no future, not together." He glanced away from the hurt in her eyes. "You know that I speak the truth, Tala."

The soft touch of her hand against his cheek startled him. "We have no future, but we have this moment in time. A moment when two worlds come together. A moment when the future is far away, and you are only a man, and me, a woman."

Her touch sent shock waves of pleasure racing through him. He couldn't deny the sizzling attraction that had always been between them. But for her sake, he must resist.

"I won't compromise your powers."

"What happened between us yesterday went unfinished."

She looked up at him with such openness, Jason felt his resolve weaken. "You won't miss what you haven't experienced."

"I already miss what I have not yet experienced," she argued. "Will you deny me the pleasure you promised?"

Denying Tala anything was difficult for him, had been from the start. If they didn't cross the line. If he only pleasured her, was it a crime?

"No," he answered. "But we must have rules, just as your tribe must have rules." When her brow creased, he added, "We can't go beyond the limits of what we agreed upon yesterday."

"This is true," she conceded, then took his hand.

Jason allowed her to lead him, he hoped, not to his ruin and hers.

226

Chapter Nineteen

Tala reached for the shoulder ties of her tunic. The outdoor hot spring where she'd once taken Jason bubbled and steamed in the warm afternoon air. Neither were as hot as his eyes upon her. She had removed her moccasins and her leggings. His gaze lowered to her bare legs, then roamed back up. Her heart beat fast inside her chest. She had never felt beautiful until he looked at her.

The smell of the tall grass that grew in the distant meadow drifted to her on the wind. She heard the sound of water rushing in the great river to the north. The sacred breath of the south wind touched her shoulders, her breasts, belly, hips, then lower against her woman's place. The tunic slid down her legs into a puddle at her feet.

The forest thrived all around her, and she was not ashamed to be in her natural state. Tala stood straight

227

before Jason, her breasts thrust forward, her eyes trained upon him.

"You're beautiful, Tala. Perfect."

He spoke the words reverently, all the while, his eyes worshipping her human form. Tala stepped into the hot bubbling water of the spring. "Will you join me?" she teased, recalling when he had asked the question of her.

In answer, he pulled his shirt over his head. It did not take him long to strip from his breechclout, leggings, and moccasins. He stood before her, as unashamed as she had stood before him.

His sex rose proud and ready to complete a union that could not take place. Tala tried to focus on more than the blatant proof of his desire for her. His skin was a tawny color, like the great mountain cat. He was as sleek and muscled as a cougar as well. His legs were long and well defined, covered in fine dark hair that almost glinted gold in the sun. The light dusting across his chest intrigued her. Her tribe's men did not allow hair to grow on their faces or their chests.

He moved toward her, stepping into the water at the opposite end of the small, shallow pool. He bent, allowing the water to cover him to the shoulders. Their gazes held across the steamy air rising up from the spring, but he did not rush to be near her.

Instead, he stretched the tension between them, staring into her eyes with the heated intensity of a wolf.

She moved toward him, realized he moved as well when they met at the pool's center. He said nothing, but his lips lowered to hers.

The contact was gentle, tender, a contradiction to

the passion she saw burning in his gaze. Her arms went around his neck, his around her waist. The afternoon heat, the steamy pool, and desire combined to make their bodies slick against each other. Jason lifted her long hair and ran his fingers through it.

Her hands moved up his back, feeling his muscles bunch beneath her fingertips. She felt alive in his arms, whole for the first time in her life . . . happy.

"Tala, you have to trust me while I pleasure you, but don't trust me to stop at that alone. Promise you'll stop me."

She would have promised him her soul in that moment. He was everything male, everything forbidden to her, and she could not get enough of his kisses, his hands moving over her skin. He cupped her breasts, brushing his thumbs against the sensitive peaks of her nipples. Tala moaned against his mouth, pulled away, and pushed his head down to her breasts.

He suckled her, as she wanted him to do, driving her mad with the skill of his tongue, his lips, the slight nip of his teeth. Her nails dug into his scalp. She threw her head back, her long hair floating around her in the water.

The strange coiling began in her belly, tighter and tighter with each pull of his mouth against her nipples. She gasped for breath, then twisted her fingers into his silky hair, pulling his mouth back up to hers.

They stood, the spring bubbling around Tala's hips. Their tongues danced, her flesh quivered in anticipation. She felt the hard length of him pressed against the soft skin of her stomach. He rubbed against her, groaned and pulled away.

Tala reached for him, but he captured her wrists.

"The rules, Tala. You make me want to forget who we are, but I can't do that."

"Do not leave me unfulfilled." Tala had never begged in her life, but their time together was short. She wanted no man but him. Would never want another. He kissed her gently, although she felt his body tremble. Jason led her to the shallow end of the spring. He pulled her down with him, settling upon the smooth warm rocks surrounding the spring. There, he took her in his arms, tasting her lips until a fire blazed between them once more.

His hands moved over her body, exploring until he reached the sensitive, pulsing place between her legs. He stroked her there, as he had done at the Sacred Waters.

He knew how to touch her, how to make her ache with need until she moved against his skilled fingers. He continued to kiss her, his tongue moving in and out of her mouth until she became too breathless to kiss him back. She dug her fingers into his broad shoulders, moaning his name.

Higher and higher he took her, and although she had flown before, looked down at the earth from a great distance above, she had never experienced the feelings Jason stirred inside her. He whispered in her ear, words laced with passion, promises he could not keep. Tala arched, spiraled upward and shattered. A rush of pleasure, intense, nearly painful, washed over her body. She shuddered and convulsed, unable to stop her trembling thighs or the words that spilled from her lips.

She mumbled words to him in the language of her people. Words she could never tell him in his own language. Jason drew her into his arms, allowing her to cling to him, to show her own woman's weakness as she had never been permitted to show it before. She felt safe, satisfied, finally at peace . . . until she opened her eyes and looked into his.

The heated glow of the beast stared back at her. It was in Jason's eyes. He made a low growling sound in his throat; then he was upon her. Tala knew what the animal inside him wanted. In her heart, she wanted it too. To complete their joining. In her heart, she wanted him to do everything, to take her powers from her.

"I can't fight it," Jason said. "Forgive me, Tala."

He thrust one knee between her legs and she felt his hard shaft waiting to enter her, to tear her flesh, to claim her for his mate. But looking into his eyes, she saw that only the beast wanted these things and that the man was sickened by his lack of control. She reached up and touched his face.

"You are stronger than he is. If you do his will, it is only because you want to lose this battle."

"I want you, Tala," he rasped. "God, how I want you, but not his way. Not because he has won."

"Then fight him. Send him away."

His jaw clenched, but she felt his sex brush against hers, slick from the juices he had brought forth with his fingers. She closed her eyes, waiting for the pain she had heard other women speak of during a first joining. Then he flung himself from her, which Tala could have done with her own powers, but had not.

"Go," he demanded. "Run while you can."

As much as she wanted to experience all there was to passion, Tala had regained enough wisdom to do as he ordered. She rose on trembling legs, snatched up her clothing, and put distance between them.

"Meet me at the camp perimeter," she called, then hurried away.

Jason fought himself to let her go. He could catch her easily, throw her to the ground, ease the ache between his legs, ease the emptiness he felt inside. Both man and beast wanted her, but for different reasons. Man would win, he vowed, taking deep breaths to bring his lust under control. Tala deserved more than he could give her. Evidently more than any man could give her. Rather than concentrate on her, his attraction to her, and the feelings that went deeper, he should be concentrating on the coming full moon.

If he fought the change each night and won, he'd be free to leave. Free to return . . . but to what? His search, he decided. All men needed a quest, either great or small. Even if Jason came to terms with what he'd become three years before, he'd never give up on the promise he had made to his brother.

He rose and walked to where he'd shed his clothing. For a moment, he allowed the sun's warm rays to beat down upon him. Tala's scent lingered on his skin. Long ago, he'd been with many women. Ironic that the one he truly wanted, he couldn't have. He bent to retrieve the breechclout to cover his nudity.

"Don't spoil the view."

His gaze shot up and scanned the surrounding area. He didn't see anyone.

"Up here."

Above him, a pair of legs wrapped in torn fish-net hose dangled from a branch. Attached to the legs was a woman, one who made his blood run cold and the hair at the back of his neck stand on end.

"I was right, under all that hair, you *are* very good looking."

"You," he whispered.

She jumped from the branch and landed in front of him. "Surprised?"

Jason stumbled back. "You're supposed to be dead."

The woman shrugged, then tore open her shirt, exposing large breasts. "She didn't cut me deep enough. See?"

There were no scars. He glanced away from her chest. What should he do? What did she want?

"Don't you like what you see?" she pouted. "I could help you with that little, or rather, that big problem she's left you with."

"What do you want?" he demanded.

The provocative twist to her lips turned into a sneer. "Revenge. You killed my mate."

Jason had thought the male had come for revenge. If not, then why? "He took one of the children."

She stepped closer. "He knew I wanted a child. But I can't conceive now, or I guess I can't. I've tried with many before I ripped out their throats and drank their blood."

A stench clung to her, as if something rotten rested beneath her human skin. "Why would you want a child?"

"To feel human again, of course. I am a female. Whether human, animal, or creature, we all want offspring. Little ones to carry on once we're gone."

They had planned to convert the boy. The thought nauseated Jason. "All you want is to spread your evil."

233

"I had my own pack," she growled. "And now you've ruined everything." Her eyes glowed for a moment. Then she blinked, and they appeared normal again. "You took my mate—I think it's only fitting you replace him." Her eyes ran over him. "You'll do."

"I'm not like you," Jason snapped.

She threw back her head and laughed, exposing human teeth, if they were badly in need of a brushing. "Not yet, but I can help you along. I can give you what she wouldn't, or what you refused to take. You want to belong somewhere, don't you? We all do. No one wants to be alone. Join us."

Nervous, he glanced around. "Us?"

"There are only a few, but soon, there will be many who run with my pack. The male you killed was the leader. You can rule with me if you take his place."

What she offered disgusted him, but he couldn't deny that part of him felt tempted. Tala had warned him about his need to belong, to be part of a pack. That need would weaken him. "Get out of here, or you'll become the hunting party's next kill."

Her gaze narrowed. "The woman. I have a score to settle with her." Long tapered nails reached out and ran the length of his chest. "And with you."

"Go near her and I'll rip your head off!"

She snatched her fingers away. "I could have killed you both while you were so wrapped up in one another. I enjoyed the show, and you, well, you are magnificent. I decided I wanted you for myself."

"That is not going to happen," he said as his gaze searched the area for some type of weapon. He could call the beast in him forth, but unless she changed, he didn't think he could kill her. Not while she was in the form of a woman. He expected Tala to return at any minute, her powers alerting her to the creature's presence. She would have her knives with her.

"Think about my offer." The blonde wet her lips with her tongue in a manner he supposed was meant to be tempting. "You might as well enjoy what you've become. You don't belong with the woman and her strange people, but you can belong with me and those we bring into our pack."

"Leave my people alone."

Sneering, she shook her head. "They are not your people. You have no people. You are alone."

Her words were true, but he'd seen what she became, what her pimp had become. Death was better than her offer. He should kill her before she raised a threat to Tala and the others. But she'd said there were more. Maybe the one who'd bitten him was among them. Maybe this was the one.

"If you join me, I'll leave your woman and her people alone. If you don't, there will be hell to pay." She backed away. "I'll give you a couple of days to think it over."

"How will I find you?"

She smiled. "Don't worry. I'll find you."

He shouldn't let her go. He should kill her here, before she hurt someone. But there was also that desperate voice in his head that said this woman might be the answer to breaking his curse. If he went with her, he might discover the identity of the one who'd bitten him. Where in the hell was Tala? He glanced around to see if she was coming, her knives drawn and ready, but she was nowhere to be seen. When he glanced back, the blonde had disappeared.

As the sun continued to beat against his skin and the forest noises returned, he wondered if he'd imagined her. Telling himself that three years before might have worked. It didn't now. He had to tell Tala, but then, surely she already knew. Maybe she was gathering forces. Jason dressed and raced toward the camp, expecting to meet a band of armed warriors on his way. But he didn't see anyone. When he reached the perimeter of camp, Tala stepped from behind a tree.

"What took you so long?" she asked. "I became worried about you."

Her dark eyes displayed concern, but it wasn't the kind of concern he expected. "Didn't you have a vision while I was gone? I expected to encounter you and most of your warriors on my way back to camp."

She frowned. "I do not understand. I had no vision. What are you talking about?"

"The female," he answered. "The one you thought you had killed. She's here."

Tala's gaze widened. She glanced behind him. "Here? But that is not possible. My powers would have alerted me to the danger."

"I saw her," he insisted. "She spoke to me."

Glancing around again, Tala took his arm. "Come. We must alert the others. Then we will talk."

She spoke to one of the guards along the camp perimeter as they passed. Jason didn't have to understand her language to know what she'd said. The man tensed, his eyes searching the area. A moment later, the guard began making birdcalls. It was a signal to the next nearest guard. A signal Jason knew would be passed along.

"We must tell Haidar," Tala said as they walked. "The whole camp must be alerted."

"Why weren't you? I kept expecting you to show up with your knives. Why didn't you see her coming?"

Tala shook her head. "I do not know. Maybe my mind had dismissed her as a threat because I thought her dead. I do not know," she repeated, her confusion over the matter obvious.

Jason was confused, too. He'd had to warn Tala about the danger, but he wasn't sure he wanted a war party storming off to kill the woman. She might be the only link to breaking the curse, and the others might escape. Then again, Tala said there were many, and this female might have no connection to him, his brother, or what had happened to them three years ago. If that was the case, then yes, the creature should be destroyed as soon as possible.

"Did she try to kill you?" Tala asked.

"No."

She drew up. "No? Why would she spare you?"

His face felt hot. He hoped he wasn't blushing. He didn't think telling Tala that the woman liked his "assets" would be a wise idea. "She wants me to replace her dead mate."

Her eyes sparked with fury. "Mate? With that creature?"

"She wants me to join her. Become the alpha male of some pack she's trying to organize."

Tala's cheeks had turned pink; now her face drained of color. "Pack? The creatures maintain the intelligence to organize? This is very bad." She took a couple of hurried steps, then stopped again. "That does not explain why she spared you. You did refuse her?"

He wouldn't lie to her. "She said she would spare you and the others if I agree to join her. She said she would give me a couple of days to think it over."

A huff left Tala's lips. "There is nothing to think over, is there?"

Jason took her shoulders between his hands. "Tala, she might know the one who bit me. The creature could be part of her pack; hell, the creature could be her. This is an opportunity for me. A chance to keep my promise to my brother."

The angry flush returned to her cheeks. "Your brother no longer needs you!"

As soon as she said the words, Jason could tell she regretted them. Her fingers flew to her mouth, but too late—her words were already spoken. His stomach made a twisting motion. "What do you mean by that, Tala?" Her dark gaze darted away from him. He shook her gently. "Tala, what do you mean?"

"Take your hands from my sister."

He hadn't noticed Haidar's approach. Jason released Tala, but he refused to stop staring at her, willing her to answer.

"What is happening?" Haidar demanded. "I hear the guards sending the signal to be alert."

"A beast," Tala answered. "The female I thought I had killed in the city has found our lair. Jason saw her."

"You saw her where?"

Haidar demanded his attention, but Jason wouldn't let Tala avoid him for long. He wanted answers.

"In the forest. Close to the hot spring." He turned to Tala's brother. "She said she had come in revenge for killing her mate."

"I thought that was the male's purpose for tracking you, sister," Haidar said, his dark brows furrowed.

"I'm sure his original purpose was to kill Tala and me, but then he saw your people," Jason provided. "The female wanted him to steal a child. The creatures evidently have maternal instincts, but they can't mate among themselves."

"A child is made of goodness, of innocence," Tala said softly. "It cannot grow from evil."

"Well, they had it in their evil heads to make a child like them, to turn him or her—I guess whichever happened along."

"Before, the creatures I have hunted were content to remain lone wolves," Tala said. "Their only desire was to feed on humans. The thrill of the hunt, the sweet taste of blood. Now, brother, they are organizing into packs. I see dark days ahead."

"Why did you not see her?" Haidar asked. "She should have come to you in a vision."

Tala shook her head. "I do not know. I saw her before in a vision, stalking our camp. I can only believe that because I thought her dead, my senses were not in tune with nature or the approach of an unnatural among us."

"I must alert The People," Haidar said. "And I will tell the women to keep the children inside of the caves until we have destroyed this evil one. Prepare yourself, Tala. We hunt."

The leader left. Tala wouldn't look at Jason. She started to move away. "Tala," he said. "How do you know my brother no longer needs me?"

"We will not speak of it now," she snapped. "I must do my brother's bidding and prepare for the hunt."

A sick suspicion churned his stomach. His hands trembled at his sides. "You killed him, didn't you?"

Her gaze snapped to him. "Is that what you believe?"

"What the hell else can I believe? Did he turn? Did you see him in your visions? Tell me!"

"It is time that you knew," she agreed. "But I will not tell you here, in the open with eyes watching us. Come to my lodge."

She turned away. Jason watched her for a moment, his emotions tied into knots. What would he do if Tala had killed his brother? For three years, his life had been about saving Rick, never really caring if he managed to save himself. He felt responsible for what had happened to them on the hunting trip.

Jason realized he was afraid to follow Tala. Afraid to hear the truth. He couldn't love a woman who'd taken his brother's life, not even if Rick had turned. And he couldn't hate a woman he loved, even if she had done such a horrible thing, because he knew she would have done it out of duty.

He took one step, then another, his feet heavy with dread, but unable to stop himself. He had to know the truth—had to know if Rick was dead or alive.

Chapter Twenty

Tala had not expected this day to come. Yes, she had owed Jason Donavon a debt, and a life taken from him. But she never expected she would come to care that his heart hurt for his brother. Before, she could not tell him without revealing her powers to him, but now, he knew of her abilities. It was time that he also knew about his brother.

She seated herself before the fire, picked up her sharpening rock, and removed her knives from the tops of her moccasins. They were once like old friends, her knives, but now they were only cold steel. Jason entered. He looked wary of her, his gaze dropping to the knives. She motioned for him to be seated.

He moved toward her, his grace as natural as any beast of the forest. She remembered what they had shared earlier and she wondered if they would share anything else together once she told him, once he un-

241

derstood that she had known his brother's fate all along and had not told him. He did not sit as she instructed, but stood, staring at her across the fire.

"Yes or no, did you kill him?"

"No," she answered, and before he finished the sigh of relief she heard slipping past his lips, she added, "But I meant to."

Jason tensed. "Go on."

"You should sit," she suggested.

"Did he turn?"

She put her knives aside. "He came to me in a vision. Unless he had drank of human blood, or eaten of human flesh, you know that I would not have seen him."

Jason did sit. He ran a hand through his hair. "He'd become a creature?"

"Not yet," she answered. "But he had bitten a woman, and therefore, he drunk of her blood. I knew he would turn completely during the next full-moon cycle, and I knew that the woman was in danger from him."

"So you went to kill him and save her?"

Tala nodded. "That was my intention. But what happened was not what I expected. The woman loved him. I tried to warn her, to make her listen, but he had claimed her heart."

"Warn her? You spoke to this woman? And to my brother? They saw you?"

"Yes and no." Tala scooted closer to him. "I took a memory from the woman. One from her childhood. A vision hidden within her mind. One she did not remember, but one that would frighten her. I had to make her listen to me. If she did not, she would stay with your brother and during the full-moon cycle, not only would he become the beast, but she would change as well."

"Because he bit her." Jason understood, then asked, "But that isn't what happened, is it?"

"The sacrifice I told you about. That was how your brother and the woman were saved."

"Sacrifice? Saved?"

She saw that he had forgotten what she told him by the confusion clouding his eyes. "One selfless act of love. Your brother knew what would happen to the woman. He loved her. He loved her enough to end his own life so that hers might be spared."

Jason drew back, his face pale. "Rick killed himself?"

"No," Tala quickly assured him. "I mean, yes. But he did not die. Or rather, he died, but he was reborn. Reborn whole again. Reborn as if he were innocent."

The hand Jason brought to his brow shook. "He broke the curse?"

"Yes. He is free."

Tears glittered in Jason's eyes when he glanced up at her. "Are you telling me the truth? Or some story you think I want to hear?"

She tensed. "I would not lie to you about your brother. He is a human again, with a woman who loves him, and whom he loves more than life."

Jason couldn't stop the tears that trickled down his cheeks. He didn't have the strength to wipe them away. Rick was safe, whole, happy. Jason's greatest burden had been laid to rest . . . if Tala wasn't lying. He didn't think she would, but to get his mind off the track it had taken with the female creature, she might.

"Describe my brother," he said.

Tala frowned at him. "White men," she muttered. "You cannot believe a person's word, maybe because you have broken your own so many times. Your brother looks like you, only your eyes are a lighter shade of blue, and your mouths are different. I watched him. That is how I knew about his bond with animals. The wolves in the wilderness where he lived accepted him as one of their own. In turn, he treated them kindly."

"You said that he saw you."

"He did not see me," she reminded. "He saw the form I took from the woman's childhood."

"Show me," he insisted.

Across from him, she straightened. Tala closed her eyes. Her image began to fade, but only slightly. In her place, he saw a weathered old hag, a woman one might see at a carnival, reading fortunes and scaring small children out of their minds. The image only lasted for a second, then was gone.

Tala's brow creased. "That is odd," she whispered. "I could not hold the shape."

"I saw enough," Jason assured her. "I wonder if Rick has tried to find me, to tell me—"

"No," she interrupted. Tala reached out and placed a hand upon his arm. "Your brother believes that you are dead, Jason. Before I left, I watched him and the woman sleep in each other's arms. I cast the sacred spells upon them. I erased what had happened to them from their minds, and for your brother, I had to erase all that had happened after you were both attacked."

A stab of pain shot through his heart. "He doesn't

remember me finding him in the city? Telling him what we had become?"

She shook her head. "For him to live a full life, he had to let go of his past, Jason. You were not his future. The woman was his future."

Jason never knew someone could feel sorrow and joy in the same instant. Rick thought he was dead, but his brother had been given a new life. "All this time, you've let me believe . . ." He shook his head. "Why?"

Her hand tightened upon his arm. "I did not care enough in the beginning to tell you. I owed you a debt, but it did not include easing your conscience. And if I had told you when you first came among us, you would not have believed me. You would have thought I was crazy."

He had thought Tala was crazy when he first met her, Jason admitted. His mind wouldn't have accepted what she'd just told him. But that was before he'd seen her powers with his own eyes. His relief over Rick didn't fade, but now Jason wondered about his own life. He was still cursed, alone, without a woman—not one that he could have, anyway. No future—not unless he found the one that had bitten him and killed the creature.

But even his own unstable future couldn't dampen the joy he felt for Rick. "Thank you," he said. "For telling me."

"I could not let you continue to punish yourself. Your brother has found his destiny. You must find yours."

She was right. But how? The blonde. It seemed like the only way. He had to find her before Tala and her band of merry headhunters did . . . but then he'd have to leave. Leave Tala. This place. It was the only way to infiltrate the female's pack.

"Today, you saw the beast in me," he said to her.

"Today, I saw you fight him. I saw you win."

"He's not gone, Tala. He won't ever be gone."

"Then you must learn to live with him."

Jason didn't speak his answer aloud. Could she live with him? That wasn't a choice. He had no place in her world. She'd be better off with him gone.

"I must leave," he said, rising.

Tala rose, too. "Of course. My brother will expect you to stay in his lodge and wait for our return later. He does not trust you enough to allow you to join us in this hunt. Besides, the excitement—were you to change in front of the others—"

"It's all right, Tala," he interrupted. Jason had his own agenda to attend, or he might have argued his right to be among the hunters of the Sica.

His heart suddenly felt heavy. He wanted to kiss Tala, one last time. He leaned toward her lips. She met him halfway. He kept it short and sweet. No sense in starting something he couldn't finish. Jason glanced around her primitive cave, which had, oddly enough, been the best home he'd had during the past three years. He stared at Tala. She was beautiful. Tough as nails on the outside, soft and sensitive on the inside. She was a woman his mother would like.

"Goodbye, Tala."

She smiled at him, somewhat shyly. "Jason. Thank you for showing me today much of what I have missed."

"My pleasure," he answered softly, touching her

face, then snatching his hand away. Then he left, while he still could.

When Jason reached Haidar's lodge, he was relieved to find the cave empty. The leader was down below, he imagined, issuing orders and gathering a hunting party. Jason searched the inner cave wall. Tala had said all the lodges had two escape routes. Now, to find this one's and make his way down the tunnels and outside on the other side of the bluffs, where he hoped he wouldn't be spotted.

An idea occurred to him. If he could change, it wouldn't matter if one the guards did see him. They would just believe he was a wolf running wild in its natural habitat. At the same time, so far, he hadn't been able to maintain his human thoughts while in wolf form for long. He might lose sight of his objective. Jason would decide what to do once he found the tunnel leading outside. If he found it.

He kept pressing against the rocks lining Haidar's inner wall, and finally a door swung open. He hurried through. Once he closed the opening, he would be plunged into total darkness. Finding the smoothest rock on the other side, he pushed against it and the secret door closed. He gave his eyes a minute to adjust to the darkness. His eyesight might be superior, but his sense of direction wasn't that great. He could roam around in the tunnels for hours without finding his way out. It was time to test himself.

Jason called the wolf. He envisioned the animal in his mind, saw the black fur, the glowing eyes. He willed it closer, demanded it merge with him. The change came upon him, but it was different from the times before. He didn't feel the pain, maybe because he didn't fight what was happening to him. The transition took place quickly. His human mind grasped that he was now a wolf. He sniffed, recognizing a scent: Tala's—that mixture of sunshine, pine, and musk that clung to her skin. He could also smell himself. He followed the trail. It wound down and around, twisting and turning, but he moved with a swiftness he could never manage in human form.

Tala had been right. He had a found a gift in place of a curse. He'd been given the skills and cunning of a wild animal with the thought and reason of a man. He emerged from darkness into sunshine. He'd found his way out. Jason would return to the hot spring where he'd first seen the female. Of course that would be the first place the hunters would search for the beast, too. He would keep his wolf form for as long as he dared, fearing he'd lose his human ability to rationalize and become a man again.

The forest moved past him in a blur of shapes, sounds, and smells. The animal became easily distracted, but Jason refused to release his control. His speed quickly put distance between himself and the camp. Soon, he would reach the hot spring. He smelled the sulfur water before he reached the spring. Jason battled whether to change back into a man, or use his superior sense of smell to track the female. He felt his control weakening and couldn't risk allowing the wolf to take over.

Jason summoned his human form to mind. He saw himself, walking upright. Two arms, two legs, skin in place of fur. Nothing happened. He tried again, concentrating harder. The sulfur smell from the hot spring brought other visions to mind: the steam that had swirled around him and Tala. Her long hair floating upon the water's surface. The beauty of her face when release found her.

A moment later, he stared down at his legs. He was naked, standing in the middle of the forest. There was a drawback to becoming a wolf at will. Clothes were not optional.

"Back so soon? And ready for action, I see."

He glanced up. The female had not left the area. She sashayed toward him. Her torn fishnet hose, short skirt and thin top tied below her breasts looked more out of place in the forest than his nakedness.

"I had to turn to escape."

"You've decided to join me." She smiled smugly. "I knew you would. You need a woman, not a fresh-faced girl."

"You were right. I do want to belong somewhere. We should leave this place now and return to the city."

She ran her nails down his chest again. "Not so fast, handsome. Your change of heart seems awfully sudden. How do I know this isn't just some sort of trick to get me away from your girlfriend?"

"I'm here. I'll go with you. What other proof do you need?"

Her hand slid up his chest and her fingers curled around the back of his neck. "Prove that you want to be my mate. Kiss me."

He'd rather kiss a toad. A toad's breath was probably sweeter, too. "We don't have time for this." Jason removed her arm from around his neck. "The woman saw you and alerted her people. They're hunting you as we speak. This is the first place they'll look."

The female frowned. "That doesn't please me. I could probably take a few of them out before they cut off my head or pierced my heart, but then, who would lead my pack?"

Jason glanced nervously behind him. "How many in your pack?"

She shrugged. "A few. Not as many as I would like. But we'll work on that, won't we?"

"Not if we don't get out of here," he reminded her. "Did you bring any of them with you?"

"No," she said with a sigh. "My mate came alone, thinking he would only have to deal with you and the woman. When he didn't return, I followed the scent path he left. I left one, too," she said, a warning note in her voice. "If I don't return, the others will come looking for me."

The thought rose hackles on the back of his neck. Tala and her people being stalked by these creatures? Of course Tala would see them before they arrived. That was at least a comfort to him.

"Let's go." He stepped around her and started walking. When she followed, he broke into a trot. It felt strange to be running through the forest naked and stranger to have a woman running alongside him wearing her prostitute's clothes and spiked heels, no less. He couldn't imagine how she ran in them.

He didn't want to think what he'd left behind. People whom he'd come to admire and respect. Tala, her uncle, and even her brother. It occurred him to question the female and learn if she might be responsible for his curse before they made it too far from those he felt certain pursued him. If she was the one, he didn't have to go with her. All he had to do was kill her.

"Where is he?"

Tala joined her brother and the hunters who waited with him. Haidar had gone back to his lodge to tell Jason to remain inside, only to find him missing. Tala had just returned from checking her own lodge. She searched the secret passages, a suspicion she did not want to acknowledge having formed in her mind. Tala did not want to tell her brother what she had found, but she must.

"He has escaped through the secret passages."

"Escaped?" Haidar's brow wrinkled. "Why would he escape?"

Tala glanced at the others, then motioned for her brother to step away. "I found his clothes in the passageway," she said quietly. "He has gone to find the creature. He believes if he joins her, she will lead him to the one that changed him."

"We both know that will not happen," Haidar said quietly.

"But Jason does not know," Tala pointed out. "Maybe it is time that he did."

Haidar shook his head. "No, Tala. You cannot tell him. He will turn on us, and we will have to kill him. Do you want that to happen?"

She could not bear the thought. But her secret ate at her heart, even before Jason had stolen it. She could not keep the truth from him. And his mission was a fool's errand—one that would get him killed, either by the creature or her own people.

"When we catch them, the others will wonder why

he is with the creature. We should go alone."

Haidar sighed. "I cannot do this for you. I cannot place his safety before the safety of our people. The creature must be caught and killed before she harms any of us. I should not have to explain this to you. We will take enough to know that our hunt will end as it should—with the creature's head dangling from a lance."

Tala knew her brother was right. "Maybe I can warn him so he will stay hidden," she said.

"Take flight. The others will expect you to shift to aid our search. If you have time to warn him, then so be it."

Nodding, Tala called the Great Spirit of the hawk to her. She would fly swiftly and find Jason, warn him to return to camp and pretend he had never left. She did not know how she would convince him without doing what her brother had forbidden her to do—without telling him the truth. She waited for the change to take her, but it did not happen.

"What is wrong?" Haidar whispered. "We are waiting."

Tala tried again. Again . . . nothing. "There is something wrong," she said. "The spirit of the hawk will not come to me."

Haidar's dark gaze hardened. He stepped closer, keeping his voice low. "You did not see a vision of the female creature stalking us, either. Tala, have you lost your powers because of the white man?"

Her face flushed. Her first instinct was to deny his accusations. She could not lie to him again. "We did not . . . there was no joining between us. He gave me pleasure, but I am still pure."

A low growl rose from her brother's throat. "Pure of mind and pure of body are not the same. What have you done, Tala?"

She had done nothing wrong, or so she had believed. Were Haidar's words true? Was an impure thought the same as an impure act? But she had thought about Jason before, had imagined him holding her, loving her. Why had her powers been taken now, when she needed them, not only for her tribe, but also for the man that she loved?

Loved? Yes, she loved Jason Donavon. The white man. The outsider. The man whose outer beauty had tempted her sister to the dark side. Jason had stolen Tala's own heart because his was pure. He had given her a sweet taste of what she had always dreamed of, always longed for within the prison of her duties. She understood now her father's actions. Why he could not live without her mother. Sometimes two hearts became one and they could not be separated, not even by death. Joy and sorrow clashed within her. To know love was the greatest gift she had ever received—but could she claim to love a man and continue to deceive him?

"Go find our uncle," Haidar ordered, breaking into her thoughts. "Tell him what you have done."

"But I want to go with you," Tala argued. "I may not be able to fly, but I can still fight!"

"I think your heart would not be in the right place. I think your heart lies with our enemy."

She lifted her chin. "Jason is not our enemy. You know this, yet you look for faults to condemn him."

"He is our enemy now," Haidar spat. "He has taken the one chosen from us. He deserves to die."

253

Before she could speak further on Jason's behalf, her brother turned his back and rejoined his hunters. He cast her a dark glance before the men moved single file from the camp.

Her gaze strayed to her uncle's lodge in the bluffs, down low for the older ones who could not climb as easily as they had done in their youth. Tala would not go to her uncle. She had to find Jason—warn him. She might have lost her ability to fly, but she could still smell. His scent could be picked up in the tunnels. She would follow him. Tala raced to her lodge, grabbed Jason's clothing, and left by the secret exit.

It took her only a moment to find her way down the passages and reach the outside. She picked up Jason's smell and raced through the forest. His trail led toward the hot spring where he had given her pleasure earlier. It made sense that he would begin his search there, since that is where he said he had last seen the creature.

Her brother would assume this also. Tala hoped she would find Jason before Haidar did. She knew her brother looked upon what had happened between her and Jason as a betrayal. One punishable by death.

Chapter Twenty-one

The forest seemed too quiet as Jason and the female moved through the trees. He wondered if it had to do with those hunting them, or if the animals sensed an unnatural presence among them. He thought they had gone far enough to get some information from her.

"What's your name?"

"My name?" She laughed, then paused to dig a rock from beneath the toe of her shoe. "I don't remember my name. I don't remember much of anything anymore. Not of the life I had. I don't care to remember. I like things fine the way they are."

If she didn't care to recall her past, Jason figured it must not have been worth remembering. "Can you remember three years ago?"

She straightened, then adjusted her breasts inside of her skimpy top. "Why? What happened three years ago?"

He shrugged. "Nothing. I just wondered if you could remember that far back."

"That was before," she said. "I told you, I don't care about what happened before. All I care about now is ruling my pack. Hunting in the streets of the city. Drinking blood."

His hopes took a nosedive. Tala had said most of those bitten turned fairly quickly. The woman hadn't been a werewolf three years ago, so she couldn't have bitten him and Rick. Of course, that didn't mean that one in her pack wasn't responsible.

"How many are in the pack?"

"Fifteen—sixteen before you killed my mate. But we're growing. We're growing fast."

A shudder raced up his spine. "Don't you feel any guilt about what you do? About hunting and killing innocent people?"

She stopped, her gaze narrowing. "No. It's just blood-sport. We're just having a little fun. We only bite those we want with us. Those we don't, we take their hearts. Do you have a problem with that?"

Jason kept his expression blank, even if every part of him recoiled. Tala was right. The woman wasn't human. "I don't have a problem with it," he answered.

Reaching out, she grabbed the sides of his face. "Good. I won't have to kill you, although I bet your blood is sweet. Makes me hot just thinking about it. That's how I get my men. I ride them, work them into a fevered state, then tear into their necks. They get theirs and I get mine, only, they end up dead." She grinned evilly.

Men, Jason supposed, were an easy mark for a woman like this. He felt certain she approached them

256

the same way she'd approached him, offering something for nothing . . . but they got more than they bargained for. She disgusted him, but he needed her to lead him to her pack.

"We'd better keep moving," he said, stepping away from her. He didn't like her touch. It felt cold, clammy, like something dead. "The hunting party won't be far behind us."

The woman straightened her short skirt. "Wouldn't mind having a party with the hunting party." She laughed at her own joke. "I saw a big handsome one among those Indians whom I'd like to have some fun with."

Haidar, Jason suspected, was the man who'd caught her eye. "He's not much for fun," he said dryly. "The last party that I saw him at, he had your friend's head swinging from his lance."

Her smile faded. "We should go," she agreed.

Jason wished he had some clothes. As they moved through the forest, he felt the female's eyes roaming his body, assessing him. He wasn't sure if he regarded him as a man, or as a meal. Probably both, he decided, and let her take the lead. He didn't trust his back, or any other part of him, to her. He let her get as far ahead as he dared.

One moment he was walking along, the next someone grabbed him and slapped a hand over his mouth. He knew her scent immediately. His heart skipped a beat. Keeping his eyes focused on the creature's back, he moved behind a clump of trees.

"Tala," he whispered. "What are you doing here?"

She shoved his clothing at him. "Rescuing you before my brother and the others find you. He will have your head along with hers."

He fumbled to place his breechclout around his waist. "I'm grateful for the warning, and the clothes, but I have to go with her. I must—"

"She is not the one," Tala cut him off. "I—"

"I know," he whispered back. "But she has a pack. I might find the one among them."

Tala shook her head. "You will find nothing with her but death. The one you seek is not among her pack."

Jason slipped into his leggings. "How do you know?"

She didn't answer for a moment. Her gaze cut away from him. Finally, she said, "I saw this in a vision. You said that I care about you, and you are right. If you go with her, I see only death and destruction for you."

"Hey! What's going on? Are you two-timing me?"

In the middle of trying to pull on his moccasins, Jason froze. He glanced up and saw the blond she-wolf standing behind Tala. In a heartbeat, Tala grabbed her knives from the tops of her moccasins and turned, slashing them in the air.

"I am Tala Soaringbird. I am the one chosen. And I am here for your head," she cried.

A low growl rose from the woman's throat. "Save the speech, honey. I've already heard it." Her eyes, which had already taken on a glow, moved to Jason. "The deal's off. I'm going to kill your little Indian girl."

"No!" he shouted, but Tala jumped into action.

She lunged forward, slicing open the creature's arm.

The blonde screamed and jumped back. Her face froze in an ugly mask. Long yellow fangs protruded from her mouth. Claws shot from her fingertips. Patches of hair sprang from her body.

Jason crammed his foot into the moccasin he'd been trying to get on and reached for Tala, his intention to pull her behind him. She moved too fast and lunged at the creature again. The blonde lunged, too, hitting Tala hard across the face and knocking her back. She slammed into the tree beside him, gasping for breath.

Prying the knives from Tala's fist, Jason charged their foe. He'd never handled knives before. His skill rather amazed him, but he had no time to think, only to act. The female continued to shift, breaking free of her clothes as her body grew stout, a thick cropping of matted hair now covering her where skin had been a few moments earlier. Her jaw jutted out. Her nose became elongated. She growled and swiped at him, all traces of humanity gone.

He circled the creature, slashing the knives through the air, thrusting forward to cut her when she came too close. Each time he cut her, she howled in rage. He felt the wolf beneath his skin, waiting, willing to emerge if he needed it. Jason held back. He needed more than animal instincts to battle this monster. He needed his human mind. Tala must be protected, and Jason still wasn't sure the wolf within could be wholly trusted.

The creature roared and charged him. They both slammed into a tree. Jason's head bounced off the trunk. The force knocked the knives from his hands. He lifted his arm to stop a blow from the creature's deadly claws, but then an arrow planted itself in the tree, dangerously close to his head. The creature stumbled back. She seemed to understand that a missile had been launched at her. At least, Jason hoped the beast had been the intended target.

Her large head swung right, then left. Another arrow flew, this one piercing her shoulder. Her scream of pain echoed through the forest. Jason scrambled for the knives he'd dropped, but Tala had already scooped them up. She grabbed his arm.

"We must run!" she called.

He tried to pull away. "It's okay. The cavalry has arrived."

She held tight. Her head jerked toward the arrow protruding from the tree next to them. "That is my brother's arrow. I am certain he did not mean to miss. He is hunting you, the same way he is hunting the creature. We must run. While the hunters are busy with the other."

The big guy was after him? "I'll explain why I went with her," he reasoned.

"His feud with you is not about the creature," she snarled. "It is about us!"

Understanding dawned. Haidar had found out about them. "Damn," he muttered. The creature had already disappeared into the forest. Jason grabbed his shirt, took Tala's hand, and ran. They raced through the woods. Usually, Tala had no trouble keeping up with him, even though his strides were longer. But this time he had to slow down a couple of times for her.

Darkness quickly closed in on them, and who knew what else, Jason thought. "Do you know a place where we can hide?"

She nodded. "This way."

He followed her, keeping an eye peeled for signs of either the creature or the hunting party. Tala led him to a small opening at the base of a huge tree. She scrambled down the hole. Jason had trouble fitting, but finally squeezed through. He fell and landed hard; jarred.

"Are you all right, Jason?"

It took him a minute to reclaim the breath that had been knocked from him. "Yeah. What is this place?" he asked, trying to get his eyes to adjust to the darkness. It smelled like his late grandma's root cellar.

"An abandoned den," she answered. "When my sister and I were young, we would hide from Haidar here. We never told him about our secret place."

"That's comforting," he said. Jason took a deep breath. "Now, tell me what in the hell is going on."

Tala did not know where to begin. Her powers were indeed failing her. She had been slow and clumsy with her knives. They did not know her anymore. "My powers," she whispered. "They are fading. I meant to take the shape of the hawk and search for you before the hunting party found you. But the Great Sprit of the hawk would not come to me. My brother saw this; he remembered that the creature did not come to me in a vision, either. He knew we had been together."

Silence. She glanced at Jason, and at least her night vision had not deserted her. He stared at her, his brows drawn across the bridge of his nose. "But we weren't together. I mean, we didn't . . ."

"My brother says pure of mind and pure of body are not the same. In my heart, I wanted to be with

261

you the way a man and a woman join together. I wanted it more that I wanted my powers."

His hand gently touched her cheek. "I'm sorry, Tala. Had I known, I would never have compromised your powers. I'm not worthy of such a sacrifice."

She covered his hand with hers. "You are worthy, Jason. Worthy of happiness. Worthy of love. Worthy of all that you desire. You came among us a stranger, but your courage, and your smile, won the hearts of my people, won my heart."

He pressed his forehead against hers. "Tala, you're blinded by innocence. You feel these things because I'm the first man allowed among your people who looked at you like you were a woman. I'm the first man who made you feel like a woman. There are far better men in the world to give your heart to and to lose your powers over. If I were honorable, I would have left you alone. I would have respected your powers and your importance to your people. Instead, I only thought of myself—my wants and desires."

Her fingers slid down to his lips. "That is not true, Jason. It was my pleasure, and only my pleasure, that you thought of today. The beast inside you, the beast inside all of us, is selfish. You fought him and won. But I would have suffered him for your sake. To give my heart to you, I must also give it to him."

She felt the light touch of his kiss against her fingertips. "I've never known anyone like you before. I'll never know anyone like you again. Seeing the creature today, how vulgar and crass she was, made me realize how pure and special you are. You duty is to search for evil in others, but your heart only wants to see the good in all."

"Not in all, Jason," she argued. "But I see the good in you."

"What happens now?"

She had to tell him the truth. "You must go far away from here to escape my brother. I can no longer protect you."

"And what about you, Tala? What happens to you?"

Tala was not certain, but she knew Haidar looked upon what she had done as a betrayal. "In the legend, Mother Earth took the powers from those females who would mate. They were no longer the chosen, but returned to what they had once been. Soon, there were few left among the chosen who were female. Mother Earth did this to keep a balance in nature. But now the balance has been upset. I am the only one left. Who will protect my people? Who will hunt and destroy the evil ones?"

His arms went around her. "My mother used to tell me things have a way of working out. I don't think your brother will harm you. He's a barbarian, but he cares deeply for you."

"My punishment will not be Haidar's decision, but decided by the tribe. It is the tribe that my sins have affected."

"Punishment?" He drew back. "Like hell anyone is going to punish you. You can come with me, Tala. I'll take you away from here."

He would not give up his search, she knew this, and she could not continue to deceive him. "This is the only life I have known, Jason. I love my people. I love the forest. I would not fit into your world. You have said this before. Besides—"

"Don't answer now," he interrupted. "Take the night to think about it."

She did not need the night. The wrongs committed against him must be confessed. A sacrifice must be made. When all was revealed to him, he would not want her with him. He would want her dead. If morning brought the pain of truth, could this night not be her own? All her life she had lived for a purpose, a duty she had not asked to receive—powers she had not asked to possess. Tonight, could she not become a normal female, as she had begged the night spirits for so often in her youth? Tonight, could she not become a woman, a whole one?

"Jason. My powers are fading and soon will be gone from me. Tomorrow, you may be gone from me as well. Tonight, will you make me a woman?"

Chapter Twenty-two

Jason's first instinct was to refuse. Not because he didn't desire Tala, but because she had been forbidden to him for so long, that shutting off his feelings for her had become natural. Her powers were fading. He sensed something different about her—a weakness, a vulnerability that hadn't been there before. She might be undergoing changes, but he was still the same. The raw lust he'd felt for her at the hot springs haunted him. He'd behaved like an animal with her.

"I don't know if I can, Tala. Not without having to battle the wolf. You know what happened earlier."

She touched his face again. "There was only a battle because both did not want the same thing—because you had made me a promise, and he did not want to keep it. Tonight, I hold you to no promises. I give you no rules to follow. Tonight, we follow our hearts."

His eyes had adjusted to the darkness. He glanced at their surroundings. They were on a dirt floor of a hollowed-out den. Tree roots hung from the ceiling like pale, twisted fingers. He saw the sky from the hole above. Saw the moon shining down upon them. Who knew what tomorrow would bring? Tonight might be all they had, Tala and him.

"I'll give you my heart," he said. "And where you lead, I will follow. You do understand that to love you this first time, I must cause you pain?"

"I know little about joining," she admitted. "Most pleasures in life are not obtained without an amount of pain. Is this not true?"

He shook his head. "You're so rational at times it's scary. I just want you to be sure."

In response, she leaned forward and pressed her lips against his. Jason opened his mouth to her. Her arms went around his neck, and she pulled him closer. He felt her heart beat against his. Her scent rose to him, firing the blood in his veins. She broke contact of their mouths to pull his shirt over his head.

The fire inside him spread as her fingers explored his chest. He wanted to touch her, too, and unfastened the straps at the shoulders of her dress. He eased the buckskin garment from her shoulders, placing a soft kiss against her neck. Her pulse leapt beneath his lips. As he pulled the dress down to her waist, she pushed his head to her breasts. He worshipped the small, perfect mounds—the dark colored nipples that hardened inside of his mouth. He let her fingertips guide him. When she pressed harder against his scalp, he sucked harder, nipped at her with his teeth.

"Jason," she whispered, then flung her head back.

He grabbed his shirt and placed it behind her, then gently lowered her to the ground. After removing her moccasins and leggings, he slid the dress over her hips and down her legs. She lay before him naked. And he sensed no shame or fear from her.

He reached for the ties of his breechclout, but she sat, her fingers brushing his aside. She undressed him, placing soft kisses against the flat, hard plains of his abdomen—innocent kisses that had his hands twisting into her long, raven hair. When he stood naked before her, she took his hand and pulled him down. He'd been with many women before the change had taken that life from him, but with Tala, the experience felt like the first time.

It was almost enough, just holding her, heated flesh pressed against heated flesh. He closed his eyes and savored the sensations. She pressed against him, demanding his attention.

"Aren't you afraid?" he whispered.

She shook her head. "I do not fear you, Jason. I know your heart is good and your touch is tender. I want this night with you."

Her trust humbled him. He kissed her again, his hands moving gently over her body, exploring every inch, every indentation, every swell. Her fingertips brushed his skin, lightly at first, then bolder as their kisses became deeper, wetter, and hotter. He ached with need for her, his body hard and ready, but he held back, determined to take his time.

She moaned when his fingers slid between her legs, stroking her until she arched against him. Then he felt her hand on him—her fingers wrap around his sex, and he nearly spilled himself then and there. He gasped, pressing his forehead against hers.

"Should I not touch you there?" she asked. "The way that you touch me?"

Once, he had thought her innocence would be a turn-off. He'd been wrong, so very wrong. "Your touch feels good," he assured her. "Too good. We don't want the night over before it begins." He removed her hand. Then his fingers took up the rhythm again, and she sighed. Her sighs turned into little moans, her moans into gasps. She arched harder against his hand. When he knew she was close, he penetrated her with one finger, not deep, just enough to send her over the edge.

Her nails dug into his shoulders. A low moan rose up in her throat. He felt her spasm and convulse, looked down and saw the beauty of her face when the climax caught her and carried her away. *Take her now*, the beast whispered. *Now, while she lies helpless and too weak to stop you. Quickly, before she regains her senses and pushes you away.*

Get out of my head, he commanded the beast. He would not go crashing into unexplored territory. For Tala, he could soothe the beast and be gentle, patient.

"Why do you not take me?" she whispered up at him. "Your heart beats as wildly as my own. Join with me. Make me your woman."

Maybe patience and gentleness were overrated. He shouldn't be surprised. His Tala was not like other women; not like any woman he had known or ever would know again.

"Whatever you say, sweetheart."

*　　*　　*

Tala wanted to give Jason pleasure—wanted him to feel the strange and wonderful feelings that she experienced. Could he? Were a man and a woman's pleasures the same? She would ask him . . . but later. He nipped at her neck and nudged her knees apart, settling between her legs. His shaft was long and thick, hot and hard, and despite her bravery, she felt a moment of alarm. She choked it back, reminding herself that she was a mighty warrior who had learned to control pain in order to fight when wounded.

She sucked in a breath when he first entered her. He moved a little deeper and she felt a sharp stab of pain. She did not cry out, although the sudden tensing of her body could not be controlled.

"Are you all right, Tala?"

It warmed her heart when he pulled back to glance down at her, his face a mask of concern. She stroked his strong cheek to let him know the initial pain had passed.

"Did you find your pleasure?" she asked.

He smiled, then kissed her lightly. "I haven't even gotten started yet."

She supposed her eyes widened when he moved deeper still, causing her to gasp softly. His giving was gentle, but she suddenly wondered if their bodies would fit together as they had been designed to do. She had not been given instruction regarding the joining of male and female. It had not been her destiny to mate, but she had changed her destiny. Her heart had changed it for her.

Slowly, he stretched her, forced her body to accept his. He moved in a way that chased doubts and fears from her mind. He moved in a way that made her blood heat, and her breathing labor. He, too, seemed to have difficulty catching his breath. It was like a dance, his body and hers moving, but together. The low words he whispered sent flames dancing over her skin.

If a fire ignited between them, she would not have been surprised. Their bodies rubbed together with the same friction required to spark an inferno. And the flame between them grew higher and higher. They became slick against one another, and still he continued. Sensation pulsed around their union. She understood the gathering, the building that spiraled her upward toward the night sky. He wound her tighter and tighter until she exploded. She called his name, died in his arms as her spirit left her body to float upward. And still he moved, keeping her to him, forcing ripples of pleasure to pour over her.

Tala's release spurred his. Jason thrust deep, felt the power of his climax building. Then at the last minute he pulled his body from hers. Pleasure ripped through him, more intense than even the pain of the change when it took him. He shuddered against her, spilling his seed harmlessly upon the ground in order to protect her. He said her name a thousand times, holding her while they both gasped to catch a normal breath, waiting for the pounding of their hearts to slow.

"I did not know," she whispered against his neck.

Jason pulled her closer. "Didn't know what?"

"That a thing said to be wrong between us could feel more right than anything I have ever known."

He kissed the top of her head. "I didn't know, either. What we share is new to me. What I feel for you is new to me. I won't let you go now, Tala. Promise me that you'll come with me when I leave."

Her silence wasn't reassuring. She snuggled closer and sighed. "We will talk of this another time. Tonight is not for talking."

"Tonight is not for making love to you over and over again in the dirt, either," Jason said dryly. "Do you think we could risk sneaking to the hot spring?"

"The camp will be quiet. Any hunters searching for us will have also settled for the night. To be certain, we will call forth the wolves in us, and slip through the darkness like shadows."

He pulled back to look at her. "I thought your powers were fading, would surely be gone after . . ."

"I still feel some power left in me, maybe enough to shift and reach the spring and then to shift and quickly reach the safety of our den when we return."

Curious, he rose and helped her to her feet. They stared at one another. Jason envisioned the wolf in his mind, called it to him. The transition became easier each time he tried. As he felt the change taking him, he saw Tala changing, as well. The form she took was that of a white wolf. He caught her scent, and he remembered it. That first night he shifted and ran wild in wolf form, she had been the other wolf he followed.

He gathered himself and sprung up, easily clearing the hole of the den. Tala followed a moment later, and together, they raced through the night. As the forest passed his eyes in a darkened blur, Jason realized that he no longer felt alone. His future no longer seemed bleak and hopeless. Tala had given him back hope. He accepted who he was because she accepted who he was. He'd found his mate. But could he talk Tala into leaving her home, her people, to begin a new life with him? Or would the dark forces he felt gathering around them tear them apart forever?

Chapter Twenty-three

For a moment, Tala did not know where she was, or why she felt sated, sore, and very happy. Jason's arms were around her, his face nuzzled against the back of her neck. She felt his warm breath, heard him snore softly. She almost giggled, but then the light of dawn chased the night shadows from the sky and all came rushing back to her.

Her powers were lost. Her brother hunted the man who lay beside her. She did not know if the beast still roamed the forest or if the warriors had slain the creature. And then there was the truth—the knowledge that she had yet to tell Jason. There was the sacrifice she must make for him. Before, she had told herself that her powers, her importance to her people, were greater than his life. But now that was no longer the truth.

She closed her eyes, embedding her every feeling

into her mind. For one night, she had lived a dream. She had been only a woman. A woman well loved by a man. Two people, ordinary for one brief span of time. Too brief, Tala realized. She was not ready to let him go. She was not ready to watch his feelings for her fade from his eyes when she told him the truth. Her deception would make him bitter toward her. He would take back the heart he had surrendered. She could not bear it—not today.

"What are you thinking?"

His voice startled her. She turned to look at him. He had dark stubble across his cheeks, and his hair was tangled.

"I am thinking I am hungry," she lied. "And that you must be hungry as well."

He nipped at her neck. "Hungry for you."

"Do you want to mate again?"

Jason laughed. "You aren't subtle, Tala. I like that about you."

His words confused her. "Am I to play the shy maiden after all we shared last night?"

He rolled on top of her. "No. I like you just the way you are. Honest. And uninhibited by what is only natural between two people who care for one another."

"You told me once, that in your world, two did not have to care for one another to exchange pleasure. I feel that I could not do what we did last night with another. Does that make me a freak?"

His lips brushed hers. "No. And I don't like the idea of you doing what we did last night with another. I don't like it at all."

She tried to bite him. "But it is all right for you? I

have never understood why males and females have different rules. I would not like for you to be with another either."

"There is no other like you."

Turning her head to avoid his kiss, she said, "Those words do not sound as good to me as they may sound to you."

"What part bothered you?"

"All are different. You should have said, 'There will be no other.'" She knew she could not hold him to that promise, but it did not stop her from wanting to hear it.

"There will be no other," he said, and the teasing had left his voice. "You accept me for who I am. I don't know another woman who could, or would."

Her head snapped back to stare up at him. "Is that the only reason you are with me? Because you believe no other would have you?"

A sigh escaped his lips. He rolled off her and sat. "I wouldn't want another, Tala. What we shared last night, that was as new to me as it was to you. What I feel when I look at you goes much deeper than a physical sharing of our bodies."

Tears threatened to disgrace her. Those were the words she had wanted, but she had no right to hear them. "Will you stay with me for a while longer?"

He didn't answer. The silence stretched. "I asked you to come with me," he reminded. "You haven't given me an answer."

She sat, facing him. "I gave you an answer. It was one you did not want to hear."

Running a hand through his unruly hair, he said, "You can't stay, Tala. You said they would punish you. I can't walk away and leave you, not without knowing what your fate will be."

"You knew our worlds were different. I must stay in mine. And you must return to yours. Haidar blames you for the loss of my powers. If you return to camp, you will be punished, as well."

"I imagine they've killed the creature. She was my best hope at finding the one who bit me. And what about the full-moon cycle? How am I to fight the call of the moon without your help?"

In two days, the full moon would call to Jason. "You could stay with me until the cycle passes," she suggested. "We could hide here together." It was a trick to keep him with her longer. When she found her courage, the strength to let him go, the moon would no longer haunt him.

"I do want to fight the call," he said. "I need to, for myself. Do you think we can stay here that long without being discovered?"

She smiled at him. "We are creatures of the forest. Haidar does not know of this place. He will not think to look for us here. But we must be careful," she cautioned. "The hunting party will continue to search for us."

He nodded. "Now, about breakfast." He pulled her into his arms. "I want to nibble on you."

Her body agreed that he should. She snuggled against him, lifted her face for his kisses. It did not take long for kisses to become more, and the morning passed in leisurely love play. Later, they argued about who would leave the safety of the den to hunt for food. Tala argued that she should go. She knew the forest and where to hide if she saw signs of the hunting party.

He reluctantly conceded. She rose, dressed, kissed him softly, and had him help her up so she could scramble from the den.

Tala moved cautiously through the forest, her mind in turmoil. It served no purpose to prolong the inevitable. No purpose but her own. She knew what she must do, but she had found happiness within Jason's arms. Happiness she would not easily surrender. What harm would there be in a two more nights together?

She had become so preoccupied with her thoughts that she nearly stumbled upon the hunting party. Tala quickly flattened her body to the back of a tree. They were some distance away, but they would spot her if she stepped into the open. The men's voices carried to her.

"We did not find the beast," she heard a tribal member say. "The creature has escaped our lances and arrows."

"This does not please me," her brother growled. "The creature knows of our camp and will continue to be a threat until her head is taken."

"We saw the one chosen and the white man fighting the beast," another man offered. "They will catch the creature and destroy her."

Tala waited, her breath lodged in her throat, heart pounding. A long silence stretched.

"My sister is no longer the one chosen," she heard Haidar finally say. "My heart is heavy to tell you this, but I am your leader, and I will not deceive you. Not any longer. Tala has given her heart to the white man.

She has chosen him over her people, over her destiny. She is outcast."

Tears moistened Tala's cheeks. She stuffed a fist into her mouth to keep from making noise. The war party remained silent, shocked, she imagined, to hear her brother's words. Tala was stunned to hear them as well. She did not have plans to return to her people. Her sacrifice would not allow her to live on among those she loved. But she'd hoped to go to the spirit world with the well wishes of her tribe. Now, that would not happen. She was an outcast, like her sister.

"We have no chosen?" a man asked. "Who will protect us from all that would threaten us? Who will help us to find food during the harsh winters, when little food is to be found? Who—"

"We must find our own strength," Haidar interrupted. "The ones chosen are few. Our ancestors have survived without one among them. We will do the same."

The tears came faster as Tala fully realized all that she had done. She hadn't meant to abandon her people, had not known that such little actions would take her purity and her powers away from her. Yes, she had wished them gone a thousand times. She had wished to be only a member of her people and not the one chosen. But her wishes might be the destruction of her people.

"Hear this, Tala, if you are listening!" her brother shouted, startling her. "If you return to our camp, you return as an outcast. The People will decide your punishment. For so great a crime against your own, death can be rightfully demanded. What the tribe decides,

I must abide. Do not face us again unless you are willing to face death."

It was a warning to stay away from the camp. One she fully understood—the most her brother could do for under the circumstances. Haidar's shame must be great. Both sisters were now considered traitors to their people. Both were marked as outcast. Both had been brought to ruin over one man. How Haidar must hate Jason, Tala thought. But she could not. He was innocent of wrong-doing—cursed by his beauty, a victim of one who lusted for things not of her world, deceived by the woman who loved him.

But Tala would not pity herself. She could only live with the path her life had taken, and die to set another's straight. For now, she would take the days until the full-moon cycle and cherish each moment. Jason would learn of her deception in the end, but before she gave him the gift of his life back, she would show him how much she loved him. She waited, listening for the sounds of the men moving away. They were silent for the most part, but the snap of a twig, the brush of a leaf, told her when they continued their search.

Tala wiped the tears from her cheeks. She snatched her knife from the top of her moccasin. Firewood must be gathered, berries picked, game killed and skinned. For what little time she had left, she would live the fantasy she had dreamed about as a young girl. The den would become her lodge, Jason, her mate. She would live her dream and not think about the end, which approached much too quickly.

* * *

Jason thought about searching for Tala. It seemed as if she'd been gone for hours. He knew boredom only made the time seem longer. He'd fashioned a ladder of sorts from pieces of wood and vine to pass the time. Now he stared at the hole above, surveying his work when it began to rain firewood. A log hit him in the head. He cussed and moved out the way.

"Catch this so it does not land in the dirt," he heard Tala instruct from above.

He moved beneath the opening and held out his hands. The skinned body of a rabbit landed in his arms. At least, Jason hoped it was a rabbit and not a skunk. Tala's legs came into view, dangling over the side. Too bad she wore the leggings and moccasins. He perched the skinned animal on a sturdy log and reached up to help her. She slid down his body, igniting a fire that hadn't gone out since the first time he'd laid eyes on her.

"Did you miss me?" she asked, her arms wrapped around his neck.

Jason pressed against her. "Does that answer your question?"

Her smile took his breath away. "I am happy to see you, too."

Their lips met, but the kiss was too brief for his liking. "We must hurry," she said. "A fog has settled over the forest, and the smoke from our fire will disguise itself, keeping us safe from detection. We will eat."

Jason's stomach grumbled at the mention of food. Tala laughed and began stacking wood. She placed the logs beneath the small hole above so the smoke would rise up and out of the den. Jason felt useless.

"Let me start the fire," he suggested. "I think I still remember how from my Boy Scout days."

Tala rose and moved out of the way. "I still do not understand why you scouted for boys."

Gathering dried leaves, he explained, "When I was a boy, I joined a club of other boys. In this club, we learned about a lot of things, one of them, camping outdoors. We earned badges for mastering certain tasks."

"Oh," Tala said, nodding her head—but he didn't think she really understood. She'd been raised in the forest and couldn't comprehend that most in the outside world considered the forest and camping out a fun pastime, not a way of life. He took a small, sturdy stick and placed it upright against a thin piece of wood, then gathered dried leaves and twigs around both. Jason began to rub the stick between his hands, creating friction. He still rubbed when Tala placed a spit holding the skinned rabbit over the wood.

He imagined she'd already have the fire burning if he'd left it up to her. Of course she had an unfair advantage in that area . . . or once had. Jason rubbed the stick harder between his hand.

"Light, dammit," he muttered. The leaves burst into flame. Pleased, he leaned low and blew softly, causing the fire to grow. The wood caught. He straightened and smiled at Tala. "I've still got it."

She smiled back. "What is it that you have?"

"A cocky attitude that is lost upon you," he answered. Jason clapped his hands together, causing her to jump. "So, now what do we do?"

"I have something for you." She untied the straps of her dress. He noticed that she'd fashioned a belt

281

around her waist made of interwoven vines. Now that he looked closely, he also saw that it appeared she'd stuffed something inside her dress. She eased the garment down and displayed her bounty—wild raspberries, most of them smashed, but they kept his attention for only a second before his gaze moved back up to her breasts.

"Those look tasty," he leaned forward and lapped at the berry juice staining one perfectly shaped breast. She sighed and curled her fingers into his hair. Jason pulled off his shirt, pushed her back and settled on top of her.

"You are smashing my berries," Tala said, but didn't sound too upset. "I worked long and hard to pick them."

"I'll make it worth your while," he assured her, then slid down her skin with the intention of removing every one with his tongue. He knew what pleased her, how to linger over her breasts, sucking and nipping at her nipples until she moaned and writhed beneath him. He moved lower, his body also slick now with the juice of the berries.

She surprised him by pushing him away. He rolled off of her. "I like berries, too," she said, smiling seductively before she began licking the juice from his skin.

He groaned and twisted his fingers into her long hair. She flicked her tongue across his nipple, causing him to jerk. "Tala," he warned when she ventured lower.

She glanced up at him. "Can I not please you with my mouth? The way that you have pleased me?"

He almost lost it then and there. "Yes," he answered, his voice raw sounding. "But I wouldn't ask you to do anything that you don't want to do."

"I want to know all the ways that please you."

Staring into her beautiful dark eyes, he thought she was too good to be true. He must be dreaming. To be with her, to hold her, kiss her, make love to her, to have her want to please him, were the greatest joys he'd ever known. His heart twisted at the honesty reflected in her gaze, the innocence of saying what she meant, of feeling no inhibitions over offering him anything that he desired.

"I'll show you," he said softly.

Chapter Twenty-four

The full moon was almost upon him. Jason lay staring through the opening above at the nearly round orb of light in the night sky. Tala was asleep, nestled next to him. Even the contentment he felt at having her in his arms couldn't command what went on beneath his skin. The nervousness and anxiety were balled up inside of him, the same way they had always been before a full moon. The beast was there, waiting to take his body, his thoughts, his soul. Could he stop it, control it—was he strong enough?

Tala murmured something in her sleep and pressed closer to him. They had to rely on body heat at night to keep them warm. Smoke from a fire would be too dangerous. He didn't mind. The flame that burned between them was hotter than any fire. In her arms, he felt like a man again, a whole one. He'd tried to tell himself that although Tala was obviously special, she wasn't the one. It had been a lie, a lie from the first moment he saw her.

He'd known then that she would not be a woman from whom he could walk away. But it seemed as if fate would force them apart, whether they wanted to be separated or not. He couldn't return to her world now, and she wouldn't go with him to his. Maybe they could find their own world. Make a life together somewhere, but not unless he could resist the call of the moon. He had to fight his battle and win, not only for himself, but also for her.

"Why are you not sleeping?"

"I'm thinking," he said, then kissed the top of her head. "Tomorrow night the cycle will begin. I'm wondering if I've come far enough, if you've taught me enough to fight the call."

She didn't respond, which surprised him. Tala had always believed in him more than he believed in himself. Finally, she said, "You must have faith, Jason. All will be right in your world soon."

"What about your world, Tala? What will have to happen to make things right for you again?"

She lifted her head to look at him. "You must not worry about me." Tala ran her finger down the side of his face. "My path has been chosen. First, fate chose for me, now I choose for myself. You must find your own path, your own destiny."

How he could not worry about Tala? How could he imagine a life without her? He loved her. Even thinking the thought seemed strange to Jason. He'd never loved a woman before—not with every breath he took, every beat of his heart. He had to talk her into leaving with him once he faced what he must.

Some way, somehow, he had to make her see reason. She had nothing to go back to—except some type of punishment, maybe death, he didn't know. He wouldn't take that chance.

"I love you, Tala," he said. "I think I loved you from the first moment I saw you."

Her eyes glittered in the darkness. She glanced away as if embarrassed by the show of tears. "You have given me what I have desired most in life. I could be happy with you, here in this den for all my days. Know this, whatever happens: I love you. All I have done in the past, or will do in future, I do in the name of love."

He wasn't sure what she meant and started to ask, but she bent and kissed him. Jason would never tire of her kisses, of making love to her. He turned her on her back and stared down at her. Her eyes still glittered in the darkness, but now they shown with desire instead of tears.

"Love me again," she whispered. "Love me as if there is no tomorrow for us."

He kissed her. She ran her hands over his skin, his back, buttocks, her nails lightly raking his flesh. She pushed him off her and onto his back, trailing her long hair over his chest, down his stomach. The sensation almost drove him insane. He had to have her, then, there, at that very moment.

Jason sat. He grabbed a fistful of her hair, turning her so her back faced him. He forced her down on her hands and knees and entered her, as a male animal would dominate a female. She gasped, but she didn't struggle. He brushed her long hair over one shoulder, nipping gently at her skin, then he pulled her up, so they both were on their knees, his finger reaching around to give her pleasure.

He stroked her until she moved against him, moaned as he thrust deep inside of her again and again. He felt her tighten around him, squeeze him as she shattered, breaking his control. Pleasure ripped through him, so intense it was almost painful. Her words were a garbled mixture of her language and his. All he could do was say her name over and over as he eased her to the ground, careful not to crush her beneath his weight.

Later, he held her again in sleep. He stirred when she crept from his arms and left the den, but he thought she needed to attend personal business and settled back to sleep, keeping an ear perked for her return.

Tala took in deep breaths of the crisp night air. She stood naked beneath a fading moon. The knife in her hand still caught its glow, sending flashes of reflected light around her. She tried to listen to the sounds of the forest, but the night was silent, as if holding its breath for the sun to rise or for her to do what she knew she must.

She said her prayers to the Sacred Winds, to Mother Earth and Father Sun, to the Great Spirit. It was a good day to die; still, her hands shook. She clutched the knife tighter. Her gifts had been taken from her. She had deceived her people for a man and deceived the man she loved. What was left for her but to give Jason back the life taken from him?

Ashamed of her weaknesses, she bowed her head. She could not tell him. She could not watch the love in his eyes turn cold for her. Death would come to her more easily if she could hold the memory of him loving her in her heart. It was a small selfishness for the sacrifice she would make. Even so, she was sad that she could not explain to him.

When the sun rose, Jason would wake. He would know the beast inside him was gone. He would feel its absence; then he would find her. He would know why he would not be asked to face the call of the moon again. Her spirit would be gone. She would not be forced to face the accusation in his eyes, the anger upon his lips. She closed her eyes and relived every moment of their days together . . . and their nights.

Power was not worth what he had given her. No power on earth was greater than love. Tala had been given her dreams, if only for a short time. Now, she would give Jason his dream. She raised the knife.

A sound woke him, or maybe it was just a feeling. Jason sat abruptly. Tala did not lie beside him. She'd gone out a minute ago, or was it longer? The night sky had faded, almost allowing the dawn to break through. He rose and hurried into his breechclout, climbing the ladder he'd made to the escape hole above. It was still dark when he scurried out, but his eyes were already adjusted. Again, he heard a sound. Labored breathing. Grunts.

"Tala?" he called, then walked toward the area where he heard the noises. His foot hit something. He picked it up. It was one of Tala's knives . . . and it was tipped with blood. His heart started to beat fast. "Tala?" he yelled, louder, then ran, his gaze searching for her.

He stumbled upon a scene that made him draw up short. Tala fought the werewolf.

"You will not have him!" he heard her hiss. "Upon my life you will not!" Then she charged the other; her arms already streaked with bloody claw marks.

He didn't think, only acted instinctively. The knife in his hand sailed through the air and landed in the beast's chest, buried to the hilt. She roared, reeled back, and clawed at the weapon. The glow faded from her eyes, and she fell to the ground. Jason joined Tala, amazed at his lucky throw. Together, they watched the creature return to the form of the prostitute.

Pushing Tala behind him, Jason approached the body. He bent and touched her cold throat, looking for a pulse. There wasn't one.

"She's dead."

The enormity of what Jason had done registered. He had killed something, but it wasn't human. There were no guilty feelings that suddenly overtook him, but something else did. He hadn't thought beyond Tala's safety. The knife had ended his chance of finding the one that had bitten him. Jason buried his face in his hands.

"Now I won't ever know if a member of her pack is the one. I could have been normal again, dammit. There was a chance at least." He wanted to raise his head and howl his anguish, but instead, he kept his face pressed against his hands. Tala touched him lightly upon the shoulder.

"There is still a chance for you," she whispered.

He heard the sound of steel being pulled from flesh. Jason glanced up. Tala stood before him, holding the bloody knife. She extended it toward him, forced it into his hand.

"You will not find the one among her pack. You will not find the one in the outside world. The one is standing before you. I give you back your life, but to have it, you must take mine."

Confusion engulfed him. His mind rejected what she'd said. It couldn't be true. Not Tala. She was of the light, not of the dark. He loved her. What kind of cruel game did she play with him?

"You're lying."

She shook her head, her dark eyes pleading. "I am not lying. I have deceived you. I am the one. Not the one who cursed you, but I took the other's sins. To be free, it is me you must kill, Jason."

Fury rose inside him. He did howl then, rising from the ground to tower over her. He grabbed her shoulders, wanting to shake her until she took back the awful words that cut slashes into his heart, into his very soul.

"Tell me you're lying!" he ordered.

"Kill me," she whispered. "Kill me and never face the call of the moon again! Do it now!"

The knife glinted, raised into the air by his own fist, as if he had no control over his rage. She did not cower in fear or cry out. Tala stood before him, proud, beautiful, willing him to take her life and save his own. His hand shook, lowered toward her breasts. Jason groaned and flung the knife away. He turned from the sight of her.

"Why did you lie to me?"

"I was the one chosen," she answered, her voice barely above a whisper. "I could not sacrifice the gifts my people needed for your life. But I sacrificed myself for my sister. I did not know that she had become a Sica. The night she attacked you and your brother, I was there. I saw what she did, and I prayed to every spirit to take her sins and give them to me. The mark on my back, it is where your brother shot her. It is a reminder that I carry her sins inside me."

Jason wheeled around to face her. "What happened to her? Where is she?"

"Finding her will do you no good, Jason. Killing her would do you no good. I saved her from the beast . . . for a time. She knows this. I know it. But I did not know what my punishment would be for taking her sins, not until I first saw you, not until I first loved you."

Too many emotions collided inside him. He needed to empty his stomach—empty his heart. Was there no end to this damned curse! No, there wasn't. There was no end because for there to be an end, he would have to kill Tala. Kill the woman he loved. Again, he roared his outrage. He knew when he faced her again, his eyes were glowing.

"Why did you let me continue to believe? How could you do this to me?"

She backed a few steps from him, he thought in fear, but then she bent, and he saw she had the knife again. "I am sorry," she said. "Do not let what you have learned tonight steal what we have shared together. I took my sister's sins because I loved her. Now, I take my life because I love you. There is nothing left for me."

He lunged, hoping to move swifter than the knife. As if in slow motion, he saw the blade descending toward her chest. He was not fast enough, but another hand suddenly gripped her wrist. She struggled, but her brother held her tightly.

The forest came alive with shapes that crept from the shadows. Tribesmen surrounded them. Dawn broke through the night. The sudden flare of pink on the horizon seemed to mock the darkness Jason felt in his heart.

"Let him go, Haidar," he heard Tala say. "We have already taken his life once! We cannot take it again."

The big man snatched a robe from around his shoulders and covered his sister's nakedness, but his eyes never broke contact with Jason's.

"They have killed Unma Kin Sica," he heard one man say.

"The outsider killed her," Tala said. "He is not your enemy. Let him go."

No one spoke. Jason kept staring at Haidar, ready to put up a fight. The leader shoved Tala toward one of the other men.

"Two of you take her back to camp. The rest of you take the body of the creature away and burn it. All of you, go."

Tala struggled against the man and broke loose. She threw herself at her brother's feet. "Do not kill him! I beg you, brother. Let him go free."

Haidar's jaw muscle jumped. "I said take her!" he thundered.

When two men came forward and dragged Tala away, Jason took a step toward them. Haidar also took a step, blocking his path.

"Do not make me kill you in front of her," he said softly.

"What will happen to her?" Jason demanded.

Haidar didn't answer until the other men took the body of the creature away. "She is not of your concern," he growled. "You have led her to this shame! I should have killed you the moment she told me who you were. You were already one sister's downfall, now you have become the other's."

"You knew," he said and then realized that of course her brother knew. It was one of the reasons Haidar hated him so much. "You both lied to me."

Haidar stepped forward and shoved him back a step. "Your people have lied to ours for centuries. Do you think I would allow my sister to sacrifice herself for you? A white man? An outsider? She should have never brought you among us. She should have killed you the night she first found you! But her heart is weak, like the hearts of our parents, one who died from sickness, the other for his own weakness!"

"I had nothing to do with your family's shame!" Jason shouted at him. "I had nothing to do with your sister attacking me and my brother, ripping my throat out! Cursing me!"

"I do not know what happened to Meka, how she became a Sica. Always she wanted things beyond our world. You tempted her. She ran away after Tala witnessed her sins. She is outcast, an enemy to The People now."

Jason ran a hand through his hair. "And is that my fault?"

"No," the big man said, although his gaze never softened. "But Tala—*she* is your fault. Do not tell me you did not want her. Do not tell me you did not

293

tempt her. She has sacrificed everything for you! She has sacrificed her own people for you!"

"She lied to me!" Jason didn't want to hear all that Tala had done for him at the moment. He was too angry with her. "She let me believe I could live a normal life, become a normal man! She let me believe that the one I hunted was still out there, that there was hope for me."

Haidar glanced away. "Did she not make you feel like a man again? Did she not give you back what you thought you had lost?"

"Yeah, she did," he agreed. "Only to rip it away from me, just like she ripped out my heart. Now you want to rip off my head." He motioned him closer. "You're not taking me without a fight. This is has been a long time coming."

The leader didn't do as Jason instructed. Instead, Haidar took Tala's knife, wiped the blade against his leggings, then slashed open his chest, and his arms.

"I can do nothing for Tala now. Her fate is in the hands of The People. I do not understand what she feels for you, why she would sacrifice anything for you. But I will do the only thing I can for her. Go, and do not come back. I hope you leave with the wisdom she has given you. You know the way now—fight the call."

Only when the big guy had turned and walked away did Jason realize he was free. He stood there, not knowing what to do. The forest was quiet. When he glanced around, he saw nothing. Not another living thing. He walked to the den and climbed down the ladder. Tala's clothes were still there along with his own. His hand trembled when he lifted her dress. He held it to his face and breathed her scent, then with a roar, threw the garment across the den.

Jason buried his face in his hands again. He didn't lift his head and howl in fury. He didn't curse her name. He did the one thing he never thought he would do over a woman's betrayal. He wept.

Chapter Twenty-five

Tala would not weep. She would not beg. She would not show fear. She stood before her people, her head held high. Only when her brother returned did her composure slip. He had cuts across his chest, upon his arms, as if he had fought. All heads swung toward him.

"The outsider will bother us no more," he said.

A moan rose in her throat. Her knees buckled, and she fell to the ground. It was her brother's hand that reached down and pulled her up.

"Do not shame me further," he said, his voice very quiet. "There is no longer a need for you to sacrifice yourself for this man. There may be honor in giving your life for another, but there is none in taking it. You may die by The People's hand, but not by your own."

She glanced up at her brother, so proud, so strong,

so unlike the rest of their family. "There is no shame in loving, Haidar."

His jaw muscle jumped. He swallowed. Briefly, he touched her face before he snatched his hand away. "I cannot interfere, Tala. Not even for you."

"I understand." She straightened. The People would not see her weakness. "It is a good day to die."

His eyes misted for a moment before he turned from her, once again the fierce leader of a tribe that would see harsh winters without the hawk to hunt for prey and dark days ahead.

Tala's people were kind, but they could also be harsh. The good of the tribe always came before the needs of an individual. She had forgotten that, had allowed her own desires to come before her duty. They would turn upon her now. She knew this, she accepted it, because it was *Oyate Ba'cho*. The way.

"Tala Soaringbird is no longer the one chosen," her brother shouted to The People. "She has given her powers away for a man. A white man. An outsider among us. What say you to her crime?"

No one spoke. They were all clearly shocked. All stared at her. Finally, Noshi's mother stepped forward.

"The outsider saved my son from the beast, and I must keep his act of bravery in my heart. But now Tala has endangered my son again. Will Noshi starve this winter when we cannot find game? Will he die by the hand of Unma Kin Sica because she can no longer see him in her visions?"

A grumble started among The People. Tala braced herself for the coming storm. She no longer cared what they did to her. She was dead inside. Her brother had killed the man she loved. Jason had died with hate in his heart for her.

"Her punishment should be death," someone shouted. "Death for the deaths she will cause us."

"She should burn!" another voice shouted.

A pebble suddenly hit Tala upon the cheek. She flinched, but she did not cry out. Others stooped to pick up rocks. They drew back their fists to throw, but a figure stepped in front of her. One with a bent frame and a mane of silver hair that fell down his back.

Tala's uncle held up a hand. "My niece has committed no crime. Our hearts do not always follow our destiny. Tala loved this man, this outsider. All things happen for a reason. We must wait and see what the reason might be."

"What reason can there be, old man?" another voice called. "Her powers are lost to us. The white man is dead. What purpose does she serve us now?"

Her uncle shook his head. "What purpose do I serve you? I am old and cannot hunt. My back is not strong. I cannot work for you. Do you turn me out to die because I serve no purpose? That is not the way of the *ba'cho*."

When some bowed their heads, her uncle continued, "Today the desire for revenge burns brightly inside of you. It is not a good day to decide what punishment Tala must face. We will not talk of this until the full-moon cycle has passed. Then her fate will be decided."

"She has acted as a lone wolf, for the good of herself, not for the good of her people," one argued. "She must be caged, put on display as a bad example."

Shouts of agreement followed. Her uncle turned and gave her a sad look. His gaze found Haidar. "You will come and talk to me when they have had their fun with your sister."

Her brother nodded solemnly.

Caged. Tala did not like the thought. Her spirit needed to move among the forest, to feel the sunshine upon her face, to run, to hunt—but she could not even find pleasure in those thoughts. She had once accepted what she could not change, but then Jason gave her the courage to want more. She had not knowingly wronged her people. But she supposed she had always wronged them. She had never wanted to be the one chosen—had never felt as if it were truly her destiny.

"Hear me," she called. "I will not defend what I have done, but I cannot say that I am sorry for loving the white man. The gifts were given to me, not by my choice, but by destiny. I never wanted them. I only wanted to be like the rest of you." There, it was out. Her secret.

"But being the one chosen is a great honor," Chandee said. "Only those with the spirit of a warrior, the purest of hearts, are given such an honor."

Tala lowered her gaze. "So the legend says."

"The legend also tells of women who chose a mate and children over the powers given to them," her uncle reminded The People. "The legend does not say those women were punished for their choice."

"But there were many of the ones chosen in the time when the legend first began," a man pointed out. "It is not so today. It was the women who weakened the numbers and the powers of the outcasts. Because

299

they chose their own needs over the needs of their people, the outcasts soon became only what they had been in the beginning, without the great powers Mother Earth had given to them to fight the evil ones."

"Enough," her uncle said, waving his hands in the air. "We will speak of these things and weigh Tala's fate carefully. Every year, our numbers grow smaller. To put one of our own to death must not be an act of passion, but an act of deep consideration. We are not animals. We are ruled by our heads *and* our hearts."

Always, her wise uncle had been able to speak well, to make The People think upon their actions. Tala realized how much she loved him. He did serve a purpose. His wisdom and his patience had always been an asset to their tribe.

"She will still be caged," someone insisted, and Tala did not care to identify the voice. Her mind had already drifted. Would she find Jason in the spirit world one day? It might be the only place they could be together.

The day was almost gone before Jason realized night approached. He still sat in the den, thoughts whirling through his mind, bouts of anger causing him to pace and curse. Then sadness would bring him to his knees again. He was free to return to his world, but he felt as if he had nothing there. Nowhere to go. No one to return to. His brother had freed himself from the curse. His family had come to accept that he was gone.

There was no reason to continue his search. He knew where the one was, and in his heart, he understood what she had done. He didn't know if he could forgive Tala for lying to him, though, for letting him believe there was a beast in the world that he might someday find and kill, releasing him from the call of the moon. Even her gift to him, her desire to save him, he suspected, had been for her sister's sake. She had wanted to know if her sister could fight the beast within her and come to terms with what she was.

Yet Tala had used him to see if she could help her sister, and he had used her for his brother's sake. Could he blame her for that? She had lost her powers because of him. He had no idea what her tribe would do to her, though he didn't think they would kill her. She was one of them. Had grown up among them. Her brother was their leader. Surely Haidar wouldn't allow them to kill his own sister.

He wiped a hand across his brow and noticed the sweat there. He glanced up at the darkening sky. No, Tala was not dead. The wolf still lived inside of him. He felt it, waiting, gathering strength. What would the animal do if he allowed it to rule him? With his heart full of anger, his emotions confused, what would the beast do? Return to Tala's cave? Seek her out? Attack her?

The thought made him shudder. Whatever Tala had done, he wouldn't see her hurt. He had to fight, fight the call of the moon as she had told him to do. Could he do it without her? There was no choice. However his days would be spent on earth, they would not be at the mercy of the moon. The wolf inside him, the one that now would live within him forever, must know that he was the alpha and the beast the omega.

The wolf would not control him, but only come at

his command. He would take the curse and make it into a gift. Jason realized in that moment, with the anger churning inside him, how easily he could use the beast within for revenge, to kill, to maim, to destroy. He pushed those thoughts away. They were the dark whispers within his soul Tala had warned him about. He must ignore them, must call upon his own goodness, the pureness of his heart to save him.

"White man . . . Jason."

He straightened, searching the dirt for Tala's second knife. It was Haidar's voice above.

"I know you are there. Tala does not think I know of this place. She and Meka used to hide here from me when we were children. They thought they were clever, but I was the clever one. As long as they were hiding, they were not bothering me."

"What do you want?" he shouted.

"Why are you not gone?"

Jason laughed, even though it was a sarcastic sound. "Where should I go? The call of the moon is upon me. The beast within will live on. You should know from your ancestors that the best plan is to pick a good location and make a stand."

Silence. He held the knife ready in case the big guy decided to scramble inside the den and take his scalp.

"Tala," the man began, then paused.

"What about Tala?" Jason demanded.

"Her fate will not be decided until the passing of the full-moon cycle. I cannot interfere with what The People decide, and their hearts are angry with her. If you face the call of the moon, and the man remains stronger than the beast, will you . . ."

"Will I what?" Jason prompted.

"Take her away."

Jason rubbed his forehead. The big guy did have a heart after all. "I don't know," he answered, because he didn't. He was still confused and angry.

"I can see where the choice would be difficult," Haidar said. "If you leave her, she will die, and you will be only a man again. The sacrifice to save her would take . . . love. The kind of love that I do not understand, but that my sister feels for you."

Haidar had known where they were hidden all along, but he had kept his knowledge a secret from the other tribespeople. He'd been buying them time, which meant Tala's life really was in danger.

"Consider what I have asked," Haidar said when Jason didn't answer. "You know the secret passages. Others will try to stop you. I cannot interfere. You may both be killed. You must decide what is worth having in your life. I must not think as one man but as the whole tribe. I leave you now. May the Great Spirit guide you and give you strength to fight the moon."

Before the other man could move too far away, Jason called, "Haidar. Choose your guards wisely during the next few nights. Tell them to be alert. If I come to your camp during the full-moon cycle, I won't be there to rescue anyone." There was something else he had to tell the leader, although it wouldn't endear Tala to the tribesmen she'd already angered. "And, the female, she left a scent trail. There are others in her pack. You'll have to watch out for them."

Tala's brother didn't respond, but Jason knew he'd heard. Jason dropped the knife he'd found back into the dirt. He was half tempted to turn it upon himself.

But besides his strong Irish Catholic upbringing having drilled that suicide was an unforgivable sin in his mind, that wouldn't help Tala. It wouldn't help anyone, except himself. The dark whispers came to him again. *End it all. End it now.* He wouldn't have to fight the call of the moon or worry about what might happen to Tala.

It wasn't in him to give up though. Jason had always needed a quest, a purpose greater than mere survival. He'd needed challenges. Rick, too, now that he thought about it. Jason would like to see his brother again, but he wouldn't undo the sacred spells Tala had cast over Rick that made him forget his ordeal with the supernatural. As long as Rick was happy, had found his life and his purpose, Jason should be grateful.

He wondered about Tala's sister, Meka. The outcast. The one who had attacked him and had let her sister suffer for her sins. Did she hunt the one who had changed her? And if Tala could see the evil ones who posed a threat to her people or those she cared about, why hadn't she seen the one who'd bitten her sister, killed the beast, and released Meka from the curse? There were questions still unanswered, he realized. Another realization found him. His skin began to itch—his gums hurt in preparation for the fangs that would replace his incisor teeth.

The night approached. The moon would rise. It would call to him, to the beast within. Could he make it through even the first night? Jason gathered his strength—summoned his courage. He needed to focus all his thoughts upon the change and fighting it. He couldn't worry about Tala now or ponder questions only she could answer. She would be safe until after the full-moon cycle, her brother had said so. At least she would be safe from the anger of her own people. He wasn't positive she would safe from his.

Chapter Twenty-six

The bars were sturdy and placed so close together that she could hardly squeeze her arms through them, certainly not her body. If Tala's powers were still with her, not even a cage could confine her. She could imagine herself as a snake and curl her way through the bars. Or a wisp of smoke. But her powers were lost. The man she loved was lost. She wondered how her spirit found the desire to consider escape. Where would she go?

Dark whispers weakened her, she realized. When all seemed lost, that was when the whispers were the loudest. But her heart was broken, and she wondered what purpose she would serve by living? If The People could forgive her, there was still much she could do for them. She was strong—not as strong as when she had been when she held her powers, but still equal to most in her tribe. She could also hunt. Not as a bird or a wolf or whatever creature best served the tribe's purpose, but as a woman.

Meka. Her sister was still in the outside, battling her own demons. Tala's uncle had said that she would return. Who would stand up for Meka if she did return? Who would speak on her behalf? In the distance, the moon sat upon a distant peak, only half risen, but soon, it would climb higher, show its full glory to the world. Her sister had battled the call for three years now, had not allowed the beast within her to control her again since that night she had attacked Jason and his brother. Had she redeemed her soul? Had she purified her heart? Or did she battle every full-moon cycle, waiting to surrender to the darkness once more?

Tala stared at the moon until a figure blocked it from her site. She jumped back, fearing it was a tribesman with a rock or an insult to hurl at her. A moment later she relaxed. "Uncle?"

"I have brought you something to eat," he said. "Now the old man must feed his children again."

He slipped some dried venison through the bars, then held a water skin up so she could drink. Her thirst was great, and she drank greedily. When she finished, she leaned back, wiping her mouth with the back of her hand.

"Have I shamed you, Uncle?"

"No, little one. You only listened to your heart instead of following what you believed was your destiny. I feel good will come of this."

Tears filled her eyes. "How can good come? My powers are gone. The man I love is dead, a man cursed by my sister and killed by my brother." She bit off the words.

"I know about the outsider," he said. "I know the man has the beast within him. Haidar told me. He told me much tonight when he came to sit before my fire. He is torn by all that has happened."

Tala bent her head. "Then you know that I have deceived The People in more than only the loss of my powers. I brought Jason among us. I hoped to give him a part of his life back, in exchange for what Meka had taken from him." A lump formed in her throat. "But I only brought his death, and now, my own."

Her uncle reached for her hand through the bars, and she grasped his bent and swollen fingers. He said, "The outsider is not dead."

She blinked. Her heart lurched inside of her chest. "But, Haidar said—"

"Haidar fears if you know he lives, you will try to sacrifice yourself for him again."

A sudden joy spread through her, but just as quickly, fled. Jason was alone tonight? He would face the call without her help? Tala pressed her face against her cage, staring at her uncle. "You must bring me a weapon, uncle. I am to die anyway. Let me spare him this night and the ones to follow."

Her uncle shook his head. "The path you would take is too simple. For him and for you. If love is strong enough, it can heal the wounds of time; it can make worlds come together. It can change destiny."

Tala gripped the wooden bars of her cage. "Uncle," she pleaded. "I beg you to let me end his suffering. I owe him a life."

He touched her fingers curled tightly around the

bars. "You owe him only your heart, which you have given to him unselfishly. Now, he must do the same."

"Uncle!" Tala called as the old man moved away. He did not turn back to her. She rattled the bars of her cage, stared up at the moon, threw her head back, and howled in anguish.

Jason ground his teeth. He clenched his hands at his side. Sweat poured off his body. I am a man, he kept repeating over and over in his mind. Then he heard Tala's voice saying, *You have two arms, two legs.* He closed his eyes and imagined her hands moving over him. For a moment, he thought he caught her scent. It was on her clothes that lay next to him, he remembered.

She had deceived him. His body shook harder, and he forced the angry thought from his mind. Instead, he brought memories back of the past days, lying beside her, making love to her. He saw her love for him shining in her eyes. She had offered him the knife, had offered him her life. Had anyone ever done more for him? Offered him more? What was true love, if not that?

The wolf appeared to him, eyes glowing, lips curled back in a snarl. "Go," he shouted. "I am master of my fate! I control my body, my thoughts, not you!" The wolf cowered, slunk down, and disappeared from his mind. Jason knew he would be back, many times before this night and the nights to follow ended. "Tala," he whispered her name, just to hear it on his lips.

Jason. If you can hear me, listen to what I say. You must go back in time, like you have done before. You must remember that you were born a human, and only a human.

The wolf is part of you, but only a small part. Your memories are stronger than his. Your will is stronger. He lives to serve you. You do not live to serve him.

He went back in time again, relived memories of his childhood and saw them as if they were old movies being played inside his head. They warmed his heart. Then Tala's memories merged with his. He saw her as a child, running with a smaller dark-haired girl through the meadows of the forest. He heard their laughter. A somber boy followed them, carrying a stick. He did not laugh, but glanced from side to side, as if making sure the girls were safe.

He saw Tala dancing before the fire, singing to the night spirits, tears streaking her small face. He understood her words, although he had not learned her language. She wanted to be a normal girl, like the others. She did not want to turn into a bird and fly away or save her people from the monsters that haunted her dreams. She was afraid, so afraid. She wanted her mother . . . her father. Why had they left her? Why did Meka leave her? Why did everyone she loved leave her?

"Tala. Don't cry," he whispered. "I can't stand to see your tears, to feel your pain. I want to hold you in my arms, kiss away your sorrows."

And suddenly he felt as if she were in his arms. He held her, kissed her lips, and wiped the tears from her cheeks. She wrapped her arms around his neck. Gently, he eased her to the ground, undressed her, kissed every inch of skin he exposed. She moaned his name and pulled her to him. Then they joined, mind, body, and soul.

It was unlike any physical joining they had shared.

A current of power rushed into his body. He felt as if he had truly become one with Tala. One person, the both of them entwined into one being. His release ripped through him, intensified by the power pulsing beneath his skin. Tala cried out his name and clung to him. He pulled back to stare down her, but it was not Tala he saw beneath him. It was a wolf. She was a wolf.

"No!" Jason shot up, gasping for breath, his clothes damp with sweat. Overhead, the morning sky blazed into his eyes. He shielded them from the brightness. A moment later, he lowered his arm and stared up at the opening above. He had made it through the night. At least the first one.

Chapter Twenty-seven

"For five nights he has resisted the call." Tala whispered.

"What did you say?" her brother asked.

He stood outside her cage, trying to act unaffected as other tribesmen passed, pausing to snarl at Tala or hurl insults in her direction. He had brought her food earlier, before the morning light revealed his act of kindness to the others.

"I know that he is not dead," she said to her brother. "Even if our uncle had not told me, I would have known. He speaks to me at times, in my mind."

Her brother glanced around nervously. His brows furrowed. "That is not possible. Unless." Hope filled his eyes. "Have your powers returned?"

She smiled sadly at him. "Do you think I would be in here if they had?"

Haidar frowned. "I do not like to see you caged like an animal."

"What are The People saying?" He would not look at her, which told her enough. "They believe my punishment should be death."

"They are not all of one mind," he said. "But I have not told them what the white man said to me. I am afraid that if I do, hope for you will be gone."

"What did Jason tell you?"

He bent, as if fixing his moccasins. "The female, she left a scent trail for her pack to follow. It will lead them to us."

Tala's heart sank. She felt ill. "And I will no longer be able to see them coming." So many at risk because she had fallen in love with an outsider. When her brother told The People this news, they would condemn her to die. "You must tell them," she said. "It is your duty."

"Never have I hated my duty so much as in these past few days," he growled, still bent before her on the ground.

If she could have reached him, Tala would have touched his bowed head. Her proud brother, always sure of his destiny, always strong in his beliefs, had been tested much by his rebellious sisters.

"What Jason told you is not something you can keep from them," she pointed out. "To do so makes you no better than me. It places them all in danger."

"I will tell them," he said, rising to his impressive height. "Tonight, when we meet again to talk of your punishment. It will not be to your favor, Tala. For this, I am sorry."

313

There were no tears left inside her. She would be strong, for Haidar's sake. "Our uncle believes good will yet come of all of this. Is he an old man who has lost his mind?"

Her brother smiled, but the expression did not reach his dark eyes. "He has a gift with words. The People still listen to him. If they did not, I would have had to fight to keep them from taking your punishment into their own hands."

"Which death do they demand?"

He glanced away from her. "I must go. I have stood here for too long."

"Haidar, which death?" Tala insisted. She wanted to know so she could prepare herself.

"Fire," he said softly, then walked away.

"Fire," Jason mumbled, blowing on his hands. The day had dawned cloudy and cold for summer. A mist hung over the mountains and crept down into the valleys. He could build a fire and probably not be spotted. First, he needed something to eat. He'd constructed a snare. Now he watched it from the cover of brush, hoping a small animal would come along and provide him with breakfast.

A rabbit scampered into view. Jason willed it toward the snare. It moved closer to the trap. He held his breath, felt the saliva gathering in his mouth. He'd been too tired to eat for the past few days. Fighting the call had taken all his strength through the nights, and he had slept during the day. Last night, it had come easier to him, but he knew he wouldn't have made it this far without Tala. It was as if she'd been with him every night, speaking to him, assuring him, giving him her strength.

The rabbit almost went inside of the snare, twitched its nose, and turned away. Jason's hand was on the knife tucked inside the top of his moccasin in a second. The next instant the knife whirled through the air and found its mark. He blinked, then stared at his fallen prey, the knife protruding from its small body.

"Damn," he whispered. "How did I do that?"

Jason walked to the lifeless rabbit, grabbed it by the ears, and retrieved his knife. He walked to the den and tossed the rabbit down the hole. Later, he would skin the animal and cook it, but before he did, he needed a bath. Waking each morning after a night of sweating made him riper than he could stand.

Always, he was alert by day if he moved through the forest. He crept on silent feet, watched where he stepped, guarded his back. His gaze moved in the direction of Tala's encampment. He saw the bluffs shrouded by mist. No one would know to look at those ragged cliffs that a civilization of people called them home. A longing rose up in him to be there, among those cliffs, inside Tala's cave, snuggled with her in her furs.

He reached the hot spring, and other visions clouded his mind. What was he going to do about Tala? He had forced the anger over her betrayal aside in order to concentrate on resisting the call of the moon. He knew he had to deal with it—also knew he couldn't leave her fate up to her people. Haidar wanted him to rescue her, take her away, but he knew Tala. She didn't belong in the outside world. She loved the forest, her people, the way of life she had always known. He wasn't even sure he still belonged to the outside.

There was nothing for him there. Not anymore. But Tala's people, *Oyate ba'cho*, as she called them, would not allow a man like him to live among them. He was fairly certain they didn't want either him or Tala to live at all.

Jason removed his clothing, pausing to rub the soft buckskin of his shirt. His fingers brushed the fancy fringe that hung from the sleeves. He could never wear shoes again. His feet had become accustomed to the soft, comfortable moccasins. He removed his breechclout, leggings, and footwear and climbed into the warm water of the spring. It embraced him, eased his stiff muscles, and he leaned his head back to stare at the cloudy sky overhead.

When he closed his eyes, all he saw was Tala: Tala fighting the werewolf in hopes of saving him, Tala offering him her knife. He allowed the anger to come. She had lied to him from the beginning. She'd let him believe there was hope of breaking his curse in the future. She hadn't wanted to save him from the call of the moon, but she'd wanted to use him to see if her sister still stood a chance of being brought back from the dark side.

She had also allowed him to believe that his brother, Rick, was still cursed until he'd forced the issue. He'd suffered over Rick's fate, and she had allowed him to do so, knowing his brother was fine— that in fact, his brother didn't even remember being a werewolf or that Jason was still alive.

But she had ended up telling him the truth, the truth about everything. Or had she? Were there still secrets she hid from him? Was she all right? Had her people hurt her? Was she suffering in any way? Even when he felt angry with her, he couldn't stand the thought of her hurt or suffering. Of course he had to save her from whatever fate her people had decided upon. If Haidar hadn't thought it would be death, her brother wouldn't have suggested a rescue.

Haidar had said it would be dangerous. They might both be killed. But what did Jason have to live for, if not for Tala? If not in hopes of finding his place in a world where he had none? What quest would drive him now? He couldn't kill Tala to end his curse. He loved her. The thought echoed through the passageways of his mind. He loved her in a way he had never loved a woman before.

Could he love her in the most important way? Could he love her unconditionally and in spite of all she'd done to him? But he couldn't examine the bad without looking at the good. She'd taught him things, impossible things. She'd shown him things, impossible things. Now that he knew the impossible existed, didn't that mean the impossible could be done? Maybe he could have a normal life. Maybe this was normal for him now.

He'd never really wanted a normal life when he'd had one, Jason reminded himself. The forest had always called to him. The great outdoors. Did he want to return to the crowded cities, the noise, the stench, the little office where he'd punched his calculator for hours a day? He couldn't see himself there anymore. Tala, she had been given a quest. Save the world from the Unma Kin Sica. But her love for him had stolen her powers. Powers she had never wanted, but important to her people nonetheless.

Of course, in the beginning she wouldn't have chosen him over her people. But she had chosen him in the end. And it might cost Tala her life.

Not if Jason could help it. What better way to go out than fighting for the woman he loved? He had to show her that he loved her, would sacrifice his life for her, the way she had offered to do for him. It was another quest. One that would begin in the morning. Tonight was the last night of the full-moon cycle. Jason felt his strength building, knew in his heart that the beast would never have him now. They would live together, he and the wolf, but the wolf would live only to serve his needs. Jason was the alpha of his spirit, and the wolf was the omega.

If Tala had never found him in that dirty alley, he would have been roaming the streets like a madman these past few weeks. He would have woken up naked somewhere wondering what he'd done and who had seen him. He'd be on a senseless search, eaten up with worry over his brother, and hating the monster he'd become. But Tala had changed all that. She had given him back a life—and no, it wasn't the one he had before, but it was a hell of a lot better than the one he'd been living for the past three years. It was a life he could live with, and that was the greatest gift she could have given him. A life, and her love. His mind reached out to her.

Hold on, Tala. I'm coming to get you.

Chapter Twenty-eight

Tala stood before her people. There were no rocks being hurled at her, no insults. Her fate had been decided, and now all knew they must live with their decision. The death of another was never easy to justify—it had not been for her, even when those she killed had lost their human side. Her punishment had not been announced, but she did not have to hear the words to understand the pain in her brother's eyes or the sorrow etched upon her uncle's face.

"Tala Soaringbird," her brother began, turning to her. When his gaze met hers, he could not continue. Then he seemed to mentally brace himself and cleared the words from his throat. "You have been judged by The People and found guilty of crimes against us. You have not acted in the ways taught, in the way of *Oyate ba'cho*. The good of all must come before the desires of one. Always, this has been the law among us, the reason we survive. To go against the law is to go against The People. Your actions have taken the one chosen from us, have placed our lives in danger. Your punishment is . . ." Haidar paused as if he could not speak, then continued, "Death."

Her knees went weak. In her heart, she knew what The People had decided, but to hear it, and upon her brother's lips, wounded her deeply. Tala had loved her people. She had fought for them, protected them, hunted for them, and now they had turned against her. Her powers were a gift and important to them. She understood their anger, but could they not understand that beneath the warrior, there also lay a woman?

No, she had never been allowed to be a woman. Instead, The People had made her a god, had expected her heart to remain theirs and only theirs. And it would have been so, had Jason not come into her life.

"How?" she whispered, but she also knew the answer to that question.

Her brother did not answer.

"How?" Tala asked louder, so The People could hear her.

Only one was brave enough to answer. Her uncle stepped forward. "Because the flame of your own desires has brought you to this ruin in The People's eyes, they have chosen fire."

They. It did not escape her notice that her uncle had held himself apart from The People. It did not escape theirs either. Despite the fear climbing up her spine, she gave the old man a warning glance. She would not cause her family further trouble.

"What say you to The People, niece?" her uncle asked.

What could she say? Nothing would change the crime she had committed in their eyes. "Love is stronger than destiny," she said softly. "Love is stronger than the greatest powers. Do what you will to me, and know in your hearts that because I also love you, I can forgive you."

Several bowed their heads. A few cried for her, but all parted so she might see what had been quickly constructed during her distraction. Several bundles of dried brush and wood were heaped beneath a large sturdy pole. Tala would be lashed to the pole, the brush and wood set on fire.

Her first instinct was to flee, but she could not escape so many. Not without her powers. Besides, her life was a sacrifice she had meant to give to Jason. He had fought the call of the moon. She knew this in her heart. He had now proven to himself that the human side of him was the dominant, the alpha part of his nature, and the wolf side the omega. He was more human than beast, could control his body, fight the whispers that would lure him to the dark side. Only the pure of heart could fight the call of the moon, continue fighting it. Only the pure of heart would use their gift for good instead of evil.

Only when the beast was fueled by selfish thoughts and self-loathing, could it become stronger than the human within. This was a battle given to all, even those from the outside. The world was descended from the Tribes Of All People. All carried the beast within, though the beast was not always in the form of the wolf. He came in many shapes.

The beast was here among her people today, hidden in the eyes of those staring at her, those who would destroy her because she had dared to love. They had forgotten that above all else, she was human. But they would remember soon enough. When they heard her screams of agony and watched the flesh melt from her bones, they would remember, and they would have to live with their decision.

There was no point in resisting. Tala walked through the crowd toward the death they had decreed for her. She refused to be dragged. She closed her eyes for a moment, her mind seeking Jason's.

Soon, it will be over. Remember always, that I love you.

A voice inside his head stirred him. Jason sat, grateful to see the morning light filtering in from above. He'd made it through the last night of the full-moon cycle without surrendering to the call. But there was one call he couldn't resist. The call of love. Tala. He had to get to her, rescue her. Jason rose, adjusted his clothing, and made sure his knife still rested inside the top of his moccasin. He had no idea what he might face when he reached the encampment. Resistance, he felt sure, maybe certain death. None of that mattered anymore.

Nothing mattered except Tala, and reaching her in time. He had to tell her that he loved her. He had to tell that he understood what she had done was in the name of love. His heart had forgiven her. Jason had accepted who he was, and his curse had become a gift. If his quest from that moment on was nothing more than to look into her eyes one last time, it would be enough for him.

He scrambled up the rope-and-vine ladder and stumbled into the pale morning light. Clouds and mist still blanketed the forest, as they had yesterday. He ran toward the bluffs, aware that if he took his wolf form he could move much faster, but unwilling to leave his clothing and the one weapon he had behind. Still, he moved with a swiftness that surprised him. It was almost as if he had wings.

The tunnels would be his wisest choice of entry. Maybe Tala would be held prisoner inside her cave, but if that were the case, there would be a guard posted inside the tunnel leading to her secret escape route. He'd have to be careful. A sudden sense of urgency gripped him—a feeling in his gut, or in his heart, that something was about to happen. Something bad.

Willing his legs to move faster, he ran, the forest now familiar to him, the landmarks he passed taking him ever closer to the tunnels' secret entrance on the opposite side of the bluffs. What if he got lost? He pushed the thought aside. No time for fears or insecurities. No time for anything. Again, something arose inside him. Fear. Not his, but someone else's. Tala? What was happening to her? The sensation of ropes cut into his arms, into his legs, causing him to stumble.

A smell tickled his senses. The smell of smoke, either real or imagined. Fire. They were going to burn her. "No!" he shouted, and he stumbled along, his arms pinned closely to his sides, his legs bound together. In his mind, he pictured the knife in his hand. He slashed the ropes that held him and picked up speed again. The secret entrance loomed before him, a gaping hole in the backside of the bluff that didn't look so secret.

The People should do something about that, he thought; then there was no room for any thoughts except making it through the tunnels. The darkness enveloped him, and the damp smell of sulfur rose from the Sacred Waters below. He tried to push that scent aside and pick up another—Tala's or his own, when he'd escaped from the tunnels before. But there were many scents inside the tunnels. Dozens assaulted him. Images floated through his mind of faces he'd come to recognize among Tala's people.

Then he saw her face in his mind, caught the scent that only belonged to her. He followed her, twisting and turning, always moving upward. The fear in his belly kept twisting ever tighter until it almost choked off his breath. Jason gasped, forging ahead until he finally reached the secret door that led to Tala's cave. His hands searched frantically for the smoothest rock and then found it, pressing against the surface. The small door swung open. He stumbled into her cave, only to find it dark and empty.

The smoke; he still smelled it. It was real and came from beyond her cave. Her scream cut into him, sharp as a blade. His heart dropped to his knees. He moved in what seemed to be slow motion toward the exit to Tala's cave. He couldn't see the smoke, but felt as if his lungs were on fire. He parted the brush at the entrance and moved to the edge of the bluff. What he saw below nearly sent him to his knees.

Tala stood lashed to a large pole, the brush and wood at her feet on fire, creating a thick smoke. He heard her cough, heard her try to drag air into her lungs. A roar rose in his throat and echoed off the bluffs. "No!" he shouted and suddenly, the fire licking at Tala's feet went out. Just like that, it disappeared. Heads swung up toward him. He didn't care to see anyone's face but Tala's, only the smoke was still too thick to see her clearly.

"It is the white man!" someone shouted. "The outsider!"

"Jason!" Tala screamed, then coughed. "Run," she choked. "Go from here!"

Fury rose up inside of him. "Release her!" he shouted down at The People. No one hurried to do his bidding, and he glanced at the group staring up at him. "I said . . ." the shout died in his throat. Jason stumbled back a step. His gaze shot to Tala, willing the smoke to clear. He saw her staring up at him, fear etched across her features . . . fear, and something else. "My God," he whispered. They were all wolves.

Chapter Twenty-nine

"He knows," Tala choked out, the wonder of it blasting the terror of moments before when the fire had come to life at her feet. "He sees us. He sees beyond our human faces, and finds the wolf within us."

"He has stolen Tala's powers!" someone yelled.

"It is not possible," her brother argued. "He is a white man, an outsider. He cannot possess the powers of the one chosen!"

"Where is it written?" her uncle shouted for all to hear. "Where does it say that Mother Earth must choose one among us?"

"The outsider is not *Oyate ba'cho*!" another argued. "He has not been raised in the ways! The power he possesses is dangerous! He will kill us all!"

"No!" Tala shouted. "The one chosen must be a warrior, must be pure of heart. Jason is these things. He has taken my destiny and made it his own!"

"He has *stolen* your destiny!" her brother thundered. "Maybe if he is dead, your powers will return!"

A lance arched through the air and bounced off the bluff wall next to Jason. Tala saw that he was still in shock—that he still tried to grasp what had happened to him, what he saw, what he now knew.

"I never wanted my destiny, or my powers!" Tala told her brother.

"Tala was only a vessel," her uncle reasoned. "She only held the powers until their rightful owner could claim them."

"I say it cannot be," Haidar snarled. "If the powers were meant for a man, Mother Earth should have given them to me!"

"Careful, Brother," Tala warned. "The beast within you rises up. We are taught not to question our destiny, but you have questioned yours, and I have questioned mine. Our sister questioned hers as well. We do not have the strength to be the one chosen."

"Your sister is right," her uncle intervened. "I have said many times that our world is changing, and we must change with it. Maybe this outsider was sent to help us upon our journey."

"And maybe he has come to destroy us all!" another tribesman shouted. "Will he use these powers he has stolen from Tala for good, as is law, or for evil?"

Tala's heart raced. She prayed her brother would keep silent, but of course, Haidar placed his duty above Jason's safety.

"The man has the beast within him. He had it in him when he first came among us."

Shocked gasps sounded around her. Tala had to fight, fight for Jason.

"He has battled the call of the moon and won!" she shouted. "He has fought the beast down! He would not use his powers for evil. Evil does not live in his heart!"

"You have deceived us again, Tala!" Chandee said. "How do we know we can trust this outsider? How can we now trust you? He has stolen not only your powers, but your heart. Sometimes a heart is blind to evil in one they love."

"I am not blind," Tala insisted. "He has been among us, saved your Noshi's life. All of you know that he is not evil. He has killed two beasts that came among us. He is not like them. He will never be like them!"

Another lance arched through the air and struck dangerously close to Jason. Tala saw that her people might kill him before they listened to the truth, before they accepted what she now knew had happened. Tala had lost her powers because they had never truly belonged to her. They would belong to the man who came into her life and taught her to love. The man who gave her what her own heart desired: a mate, and someday, maybe children of her own.

"Escape, Jason!" she shouted up at him. "Call the Great Spirit of the hawk to you and fly away!"

Jason was in shock. How could he have lived among these people, seen them day after day, and yet not have seen what he saw now? The legend was true. These people, the *Oyate ba'cho*, as they called themselves, were the original tribe of the outcasts. They were shape shifters. All except the children. He saw no wolf when he looked at them. Why?

"Jason!" Tala shouted up at him. "Do as I ask!"

What had she asked? He'd been too dazed to pay attention. The hawk—she had said to call the Great Spirit of the hawk to him and escape. But Jason didn't want to escape. He wanted to rescue Tala. A lance nearly pierced his arm and his situation became clearer to him. The People were trying to kill him now instead of Tala. He wasn't sure how to change into a hawk, but he knew how to become a wolf, so he just used the hawk's vision inside of his head instead of the great black wolf.

A ripple went through him. Another lance whizzed past his head. His body began to tingle; then he felt the change. A moment later, he was in the air, spreading his great wings and soaring into the sky. It was incredible, beyond anything he could imagine. His mind was his own, but his body soared higher and higher, freer than he'd ever felt in his life. Dying, this must be like dying and leaving all the world's problems behind him. But he could not leave one thing behind. Tala.

He turned and circled above, looking down at the faces turned up to him from the ground. Jason flew right into the thick of them, his mind now imagining himself in his true form. A moment later he stood before Tala. Shit, he was naked again.

"Jason!" she shouted. "Go!"

"No." He took a deep breath and faced her people. Several of them raised lances. "I love Tala. I don't really understand what has happened, but I know that she is my destiny. She took me from a dark place and showed me the light. I accept what I am, who I am. I can only ask you to do the same of me."

329

"Tala's destiny lays with her people," Tala's uncle said, then moved forward and handed him the blanket wrapped around his hunched shoulders. "Will your destiny lay with us, as well?"

Gladly wrapping the cloth around his nakedness, Jason said, "If you will accept me among you, I will accept you as my own."

No one spoke, which he didn't consider a good sign.

"You have lost your chosen and found another in the space of a full-moon cycle," Tala called behind him to her people. "Will you turn away from the gift Mother Earth has offered?"

"But he is not one of us," someone complained. "He was not born among us."

"My heart was born among you," Jason said. "I have no place in my world now. I have no desire to live without Tala by my side. I will learn the ways. I will do whatever you ask of me—if you spare Tala and allow us to live among you."

"He has already helped us," Annesha suggested. "He can help us learn the outside ways."

"Jason will also be able to see the evil ones, and when or if they will follow the female's scent trail to attack us," Tala reminded. "He will give back all that you believe I have taken from you."

The People nodded their heads in agreement. Jason felt a little of his tension ease. "What's it going to be?" he asked. "If you can't accept me, you're going to have to kill me, because there is no way in hell I'm letting you torch Tala. I will fight to my death to save her."

"A man who can love a woman so much, does not

have evil in his heart," Tala's uncle said.

"He will stay," someone said, which brought a smattering of agreements.

Suddenly Jason felt his arms snatched in a steely grip. He turned to stare into Haidar's dark, hard eyes. A knife flashed in his side vision. The leader bent the knife to Jason's biceps and carved five half circles into his flesh.

"Now, you are *Oyate ba'cho*," the man said.

"What does it mean?" Jason asked, trying not to wince.

Haidar smiled. "Tribe Of The Wolf."

Shouts and whoops followed. Jason's chest swelled with pride. "I am Jason Donavon," he shouted. "I am the one chosen, and I'm here for your heads . . . if you do not release my woman."

Haidar kicked piles of smoldering ash aside and used his knife to release his sister. Tala went straight into Jason's arms.

"I love you," he said, holding her close. "I couldn't live if something happened to you."

She pulled back. "You see me as I truly am now, Jason. You see again that there is a wolf beneath my skin. What do you think of that?"

He stared into her mysterious eyes. "I think that I must love her, just as I love you." He bent to capture her lips. Their mouths nearly touched when he thought of something. "The children. They're different from the rest of you."

She nodded. "We are not born with the wolf inside us," she explained. "The wolf comes when our children reach a certain age. When the girls have their first cycle and the boys are becoming young men."

"The age of accountability," he realized. "There are many things I'll have to learn about your people."

"Your people now, too," Tala reminded him. "You have been given the marks—one for each night you resisted the call of the moon. You are one of us now, and you know the days ahead may be dark."

He pulled her closer. "Whatever the days bring, I look forward to them as long as you're by my side."

"Oh, kiss her and be done with it," Tala's uncle fussed. "I think tonight we will have a joining ceremony."

"I am certain that tonight we will have a joining ceremony," Haidar said, his tone stern.

Jason bent and kissed Tala. Her arms went around his neck and for a moment, all was right with the worlds—the one he'd left behind and the one that he now claimed as his.

He thought he'd get the party started. The pile of brush and wood that were gathered for Tala's execution burst into bright flames.

"Do not show off, Jason," Tala said against his lips. "You are still only a Boy Scout and have much to learn."

"We can teach each other," he agreed. Jason pulled away from Tala but kept one arm wrapped around her. He smiled at Haidar.

"In my world, in my old world, a man chooses another to stand by his side when he takes a wife. He chooses his best friend. I choose Haidar to stand by my side during the joining ceremony."

The big guy did not smile back at him. "Bummer," he said, but then he did smile, if only a little.

Epilogue

The hawk watched the couple. The man was tall, dark-haired, and blue eyed. The woman's blonde hair and green eyes complimented her mate. They were a striking pair, even if the woman's stomach was rounded beneath her "Save the Wolf" T-shirt. The couple drew other T-shirts, like those they wore, from boxes as people hurried around them.

Dallas in July. How could he have forgotten how uncomfortable the heat and the humidity could be? It had no effect on the hawk, but the blond woman below brushed a damp curl from her forehead more than once.

"I'm not sure this is such a good idea for you," Jason heard his brother say. "You should be at my folks' house in the air-conditioning."

"Rick." The woman sighed. "I'm fine, really—and besides, this is my fund-raiser. How would it look if

333

I wasn't here to fire the imaginary pistol and get the walkers underway?"

"It would look like you listened to your husband once in a while and took his advice, Stephanie Donavon."

She grinned. "You're not a real doctor, Rick. You're a veterinarian, so lay off with all the advice-giving. *My* doctor says it's good for me to get out and stay busy. It's good for the baby, too."

The hawk's brother bent and pressed his ear against her stomach. "Hey, Jason, you all right in there, buddy?"

The hawk felt his feathers ruffle. A warm feeling spread though him. *Jason?*

"Hey you," the woman said, pulling the man back up to look at her. "Listen, it's great of you and your folks to get behind me on this project. I mean, I know it must be difficult to support a cause that . . . your brother and all."

"Stephanie." Rick placed his hands upon her shoulders. "I've told you, I don't hold what happened to Jason against the wolves. It was a freak accident. I'm sure that wolf was either rabid or it was a female that had pups in a den close by. Normal healthy wild wolves are not a threat to man, and of course I'm behind you. The kind of thing that happened to Jason is just the kind of thing that sends villagers tromping into the forest to kill the monster. Wild wolves have been hunted until almost extinction in the past, and I don't want to see that happen in the future."

"Well, remember. It was wolves that brought us together."

His brother frowned. "Yeah. I still can't figure out

whatever possessed me to move way out in the middle of nowhere to practice for farmers and their dumb sheep."

His wife giggled. "Destiny, of course. If you'd have stayed here in Dallas, I doubt you and I would have ever met."

"I guess it was destiny," he agreed, and pulled her close. "I'm looking forward to getting the new research grant and heading for the wilderness with you."

"With us," Stephanie reminded. "We'll have the little one. I can't believe your folks have agreed to come along and look after the baby while we're in the field."

He shrugged. "Mom and Dad . . . well, they've lost so much. A grandchild is just what they need to get them up and moving again. They're excited to put that RV they bought to use."

"I'll be happy to put their shower to use," she said. "I'm not much for roughing it, anymore. To tell you the truth, though, the walls in your parents' house are starting to close in on me. It will be wonderful to get out in the open again—and you're sure going to be a nice addition to my tent."

Rick growled low in his throat and nuzzled his wife's ear. "You, me, and a tent. That sounds good."

"Hey, you two, break it up." An older couple moved toward them. The hawk felt his heart speed a measure.

"Mom, Dad," Rick said. "Remember, just the first leg of the walk for you two. It's too damn hot out here."

"Listen to your son, the doctor," Stephanie said with a laugh. "They can both probably out-walk you, Rick. Have you ever tried to keep up with them at the mall?"

"True," he agreed. "Let's get you both a T-shirt." Rick unrolled a large shirt and a smaller one. He glanced at the large shirt and laughed. "Hey, Stephanie, check this out."

She frowned. " 'Save the Werewolf'? " Stephanie sighed. "Very funny, Rick. Your son has a very warped sense of humor—do you know that?" she asked the older couple.

"I can't take credit," Rick defended. "Believe me, I'd love to, but this must be someone else in your crew's idea of a joke."

"Okay, who's the wiseguy?" Stephanie called. She moved off toward a group setting up tables and refreshments.

Rick removed his shirt and slipped the one he held over his head. "No use in wasting a perfectly good joke," he said to his parents.

His mother swatted him playfully on the arm. "You and Jason, you were both always one to love a good practical joke."

The three sobered.

"You do think he'd be all right with us supporting Stephanie and her cause, don't you," his mother asked.

His brother smiled sadly. "I'm sure he would. You know Jason: He was always one for a cause, or a quest. I feel him sometimes, like he's right here beside me, you know?"

His mother and father nodded. All three put their arms around one another. The hawk was tempted for a moment to take his true form and join them, but only for a moment.

"Walkers, get ready!" Stephanie called. "Let's save some wolves."

His brother and parents moved toward her, Rick still wearing the 'Save the Werewolf' T-shirt, which received several laughs when he joined the others. Well, Jason himself had hated to waste a good opportunity for a joke. Haidar and Tala seldom got his jokes, but he was working on them.

Jason.

Tala? Is something wrong?

No, I miss you. Come home.

The hawk stared at the foursome in the distance, laughing and talking with one another. They were going to be fine. Of course, he had to assure himself. He would visit them on occasion just to make certain. He flapped his wings, took flight, and circled above, noting the traffic jams and dull smog that hung over the city's skyline.

Rick had found his destiny with the blond woman, and Jason had found his with a woman opposite to Stephanie's light hair and complexion. Jason had lost one family, but he'd gained another. And his name would live on. In this world, he was simply an accountant who'd gone on a hunting trip in Canada with his brother and never come home.

But in his world, he was Jason Donavon, the one chosen, newest member of *Oyate ba'cho*, Tribe Of The Wolf. He had beasts to hunt and a woman to protect—a *whole tribe* to protect. Heck, just because the pimp and the blond prostitute's pack hadn't yet followed their leader's scent trail back to The People's camp—that didn't mean they wouldn't. The current peace there could change in an instant, and he'd have to do something about it.

Well, he did love his quests, and he'd been given one that should prove to be a hell of a ride.

Jason.

I'm on my way. Maybe I'll swoop down and pick us up something for dinner.

Haidar says to bring Taco Bell again.

After Twilight

Amanda Ashley
Christine Feehan
Ronda Thompson

A man hunts for a woman. Yet what if he is no ordinary male, but a predator in search of prey? A dark soul looking for the light? A vampire, a werewolf, a mythic being who strikes fear into the hearts of mortals? Three of romance's hottest bestselling authors invite you to explore the dark side, to taste the forbidden, to dive into danger with heroes who fire the blood and lay claim to the soul in these striking tales of sensual passion. When day fades into night, when fear becomes fascination, when the swirling seduction of everlasting love overcomes the senses, it must be . . . after twilight.

___52450-3 $5.99 US/$6.99 CAN

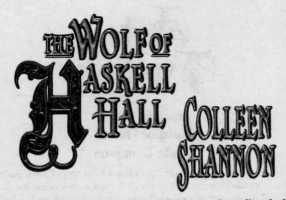

THE WOLF OF HASKELL HALL

COLLEEN SHANNON

With the coming of the moon, wild happenings disturb the seaswept peace of Haskell Hall. And for the newest heiress, deep longing mingles with still deeper fear. Never has she been so powerfully drawn to a man as she is to Ian Griffith, with his secretive amber eyes and tightly leashed sensuality. Awash in the seductive moonlight of his tower chamber, she bares herself to his fierce passions. But has she freed a tormented soul with her loving gift or loosed a demon who hunts unsuspecting women as his prey?

___52412-0 $5.99 US/$6.99 CAN

The
Trelayne
Inheritance
COLLEEN SHANNON

Women are dying, the blood drained from their bodies and two mysterious pinprick marks imprinted on their necks. Angelina Corbett cannot help wondering whether the whispers of "vampire" haunting her uncle's isolated estate might have a basis in fact — especially after meeting their enigmatic neighbor, the earl of Trelayne.

Locked in his powerful embrace, Angel feels rational thought flee. His voice mesmerizes her, his eyes silently beseech her, his touch enflames her and leaves her longing for fulfillment. She knows he is her soul mate, but will his dance lead her to the heights of ecstasy or the downward spiral of the damned?

THE GHOST OF
Carnal Cove
EVELYN ROGERS

"I am a man without conscience," claims the dark stranger who accosts her amid the pounding surf and tearing winds of Carnal Cove. Taunting her with legends of the place, Captain Saintjohn accuses her of being a seductress herself. Little does he know that Makenna Lindsay has come to the isolated Isle of Wight to escape just such temptations. But her troubled mind seems to conjure equally disturbing hallucinations at every turn: the piteous crying of an abandoned child, the silvery figure of a ghostly woman in white. But is her enemy her own imagination or the all-too-tempting promise of passion with a lover as wild and remorseless as the sea itself?
